Stay Crazy

www.apexbookcompany.com

Stay Crazy

Erica L. Satifka

Apex Publications
Lexington, KY

TPB ISBN 978-1-937009-43-4

Cover art © 2016 by Nickolas Brokenshire

Title design by Matt Davis

Published by Apex Publications, LLC, PO Box 24323, Lexington, KY 40524

First Edition: August, 2016

Visit us at www.apexbookcompany.com

For the ones who see through the thin veneer of reality, whether in the flash of a pink beam of light or the side of a box of chicken nuggets.

ONE

Dr. Atchison never trimmed his nose hairs. That was the first thing Emmeline Kalberg hated about him. There were other reasons to hate him, of course: his condescending tone, his haughty manner, the way he'd tear apart your room when you were out at group therapy — all in the name of "mental health," of course. But the nose hairs, those were Em's main complaint about the good doctor, and she trembled with the urge to leap over his weathered oak desk and pull them out herself.

"I'm not sure you're ready, Ms. Kalberg." Atchison flipped through the thick file in front of him, brow knitted. He paused for a long while before setting down the file and placing his pale, manicured hands atop it.

"Please, Dr. Atchison," Em said, "I *have* to go home today. My mother is driving all the way here to pick me up."

The doctor sighed, a little high-pitched whine that made Em want to strangle him. "Well, the other doctors seem to think you're well enough to go. They're probably right."

What you mean, Em thought, *is that my insurance ran out.* But she forced a smile, and kept her mouth shut.

"Now, Em, you do realize that you'll have to take it slow. It will take a while to recover. I want you to promise me that you won't make any sudden changes to your routine, at least not right away. Your only job right now is to get yourself well. I'm reminded of —"

As Atchison droned on and on, Em stared out the window behind him. A thicket of young trees lay beyond the chain-linked perimeter of the hospital. It looked flat and unreal, like a painting by a first-year art student with a limited range of pigments.

"Ms. Kalberg? Are you listening to me?"

"What was that?"

Atchison stood, shaking his head. "I want to speak with your mother when she shows up. When will she arrive?"

"In an hour." Em closed her eyes. "She called from the car."

"Okay, then. You can go get your things together."

Em slid from the chair and padded to her room in her too-tight blue slippers. It didn't take long to pack. She'd arrived with nothing more than the clothes on her back, and while she'd picked up a few more things in the past month, everything still fit comfortably into the lime green duffel bag her favorite nurse had brought her. She sat on the creaky hospital bed with her bag in her lap and waited for her ride.

It would be good to get back home, away from the stifling environment of the hospital. At home, nobody would tell her when to eat and sleep. Nobody would snatch a book out of her hands and tell her it wasn't a good thing for her to read. She wouldn't have to share her room with a black-clad goth named Amber whose crying jags were only interrupted by surreptitious vomiting.

Amber appeared on cue, a melancholy ghost summoned from Em's daydreams. "You're leaving."

"Afraid so."

Amber's eyes welled up. "You're leaving because you hate me, aren't you?"

"Yes, I am." Em knew Amber wouldn't believe anything else. Em slung her bag over her shoulder and went out to wait for her mother in the lobby.

Trevor the Jesus Freak stopped her. He was a thirty-year-old former meth head who had shocked himself while preaching a sermon atop an Episcopalian church and holding onto the church's weathervane for support. Before Em could smack his hand away, he anointed her forehead with a smudge of dirt. "I heard you were leaving, so I asked the Lord to bless your journey."

"Well, thanks. I guess."

"Jesus wants you to take care of yourself. When I opened my Bible this morning for my daily readings, He had illuminated your initials. When I saw the illumination I felt an overwhelming sense of peace and goodwill, and an urgent need to tell you of these things." Trevor laid one of his filthy hands — he had been anointing people all afternoon — on Em's shoulder.

Em brushed it off. "Yeah, well, like I said, thanks. But I'll tell you who's really in need of some peace and goodwill. Amber. She's in her room right now in a terrible state of despair. I'm sure Jesus can do something about that."

Trevor beamed. "You're right. I shall go visit Amber." He brushed past Em, his dirt-caked hands extended in benediction.

After perching on an uncomfortable plastic chair, Em gazed through the picture window to the concrete ocean of the parking lot. That's where her mother's midnight-blue sedan would be when it finally showed up.

Em imagined their reunion. An ecstatic Bea Kalberg would embrace Em in a hug and cover her with kisses. That alone would make these last two months worth something, to know that she would be going home to somewhere warm and safe, full of love.

When she was eight years old, Em's father had gone out for cigarettes and ice cream and never returned. A lengthy search turned up nothing, and since then, her mother was all she had. Their relationship wasn't perfect, but Em always knew her mother cared for her. Events had transpired to put her in this place — events that she still couldn't remember — but that wouldn't change anything between Em and her mother. It *couldn't*.

A shadow loomed over Em. She looked up. It was a thin-lipped woman in a gray windbreaker, a black pocketbook under her arm. Mom.

"Come along, Emmeline. Let's go."

Em spent the next week on the living room couch, covered with a blanket, while her mother worked at the bank and her sister went to school.

"Hello, folks," said the television therapist with the bald head that was always on channel 64. "I know a lot of people out there are feeling blue right now. It's a hard, hard world, and sometimes it seems there's nobody you can trust."

"You got that right," said Em.

"Some of you no doubt feel that you've hit rock bottom. That's when you've gotta take a good look in the mirror, and trust in me, Dr. Wes Summersby. When you buy and listen to my five-disc emotional healing course on DVD, a magical thing will happen. You'll feel more confident. You'll start to take more pride in your life and in yourself."

Em peeked under her blanket. She was dressed in two-day-old pajamas with a milk stain on the front.

"Buy my DVDs today, and I not only guarantee you satisfaction, I promise you a new life."

"No sale." Em flipped to a rerun of *Seinfeld*.

After months of expansion, Em felt like her life had contracted to a single dot, the space bar on a keyboard, the short silence between words. Every movement became deliberate, like punching her way through a roomful of cotton. The laugh track buzzed in her ears like feedback distortion.

She watched reruns. She laughed, but only when it was appropriate. At least, she hoped.

That night, Em's mother turned off the television. "Em, can we talk for a minute?"

Em let the fuzzy blanket fall in a pile on the floor. She was suddenly self-conscious of her greasy hair and lack of baths. "Shoot."

"I think you're spending a little too much time cooped up here. It's time you got a job."

"A job?"

"You're not too crazy to work at a store a couple of hours a week. I'll take you down to Savertown USA tomorrow. They'll hire anybody."

With great concentration, Em sat up. "I don't think I want to work at Savertown USA."

"Well, honey, we all have to do things we don't want to do. Savertown USA is a fine place to work. We'll go down there tomorrow after I get home."

"But I don't want to work there."

"I'll be home at six. Be ready." She left the room before Em could reply.

Em put the TV back on. *Law & Order: Whatever.* She took the blanket from the ground and re-swaddled it around her filthy body.

TWO

The overhead fluorescents of the Clear Falls Savertown USA hummed like the whirring of intelligent insects burrowing their way into Em's brain. The walls blazed with thick red, white, and blue stripes. Giant decals printed like cobblestones clung to the floor. Street signs, marked with names like "Electronics Terrace" and "Maternity Lane," sprouted where two footpaths intersected. Pop country droned from the overhead loudspeakers.

"Try not to blow this, Em."

"I won't have to *try* to blow it. That just happens."

Em's mom rolled her eyes. "You'll do fine."

At the back of the store, a glassy-eyed worker with a bleached-blond perm sat reading a romance novel. "Hello, my name is Bea Kalberg. My daughter Emmeline would like to see the manager about a job."

The woman looked up at Em's mom, then at Em. She then returned to her reading.

"I called earlier today. The manager said we could go in and talk to him personally."

Without looking back up at Em or her mom, the woman picked up the intercom. "Mr. Pendleton, there's some people here who say they need to talk to you."

"Send them in," a scratchy voice said.

The woman absently gestured toward the "Employees Only" door. The office was walled in clear plastic, presumably so the boss could keep a close eye on his employees as they mingled in the lounge directly within sight. The man inside — Pendleton, Em guessed — unhooked the latch to the door and gestured Em and her mother inside.

Em felt fingers digging into her back like a cattle prod. "My daughter wants a job here."

"Is that so?" Mr. Pendleton was a slight man, who wore perfectly round glasses and a shirt buttoned all the way up to the top of his neck. "Are you sixteen?"

"Nineteen," Em said.

"You ever work in retail before?"

"Never."

Pendleton gave her a hard look. "This is a serious business. We are all very dedicated here at Savertown USA. Dedicated to business. If you don't want to work hard, we don't need you."

Em tried to look into Pendleton's eyes, but the overhead lights conspired with the glasses to block them out, creating two small suns. "I'm dedicated to business."

"We have an opening in the frozen food section for a stock person. Part time."

Em couldn't stop staring at his glasses. The reflection was mesmerizing; it completely distracted her from whatever Pendleton was saying. She stared at the two white orbs until she felt her mother's elbow in her side. "Okay?"

Pendleton held out his hand. It was hairy and covered with scabs. "Welcome aboard."

Reluctantly, Em shook Pendleton's hand.

A thin black woman with a crooked smile fitted Em for a red, white, and blue Savertown USA vest. It made swishing noises when Em moved her arms, and the cheap fabric seemed designed to never smooth out completely. Somewhere along the line, she was given a nametag with "Emma" written on it.

"That's not my name."

The woman squinted, then affixed a "final markdown" price tag sticker over the last two letters. "There. It's perfect."

An elderly man sat her down at a desk and popped a DVD into a nearby player. Somehow she didn't think it would be a rerun of *Gilligan's Island*.

"You have to watch this. It's about the company. We all had to watch it." He turned down the overhead lights.

The video opened with an exterior shot of a Savertown USA store. Generic music played over the image, and the camera zoomed into the store. A pleasant narrative voice kicked in.

"Savertown USA Stores Incorporated was founded in the spring of 1982 by William St. George, a humble grocer from Lexington, Kentucky. Mr. St. George had one goal in his life: to provide affordable products to American consumers in a clean, well-organized environment, where they could get all their shopping done in one convenient location."

The narrator rambled on and on about the achievements of William St. George: about how he was the youngest self-made person to make the Fortune 500 list, about how he had gone through a string of three wives before becoming born again. The narration was underscored with photographs and artists' renderings of St. George as he progressed through life. The discussion of William St. George ended at his death, which had occurred at the tragic age of fifty-seven during a rock-climbing expedition.

Em had stopped watching the film long before St. George's demise. She instead traced the pattern of the fake wooden desktop with her fingers while humming a song.

"At Savertown USA, we respect the ideals of William St. George every day when we price our goods. We believe, as he did, that family is the most precious thing in America today, and we are dedicated to bringing the American family the very best in products and services at prices they can afford. So, new employee, as you prepare to embark on a fulfilling, rewarding career with Savertown USA Stores Incorporated, remember that your number one goal must always be customer satisfaction. Nothing is more important than the happiness of our customers. Because our customers are America, and America is —"

A scream sounded. A flash of light shot from the television, narrowly missing Em's eyes. When she looked back at the television, the afterimage of a complex mathematical formula filled the screen.

The overhead light came on. "Enjoy the movie?"

It was the man who had put the video on. Em looked him over. *He didn't hear the scream*, she thought, *or see what I saw. He can't see it even now. I must be hallucinating. Did I take my meds today?*

She stood up. "Yeah, I guess."

"Well, that's all you have to do today. You don't start work until tomorrow." He ejected the DVD and put it back in its protective sleeve. "Are you okay? You look a little sick."

"Must be the flu. Don't touch me, it's catching." Em tucked her vest and name badge under her arm and dashed through the little fake village to the parking lot, where her mother was waiting with a full trunk of groceries.

"How did it go?" her mother asked.

"It was fine. Totally fine."

Em's mom raised an eyebrow. "You don't seem fine."

"Look, I know if I'm fine or not, okay? Just drive." Em leaned back in her seat and closed her eyes. *Just a hallucination.*

§

As Em drifted off to sleep that night, she heard loud whispers through the wall behind her bed. She slid out of bed and padded to her sister's room.

"Jackie, what are you doing?"

Jackie looked up from her clasped hands. "Saying my prayers."

"We're not religious."

"*You're* not religious." Jackie quickly crossed herself and squinted her eyes at Em, like a hex.

"Just keep it down. I'm trying to sleep." Em looked around her sister's room. The walls were lined with photographs of old white men in funny suits — preachers, maybe. Thick tomes lined her bookshelf. "So you've found Christ, huh?"

"He found me."

Em considered telling her about Trevor the Jesus Freak, but decided not to. It always made Jackie nervous when Em talked about the hospital, or the other people who lived there. "Why? Are your friends into it or something?"

"I'm part of a Bible study group. We meet every Monday and Friday."

"You know we're Jewish, right?"

"That was Dad," Jackie said, with a tone that seemed to say *and that sure worked out well for him, didn't it?*

Em never understood the appeal of religion. There'd been a few Bibles in the paltry hospital library, but Em thought it was slightly improper to give people who couldn't tell fantasy from reality a book about imaginary beings. Trevor, of course, hadn't spoken to her for days after she pointed that out. "Well, that's nice. Does Mom know about this?"

"No." Jackie refolded her hands and returned to her prayers.

Em stared at her sister for a few moments before leaving the room. The whispers continued for another twenty minutes.

THREE

The next morning Em awoke to the clanging of a siren. She wandered out to the living room, where her mother was watching a game show. A man in a faded NASCAR shirt tried to stuff as much cash down his pants as he could in two minutes while tinny carnival music played.

"Do you think they disinfect it afterward?"

Em's mother looked at her. Her eyes were bleary; she hadn't had a good night's sleep. "He just keeps it."

"Yeah, but what about the cashiers at stores and stuff? Would *you* want to handle that guy's crotch money?"

Em's mother narrowed her eyes.

"All I'm saying is, if that guy comes into your bank, you should pull out the Lysol."

Mom turned up the television. "Get some breakfast and take a shower. You have to be at work in an hour."

Em went into the kitchen and poured a bowl of cereal. As she chewed, her thoughts drifted back, back to before the hospital, even before college. Things had been so much simpler once. She'd never really gotten along with the other kids in school. Partly that was due to her lack of a dad, but mostly it was her own fault. Em knew that now.

But she'd always had her art: the little comics she'd made with Jackie on their old desktop, the acrylic painting she'd completed in high school art class. Mom had forced her to major in something practical, which was probably smart of her, but Em had still worked on it at Oberlin, late into the night.

Now, of course, it was all sucked away, both the art and the 101 Poli-Sci courses, and nobody could tell her whether or not either would ever come back, or when. She suspected that the doctors thought she was faking it, her slowness, her inability to grasp either a paintbrush or a theory, but Em knew the truth. She knew she was finished.

"Em, get a move on! You're going to be late." Em scraped the bowl of cereal into the sink and went into the bathroom. After taking a quick shower, she dressed in a plain white shirt and black slacks, the only kind of outfit permitted by Savertown USA Stores, Incorporated. She pulled her red, white, and blue vest over her chest and clipped the name badge to it.

It'll only be four hours, she thought. At least that was four hours away from the tension that choked the Kalberg house like poisonous gas. It might not even be so bad, to work in that place.

But, she had to ask herself, *what was the deal with the television?* It seemed so real, but obviously couldn't be. Had she really forgotten to take her meds that day, or was their effect wearing off? Better to be safe than sorry.

Em looked over the collection of sepia vials on her bedside table. Red for paranoia, blue for panic, green for depression. She tapped out an extra red pill and swallowed it dry. Then she went downstairs and joined her mother in the sedan.

"All set?"

Em breathed deeply. "Yeah."

"Now this," said the thirty-something Vietnamese woman wearing a baseball cap embroidered with the Savertown USA logo, "is your work station. What you do is, you take a box from the pallet over there, then you open the box, then you put the stuff on the shelves." She carried a green-handled box cutter, which she stabbed in the air as she illustrated each of her points.

"Boxes, shelves. I think I have it."

"Are you being sarcastic?"

"No, ma'am."

Mrs. Nguyen handed Em the box cutter with a frown. "You can start now. Any questions, just ask."

Em began pulling boxes from the huge stack on the pallet and slicing them open with the box cutter. The work was surprisingly easy once she had memorized the location of all the items in the aisle.

Boxes, shelves, boxes, shelves. Em scanned the rows of merchandise like a stoic, thrusting her hands into the chilled cabinets whenever she found a match. She let her mind go and became a machine.

The machine didn't linger on the colorful logos, allowing itself to be overcome by associations with multinational corporations designed to keep towns like Clear Falls under their thumb. The machine didn't worry about the long-term effects of the colorful dyes and chemical cocktails present in the brightly packaged food-type products. The machine just stocked shelves, and so the machine remained happy. Or at least content.

Mrs. Nguyen tapped Em on the shoulder. "Lunchtime. Go take a break."

Em smiled, let her consciousness return, and put the green-handled box cutter in the pocket of her vest.

Em stared at a stark black-and-white sign over the threadbare break room couch that read "No Outside Reading Materials." Around it were other posters showing the correct way to lift a heavy box and what you should do if someone tries to make you sign a union card.

Two long wooden tables with benches stretched from one end of the room to the other, with employees sitting cheek-to-jowl on either side of both of them.

Screw you, sign. Em plopped down at the end of one of the long tables and pulled out a novel she had started at the hospital. She'd only read a single paragraph when she felt a looming presence behind her.

"You can't read that in here." Em could see the reversed ghost of an inside-out Tweety Bird shirt underneath the woman's Savertown USA vest. She pointed to the sign. "No reading."

"That's a stupid rule," Em said, putting the book back in her messenger bag.

The woman sat opposite her and stuck out her hand. "You're new here, right? My name's Paula."

Em accepted the slightly clammy hand. "Yeah, new."

"I'll introduce you to folks. That lady over there is May, and that older guy with the glasses is Tom —"

"I know everyone's name. We all wear nametags."

Paula's buoyant smile drooped. "Er, yeah, I guess we do." She pulled a leaking Tupperware container containing fruit salad from her lunchbox. "Want some?"

"No thanks." Em took her turkey sandwich from her bag. "I have food."

"It's fresh. And you're so skinny."

"I'm allergic to fruit. All fruit."

"Oh," Paula replied, "that's sad."

Em chewed her sandwich in silence for a time, tuning out Paula's drone, hoping she'd get a chance at a quick smoke break after she ate. Then, out of the corner of her eye, she glimpsed an enormous man. The man eased himself onto the dilapidated couch and pulled out a newspaper. When he saw Em was looking at him, he frowned and held the newspaper up in front of his face.

Em leaned in close to Paula. "Who's that?"

Paula's voice grew hushed. "That's Roger. He works in the deli. You don't pay him any mind."

"He's reading. I thought we weren't allowed to read."

"We don't say anything to him." The volume of Paula's voice grew softer still. "People say he's not right in the head. He'd be liable to kill us, we say anything to him."

Note to self, Em thought, *if they know I'm crazy, I can get away with anything.* That might prove useful.

Em washed down the rest of her sandwich with the can of pop she'd bought from the break room vending machine. She made a point of passing Roger on her way to the trash can. His bald, sickly pale head reflected the overhead fluorescent lights. His knuckles tightened around the wrinkled paper.

Em returned to the table. Paula, her seatmate, had finished her fruit salad and was now opening a stack of chocolate chip cookies wrapped in tinfoil. She gestured at the stack expectantly. Em shook her head.

"Suit yourself." Paula shoved a cookie into her maw and licked her fingers. "After work sometime you should come to my church. We have a Bible study group."

"I don't think so," Em said. "I don't believe in God."

Paula blinked. "You don't?"

"My sister does, though. You should ask her to join. I'll give you her e-mail address." *That'll show Jackie,* Em thought.

Paula swept her crumbs into a pink polish-tipped hand. "It was very nice to meet you."

With Paula gone, Em studied Roger. He turned the pages slowly, his brow intent. With practiced nonchalance, she slid into the seat next to him. Em cleared her throat.

No response.

"I'm trying to talk to you."

Roger flipped a page. "Go away."

Em frowned. This wasn't in the script. "I'm Em." She didn't offer her hand. She'd shaken too many hands that day.

Finally, Roger's beady blue eyes focused on her. "Missy, you'd better get going. Lunch break's almost over."

"I —" At that moment, the loudspeaker fired off its klaxon.

"Told you."

Em rolled her eyes. "Aren't you going back?"

Roger folded the newspaper and put it on the couch arm. "When I'm ready. You should go, though. You're new. They'll be watching."

Don't I know it, Em thought, keeping one eye on Roger as she left the break room. In return, he gave her a hard look back. His eyes bored into her like lasers on a gun sight, as if he were trying to tap her mind. Tap her soul.

FOUR

The windows in Dr. Slazinger's office were shaped like trapezoids. Em wondered idly how much more expensive it was to install trapezoidal windows than the standard variety. Then again, as she looked around the office at the high-quality synthetic leather furniture, expensive-looking wave machine, and watercolor paintings, she realized that whatever it was that trapezoidal windows cost, Dr. Slazinger could well afford it.

"Welcome back, Emmeline."

"Hi," Em said, folding her legs underneath her.

Slazinger took out a pad and pen. "I want to talk about your job. You've been there a week. Are you holding up okay?"

"Well, it's just a job. Go there, open boxes, put things on shelves. Nothing special."

"Are you getting along with your coworkers?"

"I think so. One of the women asked me to join her Bible study group. I'm thinking about going."

"I thought you didn't believe in God."

"I was being sarcastic."

"Oh." He scribbled a few lines. "So how's your family?"

She shrugged. "Okay."

Slazinger sighed. "That's not a lot of information, Em."

Better tell him something, Em thought, *or you'll get in trouble.* "Mom watches TV. That's what she does. It's like a second job, except she doesn't get paid for it."

"Does it make you sad when she watches television?"

"It's her life." Em let her gaze drift back to the oddly-shaped windows. Outside, a light rain was falling. She wished she'd remembered to put a plastic bag over her bike seat.

Slazinger snapped his fingers. "Stay with me, Em."

Em looked back at the man's tired, worn-paper-bag face. "Do you know a guy named Wes Summersby? Self-help guy who's always on channel 64 hawking shit?"

"No."

"Oh, I thought you might, since you're both shrinks. My mom loves this guy. She watches him on television all the time."

"Well, there's nothing wrong with that."

"I think there is." Em leaned forward. "He's a con artist."

Slazinger seemed to wince. "Now, Emmeline, you said the same thing about me."

"This Wes Summersby is bad news. I think he's doing something to my mom." Em's head slumped to her chest. "I don't really want to talk about it."

The doctor made a few more notes on his pad. "Maybe we should think about switching your medication."

Em wasn't happy to hear him say that, but she didn't blame him. She knew she'd sounded pretty crazy.

She was also sure she was right.

Em hit something with the door on the way out of Slazinger's office. *Hard.* Frowning, she swung it open a second time. A boy in a faded Smiths T-shirt jumped back.

"Ow. Shit." He rubbed his head. "Do you mind?."

"Sorry," Em said. "Are you okay?"

"Well, you just slammed a door into my head."

"Other than the door."

"I'm just a little anxious. I haven't been here before." He combed through his sandy blond hair with his fingers. "What is Dr. Slazinger like?"

"He's nothing great."

"My name's Kevin," said the boy. He extended his hand.

She took it. "Emmeline. But you can call me Em. So what's wrong with you?"

Kevin looked away and mumbled incoherently.

"I'm a paranoid schizophrenic with depressive tendencies."

"Um." Kevin retreated and flopped into a chair at the far end of the room. He pulled a comic book from his backpack.

Em walked over. "Is that *The Hardened Criminals*? Man, I used to love that series."

"It's still going on."

"Well, I don't read that much anymore." She slid into the stiff-backed chair next to him. "I used to draw, too."

"I guess you *used to* do a lot of stuff." He glanced away. "Sorry, that was mean."

"Maybe we should get together sometime and read comics. I'd love some recs."

His eyes shifted uncomfortably. "I don't think so. I've got this session now, and —"

He doesn't want to talk to me. He's scared of me. Why did I tell him my diagnosis? That was dumb.

"Listen," Em said, the words tumbling from her mouth. "I just want to talk to you. I think we'd have a lot in common."

"Like *what*?" He glared at her, one eye squinted. "These books?"

"That, and there's, um..." Em snapped her fingers in the direction of Slazinger's office. "Slazinger. I'm not asking for a date or anything. I just want someone to talk to."

Kevin's face shadowed over in an expression Em instantly recognized, the one that said *this person is crazy, don't talk to them.* "I don't think so."

She took a pen and piece of scrap paper from her bag and scribbled down her number. "At least take my number. Please? No pressure. I miss having friends. That's *all*."

Kevin jumped from his chair. "You're nuts." But when Em held the piece of paper up to him, he stuck it in his jeans pocket.

"Kevin Collins?" the receptionist said. "The doctor will see you now."

Kevin hoisted his backpack on his shoulder and slunk into Slazinger's swanky office. Em watched the door latch shut behind him, then went out into the cold December air.

When Em was young, before her father went out to buy cigarettes and ice cream and never came back, she would spend days sitting with him outside of the old Clear Falls Drugstore, sipping a Coke as he smoked his unfiltered Pall Malls and told her about the ways of the world.

"Big business is killing this town," he had said. "All these chains are coming in just to screw us. They want to turn us into little plastic robots, buying stuff, all kinds of things we don't need." He took her head in his hands. "Promise me, Emmeline. Promise me you won't let them take you in."

Em had nodded. "Okay."

"You don't understand now, but you will someday. You're one of the smart ones, Em. Not like your sister and mother. You'll be the one to save this town."

The Clear Falls Drugstore was gone now, driven out of business by Savertown USA and a host of other chain stores that had crept into the area over the past ten years. Em often wondered what her father would think about the town now. Would he think it had sold out? Would he think the same of her?

Maybe it's best, she thought, *that he's not here to see this. To see what I've become.* She threaded her arms through her patriotically colored work vest and went down to the carport to fetch her bike.

At the store, my knife in hand. Human machine, channel through which nothing but ritual flows. Em sliced open a case of frozen macaroni and stacked the individual packages with care, arranging them into a perfect pyramid.

She had steadily increased the number of cases she could stock from twenty-five to over a hundred a day. She hadn't even noticed what a good machine she was becoming until she saw the immense pile of discarded cardboard boxes she'd left behind.

Suddenly, pain spiked in her head and stars drifted across her field of vision. She'd cracked her skull on the freezer door.

"Dammit." Em ran her fingers over her forehead, but didn't see blood. After checking for customers, she brought a box of frozen macaroni to her aching head.

"I need your help," said a voice in her left ear. A blurred gray shape appeared before her eyes. Em threw the box down and backed away from it.

Please, not at work. Her hands shook, and hot tears pricked her eyes. She wiped them away with one insulated glove.

Em's supervisor's shadow dropped over her. "Are you slacking off, Miss Kalberg?"

"No," Em whispered, "I just have to go to the bathroom. Just let me go to the bathroom, please."

Mrs. Nguyen quirked an eyebrow. "You don't have to ask permission. Just don't be long, we have a whole other pallet to get through."

Em stumbled down the aisle and into the dinky employee bathroom with its cracked mirror and collection of five-year-old *Woman's World* magazines. She turned the water on full blast and brushed back her bangs so she could examine her forehead, which still burned. An irregular red singe mark blazed directly above her eyes, right in the center, in the place where the box of macaroni had touched her. She scrubbed at it until the toilet paper turned to mush between her fingers, but it didn't fade.

They'll think I did it, she thought. *They'll never believe that it was an accident, and they'll really never believe that the box did it.*

Because of course, boxes of macaroni didn't do that. To think that they did, well, that would be insane. After pushing the bangs over the mark, Em cautiously tiptoed back outside.

Out of the corner of her eye, something lumbered toward her. Before she could cry out, Roger's meaty hand flashed out and spun her around.

"I know what you heard." He parted her bangs. "I can see the mark."

Em screamed and wrested herself away from Roger. She sprinted down the main corridor of the store and into the frozen food aisle, where she collided with Mrs. Nguyen.

"Are you okay, Em?"

"Fine," Em said, trying to keep her voice steady. "Let's just get started on that pallet."

FIVE

*L*ift with your legs. Take frequent breaks. If you get cleaning solution in your eyes, proceed with haste to the nearest eyewash station. It was nice to know someone cared.

Em looked away from the faded safety placard on the wall to the masses of mouth-breathing Savertown USA workers before her. She waited for the company jingle to come pouring through the speakers. Every day at the start of the shift, Em's coworkers clapped their hands and sang along to the jaunty tune. It was a lot like a high school pep rally, though this time Em couldn't sneak behind the bleachers for a smoke but had to witness the humiliation first-hand.

Like marionettes, everyone's head snapped up when Pendleton entered. His face shone red behind his fogged-up glasses. Em realized he'd been crying. *Pathetic.*

"My fellow employees, I have some tragic news for you. At six o'clock this morning, Jimmy Novotny's body was found in the bed of his pickup truck. He died from a self-inflicted shotgun wound to the chest."

There was the sound of two dozen employees gasping at once, and then a low hum of murmurs.

Em leaned over to Paula. "Who's Jimmy Novotny?"

Paula's chubby face melted into shock. "You don't know who Jimmy Novotny was? How couldn't you know who he was? He worked in the lawn and garden section. He used to sit right over — there!" She stabbed a finger at the other side of the room and patted her eyes with a corner of her vest.

"This is a sad day in the Savertown USA family," Pendleton said.

"We did not take heed of the warning signs that could have alerted us to Jimmy's mental state and possibly saved his life. We can, however, make sure that nothing like this happens again. I've called the central office, and they faxed me this."

He distributed yellow fliers while the employees wailed. "These are behaviors that might indicate a possible suicide. Friends, if you see anyone in this store who seems to fit these guidelines, please bring it to my attention as soon as possible, so I can see to it personally that the employee in question receives the best possible care."

"What's this number?" one of the women said, pointing to the bottom of the flier.

"It's the Savertown USA suicide prevention hotline. It's a confidential number that we want you to call if you're feeling down, or just need someone to talk to."

Em scanned the list. Basic shit. Jimmy's suicide was far less creative than any of Amber's many attempts. Once, Amber had somehow found a way to nick an artery in the suicide-proof quiet room using a paper clip covertly hidden in her rectum. Now *that* took talent. Em folded the flier into a paper airplane and sailed it into the corner.

"We're all going to miss Jimmy very much," Pendleton said, "but we can't let his passing keep us from fulfilling our duties here at work. Jimmy wouldn't want it that way. We must all stay strong in the face of this tragedy, and not let our sadness overshadow those things that must be done. I want you to go out there and work hard, and so would Jimmy. This concludes our meeting. There will be a short prayer service out in the parking lot during lunch for all interested parties."

"What's today's stock price?" Em yelled out. All eyes swiveled in her direction. Paula looked ready to explode. *Can't you people take a joke?* she thought as the room emptied. Before she could get up too, the store manager blocked her path.

"I'd like to talk with you a moment, Emmeline."

"Ms. Kalberg."

Pendleton's face shifted from sad-red to angry-red. "Your mother informed me of your condition. I just want you to know that I'm always here, and you can tell me anything you want to. Anything at all. And you can always call the number at the bottom of the flier. It's twenty-four hours of someone who cares and is there to help."

"Will do."

He handed her another flier. "I'll give you a fresh one."

She folded it and stuck it in her back pocket. "Thanks."

"Is there anything bothering you, Miss Kalberg? You seemed troubled the other day at lunch."

"Mr. Pendleton, I'm not sure what my mom told you but you have it all wrong. I may be crazy but I'm not a suicide case. Ask my doctor, he'll tell you himself." Em pulled out her cell phone.

"That won't be necessary. I just wanted to let you know that I … care about you."

"You don't care about me. I'm just a replaceable machine."

Pendleton shook his head, the slack skin on his face swishing from side to side. It reminded Em of chicken skin. "That's not true at all."

"Course it is. Now, if we're done here, I'd like to go stock some shelves and serve America." Em saluted.

He frowned, but waved her on. "Good luck, Miss Kalberg. Stay strong."

"Oh, I'm plenty strong. Jimmy Novotny was a dick anyway."

Em sliced open another case and stocked another shelf. *At least he let me go*, she thought. She'd left him sputtering in the break room, ten seconds away from an explosion that might have shaken Savertown USA to its foundation.

She picked up a brightly-colored box of microwaveable chicken nuggets, fresh off the factory line. As she pondered where to place it, she noticed something odd about the electric blue container with its unsupported health claims.

The cartoon chicken on the box was glowing.

Em threw the box back on the pallet and pressed her back against the freezer door. She looked away, counting ten deep breaths, then peeked at the pile of boxes waiting for her.

All the cartoon chickens on all the boxes were glowing.

Don't react, she thought. *It will make you look crazy. And Mrs. Nguyen will see.* Em crammed the boxes onto the shelf and slammed the freezer door. No sooner had she done that, though, than the chicken started to dance and move its beak.

"Please stop doing that," she said, but the chicken wouldn't stop moving. Em opened the door and yanked out the box of nuggets. She held it to the side of her head. "Okay, you fucker, talk to me."

"I need your help," said the voice in her left ear.

Well, Em thought, *you sure as hell picked the right person.*

"My name is Escodex," the voice said. "I am an investigator who has been dispatched to this location to apprehend a dangerous criminal."

"What the fuck?" Em opened her eyes and looked around. A tweaker in a sweat-soaked Steelers shirt was staring at her.

"I require assistance as I have no physical body in your dimension."

"*Shut up*," Em hissed. The tweaker was still gaping at her, one hand cradling an open Mountain Dew can. She turned to the side.

"I can reward you. Anything you'd like. And you don't have to speak out loud. I can read your thoughts when you put the box to your head."

The box of chicken nuggets had grown warm and clammy against her head. Em's fingers started to shake. *I didn't take my red pill today,* she thought. *I remembered the other two, but not the important one.*

"You didn't forget it," Escodex said. "It's logged in your memory, so it happened."

Like I would believe you. You're a voice in my head. You're an illusion.

Em saw Mrs. Nguyen stomp toward her, yelling, one long red fingernail extended to the box of precious chicken nuggets. "What are you doing? Put that away!"

"Buy something at lunch and take it to the bathroom," the voice said. "We'll speak in private."

But —

The connection broke like a phone signal in a rainstorm. Mrs. Nguyen shook the box of nuggets in Em's face. "You're paying for this. It's contaminated now. And you're getting docked for the time it takes you. I'm gonna start counting right now." She shoved the box back at Em and sneered at her.

"Yes, ma'am." Em trudged up the center aisle of Savertown USA and paid for the nuggets. As the box went through the scanner, she watched the cartoon chicken. It was no longer moving.

When the loudspeaker rang out the call for lunch, Em took the box of chicken nuggets from its place in the employees' refrigerator and snuck away to the bathroom in the main part of the store. She scribbled a "do not disturb" sign on a piece of scratch paper, hung it on the door of the bathroom with a wad of gum, and locked it from the inside.

"Okay, talk."

"This store is in great danger. An unknown criminal entity from a distant point in your dimension is sucking the energy from your workers, causing them to kill themselves when their energy runs out. This entity wants to break into my dimension, which would not only be bad for us, but would also destroy your world."

Em held up a hand. "Not that. Why should I believe you're real? How can you talk to me through this box?"

"There are ID chips in all the products in this store. They are tracked via low-frequency radio waves. I hijack those waves and use the chip to broadcast into your mind. You can only hear me when the chip is very near your brain."

"Why can I only hear you in my left ear?"

"I process to the dominant hemisphere," Escodex said. "You're right-handed."

"Why do you speak English? Why do you sound like a regular person?"

"English is a fairly simple language to learn. Lots of us speak it, along with other languages from your dimension."

"And that burn I got on my forehead the other day?"

"My signal was too strong. It sparked an electrical reaction. Sorry about that."

Em sat down on the toilet. "All this stuff about 'my' dimension, what the hell is that? You have to be shitting me." The worst part was knowing that the voice could see through her sarcasm to the fear inside.

This isn't happening, she thought. *You know that, right?*

"I'm from Earth. I just come from a higher dimension."

"Higher?"

"It's the next level above yours," he said. "I'm living on your planet right now, but we can't normally interact. We exist on a plane that's undetectable to you and your machines."

"But you can see us?"

"Yes, we can. We consider it a form of ... entertainment to watch you."

Em snorted. "Well, if your dimension's so great, why can't you fix your own damn problems?"

"I need somebody who can physically collect evidence. I'm only a mental projection from my plane and cannot affect reality in your dimension. I need hands and feet. The entity has blocked my communication with nearly everyone on this plane."

"And what kind of entity would this be?"

"We have no term for it. It's something from your dimension." Em swore she could feel the voice shrug. "It's evil."

Heavy pounding rattled the bathroom door. "Open up! I gotta go."

"Just a few minutes, please," Em said, her voice trembling. "I, um, have diarrhea."

"I ain't never shopping here again," the gruff female voice said. Em stayed near the door until she heard the customer stomp away.

Em put the box to her head again. "Why did you contact me?"

"I need help."

"No, I mean why did you contact me personally? There are five dozen other people who work here. And all the customers."

"I contact everybody. Not too many listen. That's the problem with your dimension; you're so gullible about some things and so stubborn about others."

"Well, I'm no different. So leave me the hell alone." Em began pacing about the hot, stuffy room reeking of crapped-out Standard American Diet.

"My dimension is under attack." Escodex paused. "I can give you anything you want."

"All I want is for the voices in my head to shut up."

"I can locate your father for you."

She halted her pacing and dropped the box. How had he known about that? Oh yes, he'd scanned her memory. No, wait, that wasn't it — he wasn't real.

None of this was really happening.

Look at me, she thought. *I'm totally fucking loony tunes. Atchison was right, they should never have let me out of that hospital. I'm standing here in a locked bathroom holding a box of thawing chicken nuggets to the side of my head, talking to a creature from outer space about my father.*

But what about the burn? She had seen it, that creepy Roger guy had seen it.

There is no such thing as other dimensions. I'm just a goddamn schizo.

Em crushed the box with her foot, kicked it underneath the stall, and went to her aisle. Mrs. Nguyen would kill her if she were late again.

Six

"So how's work?"

"Fine."

"You don't sound fine." Kevin took a drag off his cigarette and tapped the ash into a Styrofoam cup.

"How'd you shake your sister?"

"I told her I was going to the mall with some guys. Made her happy. She let me borrow the car because I was going to do something normal."

Em laughed. Kevin's sister Margery wasn't too bright. She had no clue that he'd been spending every other day hanging out with Em. "You want to drive around for a little while? I don't want to go back to my house. Jackie's prayer circle is there."

"Okay."

Em and Kevin ground their cigarettes under their heels and got into Margery's car, a sleek new white Pontiac with leather seats. Kevin prissily sprayed his shirt with scent neutralizer, frowning at Em when she didn't do the same.

It hadn't been easy getting in contact with him. There were over a dozen listings for Collins in the phone book, and his Facebook was set to private. In the end, *he'd* been the one to contact *her*, claiming to need a day away from his overprotective sister. "Don't get me wrong," he'd said, "you're still one crazy chick. But who else in this shitty town likes good comics?"

He'd walked to her house that day, stuffed in a thick flannel jacket to protect himself from the brisk late-autumn wind. Despite the thick jacket, he was shaking.

They'd spent the next two hours talking. Em learned that Kevin's parents were traveling the country in an RV, something they'd decided to do after his dad had a heart attack and needed to de-stress. In September, Kevin had a breakdown, and had called his sister for help.

"I didn't want to call my parents," he had said. "I don't want them worrying about me. Not on their big trip."

She'd flown halfway across the country to take care of him, taking a leave from some lawyer gig in Denver. Margery had arrived just in time. Kevin had knocked back a bottle of his mom's prescription sleeping pills with a bottle of whiskey, and was waiting on his back porch for death to arrive.

"I spent a month in the hospital after that."

"And your sister never called your parents?"

"I begged her not to. I said I'd try it again if she did, but I'd use a shotgun this time." Kevin's voice had turned distant. "They're coming back in February. I don't know if I can keep it from them once they're back. They'll know something's wrong."

"Maybe not." But Em knew Kevin was right. He wouldn't be able to hide it, any better than she could.

"So, what's your story?"

"I don't know."

"No, really, you can tell me. It can't be any worse than mine."

"I mean, I really don't remember. I remember being brought to an emergency room and signing something, but nothing before that. The first couple of days in the hospital were kind of a blur. I don't really remember school at all. I was only there three weeks before I cracked up though, so it's not like I lost that much."

"What happened? Did they give you shock treatment?"

"No, nothing like that. I just can't remember."

He'd called her back the next day, inviting her to attend a book signing in Wheeling with him, which had shocked the hell out of her. Em wasn't quite sure what this was, but she also knew she didn't hate it.

She reached her hand out the car window, letting the cold wind nip at her fingertips. "Kevin, do you know who Wes Summersby is?"

"Yeah, he's that therapist guy on channel 64. My sister bought me his DVDs. She makes me listen to them."

"Do you think there's something strange about him?"

"Strange how?"

"My mom likes him. She watches him all the time. Lately she's always crying and upset, and needs to listen to Summersby to feel better again. I think he's doing something to her mind. It's like she's addicted and his show is her fix."

"Don't take this the wrong way, but that really sounds crazy." Kevin drummed an unsyncopated rhythm on the steering wheel with his knuckles. "Anyway, I listen to the DVDs, and they don't have that effect on me. I hate listening to them."

"Sorry I brought it up."

"Nah, don't be. I see why *you* wouldn't like him. You hate Dr. Slazinger and he's like the nicest guy ever."

"It's not hate. It's intense dislike. I intensely dislike Slazinger."

"Because he doesn't think much of your theories either," Kevin said, grinning. "Right?"

"I don't talk to him about this. Much."

"Whatever." Kevin pulled the car into the parking lot of a tiny convenience store. "I'm gonna go buy a pack of smokes and a pop. You want anything?"

"No, I'm fine." As her friend — her boyfriend? — went into the store Em got out of the car and stretched her legs. She lit up a cigarette.

Em never had many friends. She'd always been fixed on the future, on the places that *weren't* Clear Falls. Making personal attachments to anyone here would have interfered with her plans to leave as soon as possible and never look back. Of course, now those plans were dead and buried as the old downtown. Clear Falls was all Em had, now and forever. Maybe having at least one friend would ease the pain.

Kevin came out of the store. He handed her a candy bar. "Here, I got you this."

Em smiled and took it. "Thanks." She handed him her cigarette.

A light rain had started to fall. He took a drag and looked up at the sky. "We should head back."

"Yeah. It's getting dark."

Without warning, Kevin grabbed Em by the arm and pulled her toward him. They kissed for a long time, holding onto one another tightly to keep warm against the cold November air.

When Em showed up at work the next day, Paula wasn't there. Her lunch mate took pride in the fact that she hadn't taken a sick day since the birth of her second child. Pathetic as hell, but Em supposed even these yokels needed something to live for.

The old man at Em's side stared at her, his mustache twitching. Maybe he'd heard about the business with the box of chicken nuggets. "Boo," she said, wiggling her fingers at the old man. He turned away.

Pendleton entered the room, followed by a man in a beige polo shirt with an alligator on the pocket. The store manager cleared his throat loudly before beginning to speak. "Something very sad has happened. At three o'clock this afternoon, your coworker Paula Martin was found dead in her home of an overdose. The town coroner has listed it as a suicide."

Em gasped. The woman who'd sat across from her only a few days ago, who'd forced food on her and given her a capsule history of every employee who had ever worked at Savertown USA in the last ten years, had *killed* herself? It didn't make any sense. She looked around at the faces of her coworkers, but they remained strangely calm. Untouched.

They're not surprised, she thought. *They were expecting this.*

"As a result of this, I've hired a counselor to individually screen all employees and talk with them candidly about our two recent losses." He indicated the polo-shirted man. "This is Dr. Michaels. He will be available for anyone who needs to chat throughout today, and tomorrow as well, in the empty office across the hall. Room 109. You can speak now, doctor."

"Suicide," Dr. Michaels said, "is never the answer. No matter how hopeless things seem, there is always something to live for. Hope is always around the corner. There's nothing in your lives that's so bad that it cannot be mended. Please, for the sake of your families, your friends, your coworkers — get help, before it's too late."

"Thank you, doctor," Pendleton said. "Those are truly inspiring words. You can all go out on the floor now. Try not to overwork yourselves. You don't have to meet your quotas today."

Em couldn't even feel happy about that.

So Paula killed herself, Em thought. *Maybe she just realized how sorry her life was. I'd do the same thing if I were a middle-aged lifetime employee of Savertown USA in Clear Falls, Pennsylvania.*

But no matter how she rationalized it, it didn't square. Paula was always so cheerful, so good-natured. She loved the store. She even believed in God and everything. Em was pretty sure that Christians who killed themselves went to hell. Why would Paula, of all people, do this?

"Emmeline Kalberg, please report to room 109." Loudspeaker.

Em pocketed her box cutter and waved to Mrs. Nguyen. When she entered the room a few minutes later, she saw Dr. Michaels at one of the long conference tables. A stack of papers sat before him. "Hello, Emmeline. Please, take a seat."

"I don't need to talk to you. I'm not upset."

"Your manager Mr. Pendleton felt it would be a good idea. I agree with him." He gestured at the seat.

"I should really get back to my work. I'm behind."

"Emmeline, your manager told me a little about you. I'm sure this must be especially hard on you. Do you want to talk about it?"

"No."

"That's the grief talking. It's natural to be sad."

"I barely knew the woman."

"Your manager said you sat together for lunch nearly every day."

"*She* sat down next to *me*. I didn't care either way."

"Do you know what denial is, Miss Kalberg?" Before Em could answer, he continued on in his bland voice. "Denial is the first stage of grief. You deny your friendship with Paula Martin, because deep down you think you're responsible. That's how everybody reacts to a suicide, but it's not true. Paula Martin was depressed. You had nothing to do with it, and you have to believe that." He pushed a box of tissues toward her.

"Are you fucking kidding me?" Em slid the tissue box back to Dr. Michaels. "I *never* believed I had anything to do with this."

"Anger is the second stage of grief. You're progressing nicely."

Em stood up. "Okay, just for the record: I don't believe I had anything to do with Paula's suicide, I'm not sad about it, and I'm not going to kill myself just because she did. Can I please go unpack boxes now?"

"Your manager thinks you should take some time off." He made a note on his pad with one of his milk-white hands. "You can come back next Thursday. If you're ready, of course."

Em thought about protesting, but didn't. Maybe the talking chicken nugget boxes were a sign that she *did* need some time off.

She gathered her things from the employees' lounge and found Roger there, his gaze fixed on the OSHA placard bolted to the wall. Em considered avoiding him, but then just went for it, smiling her fakest smile at the cueballed creep.

"Hey there, Roger. I'm going to be gone for the next week. Pendleton thinks I'm a loose cannon and wants me out of here for a while. I'll see you soon though, okay?"

Roger's small blue eyes were frosted over with a glaze of terror. "We need to talk. Meet me outside the store at the end of today's shift."

Em watched the hefty man lumber back down the over-lit aisles of the store. She shrugged, left, and sat on the curb and lit a cigarette.

Em paced between the store entrance and the Home and Garden solarium, back and forth, back and forth. What could the fat man want? She grew cold when she thought of how he'd grabbed her wrist, almost snapping it. Hadn't Paula called him unbalanced?

Well, the same was true about Paula, as it had turned out. And Em couldn't exactly cast aspersions. Em stabbed her cigarette out on the curb and sunk her head in her hands. *I'll give the cretin five more minutes*, she thought, *and then I'm leaving.*

After four minutes, Roger walked out of the store, his massive frame wrapped in a huge denim jacket. He spotted Em. "Let's go," he said, jerking his thumb.

"Where are we going? I don't trust strange men."

"I don't care. I just don't want to be around the store. That pizza place, over there." He pointed to a pizza place across the parking lot.

"All right." Em followed Roger, keeping her steps short to match him. By the time they got to the restaurant, he was breathing hard.

"I'll have a diet pop. It's on him." She narrowed her eyes at Roger in the dimly lit booth. "What do you want to talk about?"

"I want to talk about the voices you've been hearing."

She frowned. "Come again?"

"Don't play dumb. I saw the burn on your forehead. The same thing happened to me a few weeks ago. First I got a burn, then I started hearing voices."

She looked out the window at the blocky facade of Savertown USA. "So?"

"You don't think this whole situation's a little strange?"

"Lots of weird things happen to me, mister. I'm a crazy person."

"But this weird thing is *actually happening*." Roger sipped at his own Diet Coke. "Listen, I didn't believe it at first either. I thought I was hallucinating again. But the same thing happened to both of us and that proves it's real."

Em rolled her straw between her fingertips. "What do you mean, 'again'?"

"I used to be schizophrenic. Haven't had an episode in twenty years. Until now. But I'm not crazy, and neither are you."

Em looked at Roger. "I think you're mistaken about that one."

Roger pouted. "I think this voice — whatever it is — has something to do with these deaths. I think whatever's behind that voice killed Jimmy and Paula."

"Escodex isn't violent," Em said. "He's just looking for information or something. And anyway, Paula was depressed."

"Yeah, I'm sure the voice would tell us if it was going to kill them." Roger said, voice dripping with sarcasm.

Em put her fingers to her temples and rubbed the sides of her head. *Nothing good can come of this*, she thought. "I have to go, Roger. This... it's too weird."

"No, don't leave. I need your *help*. I don't think the voice will talk to me again, not after the way I left it. We need to *stop* it. Together."

"I really have to go." Em stumbled up from the table, spilling her pop.

Roger wadded up a napkin and wiped it across the table. "Just be careful, Em. Don't trust anyone."

"I never do." Em left, letting the bright yellow door of the pizza place slam behind her. The sky burned orange with the setting of the sun, and as Em unlocked her bike, she felt the whisper of snowflakes on her bare hands. Winter was coming early this year.

Em spent the next week holed up in her bedroom. She blasted Fu-gazi and Bikini Kill when her mom and Jackie weren't at home, and ignored them when they came back, only entering the kitchen for an occasional snack. Kevin, for his part, was strangely distant, not responding to any of her phone calls or texts. Finally, she managed to pin him down on Twitter.

Where have you been? Em asked.

My sister doesn't want me to leave the house.

She doesn't own you. Em stabbed the screen like she was trying to shatter it. *Get your ass over here.*

I can't, Kevin replied after a fifty-minute delay. *She flipped out about you and won't let me take the car.*

Em rolled her eyes. So walk.

Another twenty minutes passed. *I'll see you soon. I promise.*

"You better." Em dropped her phone onto the carpet.

She resisted the urge to tune in to channel 64. It would only make her paranoid. Em couldn't do that to her mom and sister, and she couldn't even do it to herself. She was supposed to be taking it easy, not watching things that she *knew* would make her crazy.

Just then, she heard the roar of a car engine. Her mother was home from the bank. Em lifted the needle from her record player and waited for her mother's footfalls on the staircase.

Knock, knock. "Emmeline? Are you okay in there?"

"I'm fine. I'm reading," Em said.

"Why don't you come out." Not a question. "I'm getting Chines for dinner."

"I'll eat when I'm hungry."

The door opened with a whine of hinges. Mom slumped onto the bed with a sigh. "You're spending too much damn time in here."

Em sat up and looked at her mom, not because she wanted to, but because she knew it was what she was supposed to do. "I don't think so."

"You've gotta be feeling pretty lousy about what happened at work. Don't you want to talk about it?"

"I didn't care about those people," Em said. "I mean, I guess it's sad they're dead and all —"

Her mother held up a hand. "Your empathy is overwhelming, Em. God, you're so much like *him* that I could just spit."

Of course, Mom didn't need to define *him*. "Let me know when the food gets here. I'll come down."

But her mom just kept edging closer, until she'd put an arm around Em's shoulders. Em's body stiffened. "You know you can talk to me about anything, right?"

No, I can't, Em thought. *I can't tell you what I've been hearing in the store, because you'll lock me away again. I can't tell you that I think I'm never going to leave this place, because you'll just tell me how it's not that bad.* "Yeah."

"But you won't," Mom said, her hand sliding away. "I'll leave you alone now."

"Thank you," Em said. She rose to close the door behind her mother. It stuck, as if it didn't want to close. Em forced it shut.

When Em returned to work, she noticed a change. Wherever she walked, conversations stopped, and all eyes fell on her. When she accidentally pulled the wrong pallet from the freezer in the back of the store, Mrs. Nguyen merely clucked and ordered one of the burly men who worked in the freezer aisle to retrieve the correct one.

They know, Em thought. *Either Roger or Pendleton told everyone else about me and now they're treating me with kid gloves.* She should have felt rage. This was personal information! Mostly she just felt tired. At least this would give the chattering micro-society of Savertown USA something to gossip about until the next gay rumor.

Lunch would be a solitary activity now that Paula was dead. She tried to feel a little joy about that. Before she'd even eaten half her sandwich, she felt Roger's shadow fall over her like a penumbra.

"Go away," she mumbled through a mouthful of peanut butter and jelly.

"Has it contacted you yet? Because I think it contacted me."

"I don't know *what* you're talking about." She hunched down.

"It jumbled the letters in the nutrition information panel on the side of a box of cereal. It only happened for a second so I couldn't read it. But it was *there*."

"Maybe you need some new glasses. Or new meds, you schizo."

Roger plopped down in the chair opposite hers. His stare ground into her like a drill bit. "It'll contact you soon," Roger said. "I know it will. And when it does, you can slip me a note."

"I'm not slipping you anything. You're delusional." She wadded the rest of her sandwich into its brown paper bag and tossed the bag into a nearby trashcan. *Three points*, she thought, *and the crowd goes wild.*

Roger began the laborious task of rising from his chair. Em could almost see his sweat run in rivulets down his hairy back. "Fine, I'll leave. God forbid I tarnish your reputation. But if anyone else dies, it'll be on *your* head, missy." He jabbed a finger at her.

Guilt doesn't work on me, she thought, letting him have the last word. A minute later, the loudspeaker sounded, and Em and the others were called to the sales floor.

Work made Em feel like a real person. She certainly didn't feel that way at home. Even when she could steal away a few minutes for herself, as she walked down by the abandoned train yards or rode her bike into the dead downtown, she was acutely aware of the things which made her different from most people. Em always felt as if there was a haze separating her from the world.

This, though, this made sense. Routinely slotting items into their respective holes made her feel like a useful machine. She didn't have to think to do this job. All she had to do was move.

As she loaded ultra-high fructose ice cream into the freezer, she thought about the two-year plan she and Slazinger had devised. If she could go that long without a break, and stay medication compliant, Slazinger would talk to her mother about allowing her to resume college. Em wanted that to happen, she wanted it so badly... or did she? If she graduated college, she'd have to get a better job. Which meant more stress. Which meant going crazy.

Maybe by then they'll make a better pill, she thought. *Something to remove the haze once and for all, to truly make me part of reality.* Em wasn't about to bet on that, though. The more likely outcome remained failure.

As if in answer, the label atop the carton of ice cream she held in her gloved, cold hand started to melt and reform into a sinister pattern. Em shoved the ice cream into the case and covered it with a carton of fruit-shaped popsicles.

Em found the tract in her underwear drawer, folded underneath a neatly stacked pile of bras. She turned the bright pink pamphlet around in her hands a few times before bursting into Jackie's room.

"Did you put this in my drawer?"

Jackie looked up from the book she was reading. "Jesus saves, Em."

"I don't want you touching my stuff. Especially not with this trash."
Em threw the tract down on the hardwood floor of Jackie's room. It
landed softly, like a feather.

Jackie's lips fluttered in what Em took to be a silent prayer. When
she spoke again, her words were measured. "Why are you so dismissive
of the Word? I only want to help you, Sister."

"What's the deal, you get a toaster for every new convert you bring
in?"

"Lord, bless this sinner. She knows not what she does."

Em shook her head. "You've changed, Jackie."

"You should talk." Jackie lifted a copy of the *Teen Guide to the Bible*
in front of her face.

"News flash, Jackie: there's no God."

"I'm not listening."

"Think about it, kiddo. What kind of God would make me sick this
way, huh? And why did God send Dad away? Why don't you ask him
that one?"

"You're just making fun of me."

"That's right. Your views are ridiculous."

"Please go away, Em. I won't put anything else in your room. Just
leave me alone."

Em picked up the tract and laid it atop a stack of identical ones on
her sister's dresser. "Do you ever think about him, Jackie?"

"God? All the time."

"No, Dad."

She could see Jackie's head shake even through the barrier of the guide. "Never."

"You're lying." Em left the room, quietly closing the door behind her. *Fuck this place*, she thought, *I'm going out for a smoke.*

In the kitchen, Em ran into her mother, who was wrist-deep in bread dough. "You don't cook," Em said as she fumbled in her bag for her cigarettes.

"You know a lot about what people don't do, don't you?"

"What?"

Her mother's expression softened. "Here, help me," she said as she thrust one of Em's fists into the dough.

Em kneaded, squishing the rubbery substance between her fingers and palms, hearing the faint pops and sighs of the yeast at work.

"Put some more flour in it," her mother said as she wiped her hands on her apron front.

Yes, Em thought, *she likes this. She's found something her crazy daughter might not screw up. Whoop-de-doo, I can knead bread. At least if my next try at college doesn't go well I have this to fall back on.* "Thanks."

"So, what are you doing today? Any plans?"

"Um, I have work. From three to ten. I thought I told you that."

"Oh, that again. You know, Em, maybe I was wrong about that job. If you want to quit, it's fine with me."

"You just don't want to drive me there," Em said, letting her gaze fall back down to the lump of dough. *Because it's twenty minutes each way through the snow, twenty minutes that would be better spent watching reruns of sitcoms and staring into space.*

"It's up to you."

"I don't want to quit."

"Fine then." Her mother slopped the dough into a pan and slid it into the oven so hard it hit against the opposite side with a clang.

Em sighed and washed her hands in the kitchen sink. "Mom, do you ever think about Dad?"

"Your father is dead. I'm not wasting my life on a dead man."

Yeah right, Em thought. "The police never confirmed that. They never found a body. He could still be alive out there."

Her mother's lips became a pencil-thin line. "You are not to mention that man in this house again, Emmeline Kalberg. You are not allowed to talk about him to me. You are not allowed to talk about him with your sister. He's *dead!*" Hot spit rocketed onto Em's eyelid.

Em blinked. "I'll ride my bike to work today." She banged the screen door behind her. She'd be early, but for once she'd rather be at Savertown USA.

Em scanned the aisle until she knew the coast was clear. She pulled her box cutter from her pocket and sliced open a case of frozen turkey dinners. She took one last look around before pressing the ice-encrusted dinner to her ear.

"I'm in."

EIGHT

"I'm glad you've decided to come to your senses," Escodex said. "I suppose you finally got tired of seeing your friends die."

"I don't care about these hicks. I want to find my father."

"It doesn't matter why you help me, as long as you do it."

A pragmatist, Em thought. *I like that.* "I'm going to help you, but if we're going to work together, you need to follow some rules."

"Okay," Escodex said. She could have sworn there was a mocking note in his flat tone.

"First of all, I don't want you manipulating what I see or making me hear you when I don't want you to. When I want to talk, I'll put the box up to my ear, like now. None of this 'freak out the crazy girl' shit."

"What if it's an emergency?"

"I have the upper hand here, Escodex. Deal with it."

"Okay, fine. I'll only hijack your brain when you're within three centimeters of the box," he said. "That's about one inch."

"I *know.*" Em sensed a customer nearby, and switched her method of conversation over to thought. *Second, nothing illegal.*

"You'll have to. This job requires breaking into offices and gathering information."

Well, okay, I can do that. But no killing.

"That's fine. More than fine. I'm trying to *prevent* killing."

Third, I can quit any time I want.

"No. I've had too many partners give out on me before. If you go in, you're in for the long haul."

No deal. She started to peel the box away from her head.

"Then you'll never find out what happened to your father."

"You bastard," Em said aloud. "You know where he is right now, don't you?"

"I'm not authorized to reveal that information."

"I *have* to be able to walk away," Em sobbed. *And you might turn out not to be real.*

"I've agreed to two of your demands," Escodex said. "And I *am* real, Em, and so is this being that's trying to destroy your world. You know what happened to those two people."

And I know what happened to Roger, she thought. Even if Roger was crazy, which he was, it was beyond coincidence that they would both be contacted by the same voice, with the same unusual name. "Okay. It's a deal. I'll help you until the case is closed. How long will that take?"

"It depends on multiple factors."

"So in short, you don't know."

"Could be weeks, could be months. It's complicated."

I'll bet.

"You really don't know how important you are, Em. Right now, you're probably the most important person in your dimension."

Delusions of grandeur, Em thought. She tore the box from her ear and shoved it onto an ice-encrusted shelf, muffling it with several other boxes. The most important person in the world doesn't stock shelves at Savertown USA. *The most important person in the world doesn't need her mom to drive her to work, and she doesn't need to drop out of college after three weeks. She doesn't need to make covert plans to see her own boyfriend.*

Em wasn't the most important person in the world. She was just a girl looking for her father.

Escodex gave Em her first assignment later that day. "I need you to break into Mr. Pendleton's office," he'd said. "Search for anything weird."

"Like?"

"Just things out of the ordinary. Unusual notes. Write-ups for employee behavior. Based on incidents in other dimensional planes, the entity starts by infecting one person, one nerve center through which it will recruit others. It's often the last person you'd expect."

Wouldn't that person be me?

"It's not you, Em."

She broke communication.

Remember, she thought as she pulled a straightened bobby pin from her khakis, *you're doing this for Dad. What if he's in trouble?* Em had not ever believed that her father had just abandoned the family. Her father loved her too much to just run out. When she was a child, she used to fantasize that he had been kidnapped by terrorists, or recruited into some covert government spy program. But as an adult, she'd arrived at an even better explanation.

Fugue states. That was what they were called — long bouts with amnesia often resulting from a bump on the head or gross psychological trauma. A fugue state explained why her father had never contacted her.

Of course he wasn't dead.

But Em couldn't think about her father right now. She had to get in and out of Pendleton's office before the pep rally was over, while everyone was distracted. At least she'd learned how to pick locks in the hospital, under the tutelage of Trevor the Jesus Freak.

"All those poor little babies," he'd said with a sad shake of his head. "They were just begging me to liberate them."

"Babies?"

"The government denies their humanity. They call them genetic waste. Every life is sacred." Em later figured out he was talking about looting the surplus frozen embryos from fertility clinic dumpsters.

Pendleton's lock sprang even more easily than she thought it would. *They probably took this lock right off the Savertown shelves*, Em thought, *that's why it's so crappy.* She eased open the door, bracing for a squeak.

It didn't. Em stepped inside, hunkering down low so nobody could see her through the scratched Plexiglas walls. As the Savertown morale song rang through the break room, Em spread the contents of Pendleton's desk out on the blotter. "Low prices, all the time," then two hand claps, "low prices, for yours and mine." Em shuddered and pulled out her cell phone.

She finished just as the final round of rhythmic hand clapping ended. Em tucked her phone into her vest pocket and slipped out of Pendleton's office. She stumbled a little on the way out, sending the door crashing into the frame with a rattle. *Shit.* Em put the lock back on, not caring whether she made any noise or not. The goal now was speed, not silence.

She joined the stream of workers leaving the break room. Some of them gave her the evil eye — missing the daily pep rallies was a major violation of the employee handbook — but she ignored them. Em wasn't so lucky, though, when Mrs. Nguyen caught her eye.

"Where were you?"

"Bathroom," Em sneered as she went back to the sales floor and a waiting interdimensional detective.

The neon lights of the gas station shone off Kevin's full lips and rosy cheeks in what Em thought was kind of a really attractive way. She leaned over, across the pile of discarded food wrappers between them, and kissed his earlobe.

"What was that for?"

"I really like you, Kevin."

"I really like you too, Em." He smiled, revealing a row of slightly crooked teeth. Em loved his smile. She could look at those imperfect teeth all day and never be bored.

Two weeks had passed since she last saw Kevin. His sister was being more overprotective than ever. According to Kevin, she had hidden the keys to the car in the shed, and he had only found them when searching for the backup snow shovel after the handle broke on their first one. Em wondered why he didn't hot-wire the car, or better yet just walk to Em's house, but she didn't want to get into a fight with Kevin on one of their stolen moments together.

Across the parking lot sat high school students in their parents' cars, top 40 radio fuzzily blasting from the overextended speakers. This was the main hangout spot in Clear Falls, a place where every person of high school and college age and even some older people went to socialize, eat terrible food, and make out. It made Em nervous to be around so many people and so much noise, but she didn't let it show.

"What are you thinking about?"

"I'm not thinking about anything. I'm a guy."

"Hilarious. But I'm serious. You're so quiet."

"I'm just enjoying the moment, being here with you. Even when there's people around, I feel so alone when I'm with you. It's a nice feeling."

Em took one of Kevin's hands in hers and traced the lines in his palms. "You know, we could just leave."

Kevin looked at the milling crowds. "Too many people?" He reached for the gearshift.

"No, I mean… completely. We could, I don't know, run away."

"And go where?"

Em shrugged. "Pittsburgh? Columbus? Ecuador? Any place would be better than this dump."

Kevin pulled his hand away. "Clear Falls isn't so bad."

"Says the guy who almost killed himself to get out of this hellhole."

"Clear Falls had nothing to do with that."

Em rolled down her window and lit a cigarette, ignoring Kevin's frown. "I mean it. We don't have to stay here. We're both adults and there isn't anything keeping us here. Legally, I mean."

Kevin shook his head. "I'm not leaving my sister. She needs me."

Em took a big drag. "She treats you like shit."

"Hey, just because you don't care about *your* family —"

Em held up a hand. "Drop it. Why don't we drive back to my house?" She saw Kevin tense up. "I don't know."

"I have *needs*, Kevin."

He swallowed. "I'll just take you home."

Em blew smoke directly on Margery's white upholstery. "Don't bother. I'll walk." She slammed the car door behind her and headed into the night.

NINE

Em adjusted the volume on her stereo, turning the treble all the way up so that she could better hear the high tones in the Wes Summersby DVD she had borrowed from her mother's bedroom.

God, she hated the sound of the man's voice. Summersby struck a tone between Dr. Slazinger and Cotton Mather: faux-caring most of the time, but occasionally breaking into fire and brimstone. He was in a fire and brimstone mood at the moment, and the signals were coming in thick and fast.

Em had detected a high-pitched whine that ran throughout Summersby's sermons slash healing sessions. The whine wavered in strength and pitch, sometimes loud enough to make Em's eardrums pound, other times fading out altogether. It followed no repeating pattern that Em could detect, though she hadn't analyzed many of the DVDs yet. There were a lot of them to go through, and she could only take Wes Summersby's voice for so long before needing a break.

There was a certain speech that Em had reviewed a number of times. It was the five second pause right after Wes had finished his spiel about the five Cs of caring: compassion, consideration — Em knew it all by heart by now. He was just about to take scripted questions from the studio audience when the whine came in. This one was different, more "literal-sounding" than the rest of what she'd heard. It almost sounded like words.

"Trust … me … kill yourself … I know … take …"

Em tore the headphones from her ears. This was getting to be a little too intense. She kicked her headphones to the other side of the room and went to get her bike.

She slowly made her way down the potholed suburban streets to the abandoned tire factory on the shore of the Monongahela. Frigid air tunneled its way into her coat sleeves, biting into her skin with bitter teeth.

The tire factory was Em's favorite place in town, maybe the *only* place she liked in town. Once, the factory had provided work for almost a quarter of the town's population. Clear Falls had once been the tire manufacturing center of the eastern United States. Now it sat empty, only used occasionally during the summer as a meeting ground for the town's homeless population. And even most of them had set out for Pittsburgh. *Lucky them.*

At times like this, when there were no people in sight and no walls to block the view, the world felt so big to Em, so complex. When she was alone, outside in the elements, Em could sometimes swear that she saw God.

Religion in Em's family had been a lot like donating to public broadcasting: her mom considered it a nice idea, but she didn't participate in it. Religion was for other people, the ones who needed it. Which made Jackie's conversion all the more perplexing.

Em dropped down on the broken curb of the tire factory and lit a cigarette. If she could only find a way to connect her twisted mind with the minds around her, maybe she could tell people once and for all about the dangers that surrounded them. As if on cue, blueprints flowered into her head, a machine of wood and brass, a transceiver —

A machine like that had existed once. She had built it. That was all she knew.

I'm starting to remember, Em thought with giddiness. *I'm start-*

*ing to remember the events of my breakdown, the reason why I was
sent to the hospital and had to leave school.*

She was emerging from her own fugue state.

Should she think about it? It might cause her to go crazy again.
Could she think about it? This machine, whatever it was, had been
totally wiped from her memory for months. Even now, the details
were being plucked from her mind one by one. All that was left was
the memory of remembering it.

And even that memory might be faulty, Em thought. She was living a fiction that felt like fact. A 3-D movie full of exciting sights
and smells and especially sounds and voices, being broadcast 24/7
to her cerebral cortex. It was realer than real. But it was all fiction
nonetheless.

Em stubbed out her cigarette and mounted her bike. With the
wind at her back, she rode away from the abandoned factory, guiding her mint-green Huffy around banks of leaves and patches of ice
which glinted like plates set into the road. The universe was speaking to her again.

There must be a million things that cause cancer in this stuff, Em
thought as she looked at the can of fake snow. *Awesome.*

In three days it would be Christmas and Em really didn't care.
Christmas had never been a big deal in the Kalberg household even
when her father was still there. Presents were rarely exchanged, and
their parents only put a tree up when Em and Jackie begged for one.

"You know," her mother had said, "we're actually supposed to be
Jewish. Kalberg is a Jewish name." But she'd bought the tree anyway.

Nowadays, Jackie would have a fit if Em put up the tree. Secular
blasphemy, she'd say. Not in keeping with Christ's spirit. Which is

exactly why Em was hunkered in the crawl space, dusting the spiders off the water-damaged cardboard box.

Em dragged the box upstairs, leaving a trail of dirt on the carpeted stairs. As she sliced open the box with a pair of scissors held flat she was overcome by a blast of disintegrated tinsel billowing off the tree's plastic boughs.

She assembled the tree, sticking the pipe cleaner-like branches to the stark metal pole that served as the trunk. Then she started putting on the ornaments. They were kept in old shoeboxes, the more fragile ones wrapped in newspapers dating back to before she was born. Her mother's old ones, she deduced. She handled the transparent bulbs and blown shapes with a light touch, placing them on the artificial twigs carefully so they wouldn't fall and shatter on the steel disc at the base of the tree.

Em thought back to the last Christmas present she had received from her father. It was a children's microscope. She hadn't been interested in science then, not like he was, and she still wasn't — conversations with interdimensional detectives notwithstanding. But she had loved it, because it came from him. It had been the last present her father had ever given her. He'd gone into his fugue state in mid-January the next year.

After the ornaments were up, she dusted the tree with a light coat of fake snow. Em coughed as the vile chemical cocktail trailed up her nose and into her lungs. *This is way more dangerous than smoking,* she thought. *Has to be.*

Just then, she heard rustling behind her. "Hello, Jackie," she said, turning around.

"Mom's going to kill you when she sees all this dust on the floor."

"So I'll clean it."

Jackie sniffed. "The commercialization of Christmas is a direct affront to our Lord. I find this display to be revolting and offensive."

"Cut the crap. You're not even supposed to be reading that," Em said, pointing to the Bible in Jackie's hand. "We're Jewish."

"Jesus was a Jew, too."

"Well, you saw what happened to him. Now get out of my face before I crucify your ass."

Jackie slunk away.

Her sister may not have been game, but everyone at Savertown USA had been in the Christmas spirit since roughly mid-October. Tinny carols squeaked out of the locker-sized speakers at the four corners of the store, and the ceiling was festooned with a canopy of red, white, and blue tinsel from which dangled many oversized inflatable ornaments. Paper Santas and menorahs were tacked haphazardly to the patriotic walls.

Em hadn't heard from Escodex in a week, though she pressed her ear to a frozen dinner at the beginning of every shift. She allowed herself to enjoy the silence. Roger, meanwhile, was nowhere to be found.

She was busy standing up all the boxes of food so they would face the customers — an exercise in futility if ever there was one — when there was a tap on her shoulder.

"I wanted to give you your Christmas present a little early."

"Shit! You startled me," Em said, crossing her arms over the ugly vest. Kevin recoiled, but she calmed him with a touch to his cheek. "I didn't want you to see me like this."

"I know you work here, Em," he said, rolling his eyes.

Worlds colliding, Em thought. *Not good.* "At least let me get out of this vest. I look like such a dork." There were fifteen minutes left in her shift, but Mrs. Nguyen was off today so there was nobody watching her. Em stripped off the vest and bunched it into a tiny ball.

Kevin handed her the package. It was wrapped in silver paper so shiny that she could see ghostly reflections of her face on the surface. The top was decked with a miniature red bow. "For you," Kevin said.

It was a deluxe hardcover omnibus of *The Hardened Criminals*, signed by the artist. "Where did you *get* this?"

"Pittsburgh Comics Expo. You couldn't go because you had to work."

She kissed him on his full lips, and ran her hand through his blond hair. "Thank you. I'm sorry we had a fight."

He waved. "It's nothing."

"Come on, let's get something to eat."

"Don't you have to finish your shift?"

Em looked around at the shelves of boxes still askew, the floor tracked with the black lines of countless feet, the sticky-fingered children waiting in line by the Santa throne near her aisle, scream-ing their heads off.

"Screw it." She took Kevin by the hand and together they raced out of the store, a synthesized boy-band version of "O Holy Night" at their heels.

Em awoke on Christmas morning with her feet frozen solid as bricks. She pulled on a pair of thick socks and padded down to the living room.

No presents, of course, just the tree with its cloud of carcinogenic snow. Em fixed herself a bowl of cereal and sat underneath the tree. She propped open the copy of *The Hardened Criminals* Kevin gave her and started reading.

The plot, stretched out over twelve issues, involved the escape of a convict of indeterminate gender from a sentient prison. Drawn in black and white with random drips of color, it wasn't anything you could pick up at the Clear Falls Books-A-Million. Em related to the nameless, featureless escapee. Although the prison doors formed out of two giant breasts were just *weird*.

The front door slammed on its hinges. Jackie came in, her face wrapped in a scarf. "Cold out there," she said.

"Sure is. That's why I'm in here."

"Oh, it's you. I thought it was Mom."

"You know she never gets up before noon on her off days." Em drank the remainder of her milk and set the bowl down. "How was the Bible meeting?"

"Like you really care."

"Honor thy sister."

"That's not in the Bible." Jackie peeled off her coat. "It was fine."

"Hey, I got you something." Em took a small package from a hiding place behind the couch. "I know you think it's blasphemous, but I saw this —"

"It *is* blasphemous. And why would I want anything from you anyway? You don't even like me."

"That's not true."

"I'm going to my room. If Mom comes downstairs, tell her I'm back." Jackie stomped up the stairs and slammed her door. Em heard the lock click behind her.

Where did we go so wrong? Em thought. Sighing, she took her bowl and spoon into the kitchen and put them in the sink.

She had to get out of the house. Shrugging on her thick parka, she made her way down the icy sidewalk. Snow fell hard against her hunched shoulders, and the wind bit at her nose and ears, but still she trudged on. Every house save hers was decorated to the nines with rows of colored lights and plastic Santas in the front yard. Inside the houses, happy families were congregating around over-decorated trees and neatly wrapped presents. Em wondered just how many of those presents had been bought at Savertown USA. *Probably a lot*, she thought. *So many conduits for Escodex to communicate through. Too bad his influence doesn't reach beyond the store, or I could talk to him at least.*

"Emmeline?" a voice behind her said. Em jumped, spinning around. "Is that Emmeline Kalberg, Bea's kid?"

"I'm sorry?" Em said, scanning the unfamiliar woman who'd just stepped off her front porch.

"It's me, Mrs. Arroway. Denise's mom. Why, I haven't seen you in ages. You haven't been over at the house since what, eighth grade?"

"I've been a little busy."

"What are you doing out here? You'll catch your death."

I wish. "Oh, just enjoying the lights," she said, before realizing it was daytime.

"It's Christmas. You should be at home. Come on, I'll drive you back to your house."

"No thank you, Mrs. Arroway. We don't celebrate Christmas. We're Jewish." *Well,* thought Em, *that's almost the truth.*

"Oh." Mrs. Arroway rubbed her gloved hands together against the cold. "So how do you like college? I heard you got into Oberlin."

She doesn't know. Mrs. Arroway hadn't heard about Em's breakdown, and she didn't know Em worked at Savertown USA. Maybe she drove an hour to the Whole Foods instead. Em wrapped herself in a thicker web of lies. "I like it fine. I'm majoring in political science."

"It's pretty cold out here, Em. Do you want to come inside and warm up? Denise will be back soon. You two used to be so close."

That was true, they had. But then they entered high school, and while Denise had plunged full-force into the banquet of social opportunities that were available — student government, cheerleading, French club — Em had spent her days writing poetry and sneaking smokes behind the auxiliary gym. They'd never really spoken to one another since, save muttered hellos in the halls between classes. It *would* be good to see her old friend again, to see if the distance of graduation had healed the rift. "If it wouldn't be too much trouble —"

"Not at all. Hurry, though, my fingers are freezing."

Em walked underneath the mistletoe above the Arroways' door and breathed in the spicy scent of eggnog. In the corner, a CD of Christmas carols was playing in an old boombox. A tree — so imperfect under its trimmings that it had to be real — stood in the opposite corner.

"You have a lovely house, Mrs. Arroway," Em said, hoping she didn't sound like too much of a suck-up.

"Call me Linda." The friendly woman went into the kitchen. "I'll make us some cocoa. The others are taking a drive, but they'll be back soon."

Em sat down on the overstuffed couch. Mrs. Arroway's house looked like a picture in a magazine. It was neat as a pin, the coffee table covered with fashion and lifestyle magazines whose spines weren't even cracked. The smell of potpourri was practically baked into the paneled walls. And although Em didn't know for sure what did or did not constitute "good" furniture, she figured that everything in the house would count, if one were counting.

You know what they say, Em told herself. *Their house might look nice, but really they're the most dysfunctional family that ever lived. Linda probably beat Denise and her brother every day of their lives. She fed them rancid meat and spoiled milk.* But as she heard Linda humming away to the music in the kitchen, she knew that wasn't true. That was just a lie that people who come from real dysfunctional families told themselves.

Linda came out of the kitchen, a steaming mug in each hand. "This'll warm us up."

"Thanks." Em sipped at her cocoa.

"So what classes are you taking?"

Just what Em needed. She spun another lie. "Oh, you know, political classes. An introduction course, and also I'm taking this class on Marxist rhetoric in the age of machines. The semester's over, though."

"How were your grades?"

"As and Bs."

"Good." Linda shot a few glances at the window. *She's waiting for them to come back*, Em thought, *because she's scared of the crazy person.* No, wait, that was just paranoia. Linda didn't know about Em's condition. And if Em was smart, she never would.

Em made small talk with Linda until Mr. Arroway, Denise, and Denise's brother Sam came home, then fell into conversation until early evening. They gave her a plate of Christmas dinner and begged her to have seconds, and when she refused they shoved Tupperware into her hands. None of them knew, or they were all too polite to mention, that Em worked at Savertown USA. They all thought she was a normal college student home on break.

And best of all, Denise had changed. She wasn't stuck up anymore, and the two of them made frenzied plans to hang out on New Year's Eve.

This can't last forever, Em thought as she walked home through the blustering wind. *They'll find out eventually. Clear Falls is a very small town.* But right now, she had friends, and it felt so good.

*B*owling: *It's Right Up Your Alley!* Em groaned and tore the flier from the wall.

For the past few weeks, Mrs. Nguyen had been blanketing the Savertown USA break room with photocopied fliers for the store bowling championship. Em wasn't about to spend her off-hours hefting ten-pound balls in some beer-reeking bowling alley. Lately, though, she had the feeling that her supervisor had been scoping her out as a possible addition to the team.

"Come on, Em," she'd whined. "Don't you want to get those jerks in general merchandise?"

"Not really. I don't even know them."

"We've got a good shot this year. Old Lady Walker isn't playing, and I just bought myself a new ball."

"I *hate* sports."

Mrs. Nguyen had made a tsk-tsk sound. "Bowling's not a sport. Anyway, this is a store tradition. We'd all really like it if you played. Won't you consider it?"

"Fine, I will."

A roll of the eyes. "No, you won't. But I'll keep working on you, missy."

At least there hadn't been any more deaths since Paula's suicide nearly a month ago. Was Escodex's work coming to fruition, or was it a coincidence? Em didn't care about these people, but she was glad they weren't falling over dead every other week. Who knew what the store counselor would say to her — or accuse her of — the next time some hick bit the dust?

"Attention, people," Mr. Pendleton said as he clapped his hands.

"We're three minutes behind schedule. Time is money."

As the rest of the workers sang the Savertown USA jingle, Em watched Roger, his mouth silently echoing the vapid words. Nobody had asked *him* to join the bowling team. *Well, who wants a fat, bald, creepy schizophrenic on their bowling team? At least I have all my hair.*

At the front of the room, Pendleton clapped his hands together. "Now, as you all might have read, Savertown USA stock is up a phenomenal two points. Let's all give ourselves a hand! Great job, team!"

Yeah, Em thought, *the work effort of a bunch of small-town rubes is sure going to impact the stock price. Will these people see any of that money? Didn't think so.*

"As a bonus for our dedication, the regional manager is going to make a surprise visit to our very own store sometime in January." Em rolled her eyes as the rest of the workers oohed and aahed. "He'll be personally handing out that month's Employee of the Month prize, so I'm sure you're all going to work extra hard for that."

Sure thing, Em thought.

"But we'll have to pitch in to get this store ready. We'll be carrying in a lot of new products, and we'll be bleaching the floors. I want those products to be neat and organized on the shelves so every customer has access to them. I'll be setting up special teams to get us in shape, and I may offer some of you extra shifts."

Em shut her eyes and daydreamed, taking herself far away from the store into what Dr. Slazinger had called her "happy place," a zone that she could escape to whenever the outside world was too much for her fractured mind to handle. Slowly, Pendleton's chatter faded into a low hum as she blocked out all external stimuli and forced herself into a place of stasis.

Em's happy place was bursting with the best memories from her youth and the projected memories of things that had not actually happened, but should have. There, her father was alive and well. There, she was still in school. She had never lost her mind. She had never been forced into servitude at Savertown USA.

The happy place was infinitely better than real life.

She couldn't totally block out Pendleton's speech. It rose and fell like the ocean, occasional words like "profit" and "point of sale" pricking the extreme ends of her consciousness. Em coped as well as she could with the intrusions, but Pendleton's words kept sucking her back, until she couldn't stay in fantasyland for more than a few seconds at a time. After a while, she realized the problem: there was a pattern to Pendleton's speech.

She followed the pattern. It moved around curves and bends, a very complex pattern, faintly repeating. She dove into it, searching for the deeper meaning that could only be found with intense rumination.

I am here, the pattern said, *and I am waiting. Waiting to ascend, waiting for my energy to expand to the level I need to rise upwards. I am so close. I am so close to where I need to be.* All of a sudden, a grotesque image of nothing and everything at once, a black-white figure of immense size and infinitesimal proportions that reached its fingers into her brain, gnawing at her, forcing her to open her eyes and rejoin reality.

"So let's get out there!" Pendleton said.

Em staggered out into the fluorescent lights of the sales floor. After fetching a pallet from the freezer in the back room, she ripped open a case of food and held a box to her ear.

"Hey, Em. Great job on that last assignment. I have something new —"

Of course you do, Em thought.

Escodex's newest assignment would require Em to be in the store until after midnight. He wanted to monitor the movements and actions of the night workers, to see if the entity's nerve center was among them.

"You day workers have to be presentable since people in the outside world see you," Escodex had said. "You have to function as reasonably normal human beings. The night workers don't have that problem. Most of them don't have families or friends. They're the perfect breeding ground for the entity. I haven't been able to get any sort of picture of what the store looks like after hours. It could already be recruiting."

I don't want to waste my nights at this shitty place, Em protested. She didn't want to waste her nights at the store. *And anyway, I have New Year's plans.* "If the entity takes over your dimension," Escodex replied patiently, "your friends will no longer exist."

Fine, Em thought, putting the box on the shelf. She turned to her supervisor. "Mrs. Nguyen, I'd like to work a couple of nights this week."

"Nights?" her supervisor said. "Nobody wants to work nights."

"I need some extra money. Please? Just two or three shifts. Mr. Pendleton said he needs additional help anyway."

"I'm not supposed to give out shifts. That's Pendleton's job." Mrs. Nguyen chewed her lower lip. "I *could* be persuaded to talk him into it if —"

"I bribe you?"

"The bowling championship. We need you. Do that and I'll let you work a couple nights."

"But I've never bowled before in my life!"

"You're young, you're strong, and you're the only person in this store besides me who isn't morbidly obese. You'll be quick on the lanes. And we need another woman."

The thought of participating in social activities with her coworkers made Em want to vomit. She started to shake her head no, but an image of her father surfaced. *Remember*, Em thought, *I'm doing this for him. I have to find him, whatever it takes.* "Okay, I'll do it. I'll be in your stupid bowling tournament."

"It's not stupid," Mrs. Nguyen said. "It's tradition."

"So how was your weekend?"

Em slouched down in the uncomfortable faux-leather high-backed chair and glared at Dr. Slazinger. *Too bad shrinks don't use couches anymore,* she thought. *I need a nap.* "It was okay. I worked, mostly."

"And how is that going for you?"

"Oh, you know, work is work. Certainly no alien beings broadcasting messages into my head."

"Uh-huh." Slazinger made a notation on his chart.

"I was being sarcastic."

"I'm supposed to help you, Em. When you say things like that, I'm not totally sure whether you're joking or being serious."

She lowered her head. "I was joking."

"I heard something very interesting. Is it true that you're in a relationship with a boy named Kevin Collins?"

"What's it to you?"

"Kevin is a client of mine. Did you know that?"

Em met Slazinger's gaze. "Yes."

"Well, how are you getting along with him? Is everything going smoothly?"

Em shrugged. "I guess. I don't really want to talk about Kevin with you."

"That's what I'm here for, Em. To listen. Where did you meet Kevin?"

"Here. Well, out there," Em said, pointing toward the door and the waiting room beyond.

"Do you have things in common?"

"There's *you*." Em gave Slazinger her best sneer, but still her therapist retained the same calm, calculating demeanor. *I really do hate him*, she thought.

"Besides me."

"Yeah. I mean, we like being around each other. At least, I like being around him. The sex is pretty great, and anyway, we have something in common. Both of us are consistently put down by a society that seeks to tear us down at any turn. Are you laughing at me?"

"No," Slazinger said, his long-fingered hand over his mouth. "Why would you say that?"

"You *are* laughing at me." Em crossed her arms. "I know what you're thinking. You're going to try to break us up."

"Em, is Kevin your first boyfriend?"

"I don't see how that matters."

Slazinger put his notebook on the table near his chair and leaned forward. "I believe that part of the reason you are so protective of this relationship and want to preserve it stems from the novelty of having a relationship. I'm not saying you don't love Kevin —"

"You better not be saying that," Em spat.

"— I'm just saying that this is a new experience for you. Don't get so wrapped up in this relationship that you lose sight of your own recovery. You need to focus on yourself, Em, not on Kevin."

Em stared out the window. A full foot of snow blanketed the medical plaza where Slazinger's office was located. The plaza also housed the offices of an eye doctor, as well as a dentist. As she watched, a woman exited the dentist's office, dragging a small boy behind her. Em wanted desperately to be that little boy with his simple toothache. Em reached her hand out to the window as if to draw herself into their scene, into their reality.

"Em, are you listening to me?"

"What?"

Slazinger snapped his fingers. "I'm over here, Em."

"I know where you are," she said, tearing her eyes away from the parking lot. The little boy and his mother had vanished and a thick carpet of footprint-studded white spread out in the space where they had been.

But, Em thought, *do I know where I am?*

Savertown USA became a different place at night. Without the bustle of customers, it was quiet, almost peaceful. A girl could get a lot of thinking done in a place like this.

Mrs. Nguyen's night shift equivalent was a sixty-year-old named Fred. He never spoke, except to tell Em which pallet to pull from the big freezer in the back. Fred didn't know about Em's "condition." He left her alone. Em liked Fred.

Roger wasn't there either, and that was an even greater blessing. Even though he hadn't hassled her in weeks, he emanated a creepy vibe that surrounded him like a living cloud.

Am I that creepy? Em wondered, and shrugged. She couldn't help it if she was.

Escodex had told Em to report in at three a.m. She checked the large clock on the wall. One-thirty. *Damn.*

She returned to the comfort of the stocking routine, letting the time roll by. Without small talk from customers or workers, or Mrs. Nguyen's screeching, work went by a lot quicker. She was actually surprised when she looked up from her work to see the clock reading three.

After making sure Fred wasn't around, Em picked up the nearest box and held it to her ear.

"What do you have for me?" It was barely a question.

"*Hello*, Escodex. Or are my Earth pleasantries too much for you to handle?"

"Any odd behaviors? Strange smells or visions? Perhaps you should take some pictures or video, like you did in Pendleton's office."

"Why don't you just dip into my memory? I've already seen these zombies up close and personal."

The word "zombie" didn't describe half of it. The night workers all had a gray pallor to their skin. Em could almost see dust in their pores. Their dead eyes rolled around in their sockets like marbles. Either they were ground zero for the great entity invasion, or their poor health was the natural result of years of night-shift work.

"The beings on your plane of existence don't have very clear memories. They are tainted by your preconceived notions and prejudices. If I took from your memory, it would be a picture of what Emmeline Kalberg thinks the world looks like, not what the world actually looks like. My evidence needs to be objective."

"Do you think I'd lie to you?"

"It's not lying. Lying is deliberate. This is a necessary delusion, and you all do it. Human beings — at least the ones in your dimension — don't possess the mental faculties necessary to face true reality. If you saw how insignificant your individual lives really are, you would fall into a deep depression, and be forced to self-destruct. The only remedy is an egocentric worldview."

Enlightenment is suicide, Em thought.

"Exactly."

"I'll get your pictures. I'll take them at the break." She checked her phone. Almost time.

"Thank you, Em. Is that enough pleasantry for you?"

Em rolled her eyes, hoping that Escodex could detect and interpret it, and tore the box from her ear. She stocked the rest of the case, then went to the back room, where she fetched her phone and brown paper lunch bag from her locker.

In the break room, she huddled in a corner and pretended to be engrossed in a copy of the company newsletter, *Newstown USA*. Stealing glances over the top of the pages, she took out her phone and started snapping pictures.

None of them paid any attention to her. If they saw the phone, they didn't care. Em took stills interspersed with the occasional thirty-second movie until the phone was almost out of charge. Then a beefy hand covered with black fur clamped on her arm.

"Who are you?" Em said before she realized that the man wore a nametag reading "Tony." Idiot.

"I'm Tony, the night manager. What do you think you're doing?"

Think fast. "I'm writing an article about how great our store is. For, um, this," she said, indicating the copy of Newstown USA.

"No, you're not." Tony snatched the phone from Em's hand. "You're being weird."

"Give it back!" Em made a desperate grab for the phone.

"I'll bring this up with Lars when he comes in. You're off nights. Lars told me to keep an eye on you." Tony shook his head. "I should have listened."

"Lars?"

"Pendleton." Tony slid the phone into the pocket of his Dockers. He shook his head. "Writing an article. Did you really think I'd buy that, Em?"

"Ms. Kalberg," she said, as she cast her eyes at the dirt-streaked tile floor. *His name is Lars?*

ELEVEN

"Let me in, Em! You've been in there for almost an hour!"
Em turned on the blow dryer to drown out her sister's yelling. It worked, at least until her sister barged in, rage smeared over her face.

"I'm getting ready for tonight."

"I need to get ready too. I'm going to a midnight prayer circle."

Em put down the blow dryer and picked up a bottle of blue nail polish. "That sounds like a lot of fun."

"Do you *always* have to be sarcastic?" Jackie shimmied her way between Em and the sink and turned on the faucet.

"Whore of Babylon." Em stamped off to her room to try on outfits. This evening had to be perfect. Denise was Em's only pre-breakdown friend, and she intended to keep her. Em had already coached Kevin on what he should and should not say with regard to her situation.

"I'm going to say that I'm thinking about doing the next semester as independent study," Em had said. "That'll cover me in case her family ever sees me around town." Unless they saw her at Savertown USA. She'd cross that bridge when she got to it.

"Should I tell them you're on the Dean's List?" Kevin had said, rolling his eyes.

"That might help."

While Em looked through her closet for something suitably festive — did she have *anything* except shapeless dark sweaters and jeans? — her mother came into the room.

"Big night for you, huh?"

"Does this look okay?" Em held a low-cut purple blouse up to the black linen skirt she had salvaged from the back of her closet.

"It looks fine."

"I think it might be too small now. I've gained some weight. You know, from the —"

Em's mother took her by the shoulders. "You know I love you very much, don't you, Emmeline?"

"Okay."

"And I'm very proud of you for putting yourself out there and going to this thing."

"It's just dinner, Mom."

"You never had a lot of friends. I thought you were just being difficult on purpose or something. But now that I know why ... there were so many wasted years. If I would have been more ob-servant —"

Em pulled away from her mother. "This is making me a little uncomfortable."

"I'm sorry." Em's mom said, backing up a few paces. "I'm just feeling emotional right now."

"What are you doing tonight?"

"Oh, I'll just stay here. I'm bushed," she said, though she didn't seem all that exhausted.

"Gonna watch some Wes Summersby DVDs?"

A raised eyebrow. "So what if I am?"

"I'm not saying anything. Have fun." Em started packing her bag, hoping her mom would get the hint and leave.

Mom seemed in no danger of going anywhere. "If you need me to pick you up, just call."

"Kevin will drive me home." Em zipped the bag closed. "I need to get dressed now, Mom."

Her mom shook her head as if clearing it. "Of course."

Finally. Em propped her desk chair under the doorknob and slipped into the too-small party clothes.

Em and Kevin met Denise and her boyfriend Ben at the all-night diner in Clear Falls, the one that was not a Denny's. There had been talk of meeting up at an all-ages club in Pittsburgh, but the seven inches of snow on the ground dictated otherwise. As Kevin guided his sister's Pontiac into a parking space, Em fidgeted with the cuffs of her blouse.

"Remember what I told you to tell her," she said. "No getting into specifics. You don't know a lot about me because we just met a few weeks ago. Anything you say might conflict with what I told them on Christmas. In fact, you probably shouldn't talk unless one of them asks you a question. Let them think you're the strong silent type."

"Yes, ma'am," Kevin said, rolling his eyes.

"Oh, come on. It's only one night."

"Yeah, until the next time. Right?"

Em brushed back his hair. "Don't be upset."

They sat on the low wall near the restaurant and waited for Denise and Ben to arrive. When they showed up, Em was embarrassed. Denise had wrapped herself in a very flattering wine-colored dress, and her boyfriend wore a nice-looking sport jacket without tie. All four of them were overdressed for a diner, but all Em could think about was how much better Denise looked. She shifted her bag in front of her gut.

"You look great," Em said, trying to smile.

"Thanks."

The hostess seated them under a chrome grill pried from the

front of a '57 Buick. After ordering, Denise and Em huddled in close together, leaving the men blinking at each other across the mosaic-covered table.

"Remember that Mr. Foster in art class?" Denise said. "Did you hear he got busted for indecent exposure last year?"

"No, *really*." High school gossip didn't filter through the Saver-town USA retail-industrial complex.

"I'm sure glad I only have to be in Clear Falls for vacations and summer. This town is so constricting. Don't you think so? I mean, there are worse places than this, but smart girls like us don't belong here."

"Ain't that the truth." Em played with her straw.

"So where do you go to school, Kevin?" Denise said, directing her gaze at him.

"I, um, don't. I'm taking a year off."

Em wanted to hit him. Sure, she hadn't coached him in advance — who could have guessed that Denise would want to talk about him? — but it wouldn't have killed him to blurt out "Penn State" or even "Harvard." She gritted her teeth and fumbled for an excuse. "Kevin's doing independent study. He's a very self-directed learner. In fact, I'm thinking of doing the same thing next semester."

"Oh, I see." Denise's smile drooped slightly. "So where did you two meet?"

"Laundromat. Hey, look, Galaga!" Em said, pointing toward the video game cabinet at the back of the restaurant. "Kevin, let's go play a game."

"But the waitress is here."

"Give us a few minutes," Em said, smiling at the waitress in what she hoped was a sweet way, although it probably just looked creepy, like everything Em ever did.

Once they were over at the machine, Em bared her teeth at Kevin, and punched him in the arm. "What are you doing? You're going to give us away!"

"If anyone's going to give us away, it will be you and the way you're acting right now."

"You take that back!"

"Is everything okay over here?" a passing busboy said.

"Everything's fine," Kevin said. "Come on, Em. Let's go back to our table."

He didn't even want to be here, Em thought. *I dragged him into it.* She hid her face in her palms. "I'm sorry," she whispered.

"Em, are you okay?" Denise said.

Em nodded. "Yeah."

After a few sideways glances between Denise and her boyfriend, the meal resumed. The waitress dropped off the bread and took their orders.

"I just love the atmosphere here," Denise said, twining her hands with Ben's. "It's so retro."

Em could barely breathe with all the carefully constructed artificiality pulsing around her, but she forced herself to nod at her friend's statement. "Yeah, far out."

"So, how long have you two known each other?" Ben said, the first words he had spoken all night.

"Oh, Em and I go *way* back," Denise said. "Since kindergarten, isn't that right?"

"I think so. We were both in the afternoon session."

Moment of silence. "I didn't go to kindergarten," Kevin said quietly.

Well, thank you for that stirring piece of information, Einstein, Em thought. But she shrugged, smiled, and laced her fingers with Kevin's, the mirror image of the Denise/Ben tableau.

"Ben and I met at the Museum of Modern Art. I was feeling awfully lonely, so I took the train down into the city —"

Christ, Em thought, *she's been away for one semester and already New York is "the city."* She squeezed Kevin's hand a little tighter.

"And I heard this man with a Pittsburgh accent asking for directions. So I look over, and what do you know, he's *cute!* So we got to talking, and one thing led to another, and it turns out we grew up two hours away from each other. Isn't that funny?"

"That's really, um, awesome," Em said.

"We're going to rent an apartment in Brooklyn next summer if we can find people to room with."

The food arrived, steam rising from the plates like mountaintop mist. "Uh huh," Em said, unrolling her silverware set. She smoothed the napkin across her lap.

"Boy," Kevin said, "this looks good." Em shot him another warning glance, but he seemed not to notice.

"So," Denise said, after taking one dainty bite of her food. "How are things at Oberlin? You know, a lot of people from high school are really jealous of you for getting in."

"Oh, it's great. Totally cool."

"Yes, but what are you *taking?* And how many credits?"

"Um, twelve. Mostly basic classes."

"Honey, you'll never get ahead taking that kind of a load. Now, look at me. Right now I'm taking eighteen credits. You have to want to work, Em. After all, you only get one shot at this."

"I'm happy with my course load." Em took a bite of her sandwich.

"You may not be a few years down the road."

Ben clapped his hands together. "Hey, I know, why don't we stop talking about this? All in favor?" He raised his hand.

Em smiled and raised hers too. She kind of liked Denise's boyfriend, even if he dressed like a prep school student and lived in New York City. Kevin, meanwhile, stared at the table in silence.

Denise playfully rolled her eyes. "I can see my advice isn't wanted."

Em reached for her fork to scoop up a bite of Kevin's pasta primavera. And that's when she saw them.

There were bugs swarming over the silverware.

Not real bugs, Em could see that much, she wasn't an idiot. They were gleaming, silver bugs, with long segmented legs and feelers tipped with grain-sized transmitters.

They beeped at her and talked amongst themselves.

Kevin's hand clamped on her shoulder. "Em?"

She glared at him. "What?" Couldn't he see that he was embarrassing her?

"You dropped your napkin."

"Oh." Picking it up, Em thought she detected a feeling of tension in the room, a rubber band strung tight over Denise and Ben's heads, ready to snap! She smoothed the napkin over her lap and smiled with her lips screwed tight. "Thank you."

Denise sat frozen, but Ben started to eat. As he raised his loaded fork to his mouth, one of the silver bugs took a swan dive onto his lower lip, and scurried into his oral cavity. Ben swallowed.

"Did you *see* that?" Em hissed at Kevin. She hunkered down so Denise and Ben couldn't see her. *This is disgusting.*

"Maybe we should leave," Kevin said, his voice so low Em could scarcely hear him. "I'll get the check." He stood. Denise and Ben were oblivious, lost in a private conversation.

Em pulled at Kevin's arm and hissed in his ear. "No! I do *not* want to leave now. We are going to have a *nice* dinner, with my *friends*, and I am not going to let you or *him* —" she pointed in the general direction of a waiter, "— ruin this for me!"

"You need to chill out, Em."

"Fuck you." She pushed her plate away; even someone as low-class as Em couldn't be expected to eat food filled with thousands of microscopic bugs.

"Except they want me to eat it," she said, replying to herself. "Maybe that's how they want to control me. Do you think that's true, Kevin?"

Kevin sighed. "No, I don't think it's true."

"I mean, look at them. So pretty and perfect. How do they get that way, hmm? By *poisoning* me. With *science*."

"You need to keep your voice down."

Em's fist hit the table before she was aware she'd even raised it. "Don't you tell me to shut up!"

Denise and Ben looked up. Their eyes shone silver like the carapaces of the insects positively swarming over the dinner plates. Shrinking back into her chair, Em drew her hands to her chest and her knees to her hands. *They can hear me. I'm speaking out loud.*

Denise met Kevin's eyes, a conspiring glance. "What's going on?"

Kevin shook his head. "She ... she's not well. I think we should go —"

"Yes, I understand." Denise ran to the front of the restaurant for the check, while Ben sat dumbfounded like a wax mannequin.

Kevin gripped Em's wrists in his hands, but she kept them

crossed corpse-like over her body. *Like I'm in a coffin*, Em thought, *like I'm already dead.*

"You've fucked it all up, Kevin."

"You're welcome, Em," Kevin said, a slight frown on his face. Em closed her eyes, the afterimage of the insects still burning on the inside of her lids, in a place where she could never, ever wash them away.

TWELVE

"**B**ut you *have* to give me my phone back!" Em yelled. "It belongs to *me*."

"You were taking pictures of your coworkers without their consent," Pendleton said as he fiddled with his red, white, and blue tie. The cell phone sat between them on his rusted metal desk. "You know that's not allowed under the rules of the Savertown USA employee handbook."

"I think American law trumps the handbook."

"Why were you doing this, Em?"

Em twined her fingers around one another. "I told you. Well, I told Tony. It's for a project."

"The employee handbook says I am to confiscate personal devices being used on company time," Pendleton said. A copy of the handbook was spread out over his desk. "It doesn't say anything about giving them back."

Hot tears poured down Em's face despite her best efforts. "I can't afford another one."

"You should have thought of that before." Pendleton sighed. "I'll give it back this one time. Don't let it happen again, or I'll fire you. With or without your 'special needs'. We have rules here at Savertown USA."

"Thank you, sir. It's more than I deserve, really."

Pendleton handed the phone back. "Cut the crap. I know what you think of me and everyone who works for this company."

Em slipped her phone into her pocket, holding a hand on it to make sure it didn't get away. Should she thank him again? She settled for meeting his stony gaze across the table. As she got up to leave, a loud *bang!* rang out from the other side of the store.

"What was *that*?" Em said, as all the blood rushed from Pendleton's face and he burst from the office. But somehow, she already knew.

They found the manager of the Sports and Outdoors section slumped over in a folding campsite chair on display, his lower jaw ripped from his bloody face. Yellowed teeth peppered the aisle like candy corn. His eyes were open, vacant, his soul a snuffed candle. A nametag reading "Doug" remained pinned to his ruined vest. Pendleton jumped into action, ordering a cordon drawn around the scene and the customers evacuated.

Em ducked behind a shelf. Bile rose in her throat as she spotted a loose tongue out of the corner of her eye. She felt detached, apart from the blood-spattered wreck of a human in front of her.

Cry later, she thought. *Act now.*

"He shot himself," said the stammering, pale stock girl who worked alongside Doug. "He just — picked it up and ... and ..." Her teeth rattled loud enough to drown her words.

"What do you mean he shot himself?!" Pendleton screamed, pointing at the display of AR-15 rifles with a "Great for Holidays" banner over them. "These guns aren't supposed to be loaded!"

The woman looked up at Pendleton through a haze of tears. "Well, it was."

"Take her outside," Pendleton said to the security guard who had just shown up. "She'll have to talk to the police when they get here."

"Will do," the guard said, leading the shrieking girl away.

"Get back to the break room." Pendleton said to nobody. His voice cracked as he spoke. "Nothing to see here."

Em pressed her ear to a can of tennis balls. *Escodex, it's happened again!*

"I know. Just now I noticed a concurrent rise in the entity's energy level."

You didn't stop it?

"What could I have done? I'm only a voice here, Em." There was a break in the transmission, which felt almost like a sigh. "We need to speed things up. You'll have to work extra hard for me if you don't want your friends to keep dying."

I've already told you they're not my friends, Em transmitted.

Escodex barreled forth without a pause. "We must find the nerve center. I need you to get me some of the surveillance footage. Perhaps the nerve center reveals itself when you're not around."

"I don't know if I can get them," Em said, momentarily lapsing into speech. "I got in trouble for taking pictures."

"You'll find a way." He cut the connection.

Em peeked back around the shelf. The police had arrived and backed Pendleton into a corner. A team of medics and police officers were dealing with the body, as other officials scoped out the scene.

"There's no mystery here," a nervous Pendleton said. "A dozen people saw the guy kill himself. Just get that body out of here!"

The police shook their heads and conferred some more. Em held her breath and made a break for it. She winced when her sneakers squealed on the tile floor, but none of the cops looked up. She opened the door a sliver and slipped inside to join the other exiled employees.

Em threaded her way through the ranks of shell-shocked coworkers to the fat, bald man standing by a light pole, newspaper before his face like a screen.

"Roger," she whispered, "help me."

Roger's eyes narrowed. "Look who's come crawling back."

"Can the tired movie clichés, Roger," Em said. "You know as well as

I do that these aren't suicides. Escodex wants to stop it, and I promised to help him. But I can't do it alone. You're the only other person he's successfully communicated with."

"You have it backwards, sweetie. Escodex is killing them."

Em shook her head. "Escodex is a detective, or whatever the equivalent is in his dimension. He needs to gather enough information so that he can take this *thing* down."

Roger snorted. "You're going to believe an alien who lives in boxes of food before you believe me?"

He's a lot less creepy than you, Em thought. "What exactly did he say to you when you talked to him?"

"He said some people were going to die. Figured he was confessing."

"Well, he wasn't," Em said. She looked around at the other workers, but none of them were paying attention. "Just give him another chance. Open communication with him and keep it open until he tells you his side of the story."

"I'm not talking to some alien," Roger said, a faraway look in his eyes. "You're trying to make me crazy again."

"I would never do that, Roger."

"Go away," he said. "I want to be by myself."

"But —"

"Go!" He snapped his paper back open so loud that some of the other workers looked their way.

Em sighed and went over to Mrs. Nguyen. "You okay, honey?" her supervisor asked.

"Fine."

"Thank God, I was in the bathroom at the time. I didn't see anything. Did you see it?"

"Yeah," Em said. "I saw it."

"I'm just grateful it wasn't one of us," Mrs. Nguyen continued. "You know, on the grocery side. Of course, it's very sad, so sad, but those general merchandise people aren't right in the head. You know that, right?"

Em's mouth dropped open. "You're fucking sick."

The older woman drew back. "You got no right to talk to me like that." She stalked away, her arms crossed around her Savertown USA vest.

Em looked back at Roger. His eyes were crossed; one small eye on his paper, the other one squarely focused on her. She glared at him for a few seconds before saying:

"By the way, he's not an alien."

Em stood under the carport and smoked a cigarette, watching the smoke curl from her fingers like dirty angel wings. The snow fell thick on the slate roof of the carport. As Em shivered inside her heavy pea-green winter coat, a clump of gray sludge fell right in front of her, hitting the hole in the tip of her sneaker. She groaned and wiped the sludge from her feet.

"Oh, Em, I wish you wouldn't smoke," her mother said as she sidled up beside her.

"Shit! You startled me."

"Sorry." Her mother's teeth chattered. "We need to have a talk."

Em took a long drag on her cigarette, pointing the smoke away from her mother's face. "Okay."

"I found this … place where you can stay. It wouldn't be forever. It would only be for a little while."

"I don't need to go to a place. I'm fine right here." Em stubbed out her cigarette. "I have a job."

"I was scared last week, Em. I've never seen you so confused. You probably don't remember any of it, but I had to hold you down to the bed and force pills down your throat. I thought you were going to strangle me."

Em *did* remember all of it, or at least, a lot of it. She could usually piece together her "episodes" after they had happened. She'd seen her mother and sister as angels of the fiercest light, and the bed as some sort of primordial womb. Above it all, in the background, had hummed the mysterious machine. "Someone died at work today."

"I know. Mr. Pendleton called me."

"And I didn't kill him. Isn't that surprising?"

Her mother rubbed her hands together. "I knew you'd take that the wrong way."

"What other way should I take it?" Em reached in her pocket for another cigarette, but decided not to when she saw her mother's frown. "I'm not going back to the hospital."

"It's not a hospital. It's a supportive living environment."

"Do I even have a choice in this?"

"Of course you have a choice," her mother said. "I have to head in. My lips are turning blue."

Em looked out at the grimy snow drifts that piled up on the patch of grass right outside the carport. Then she leaned back against the aluminum siding and lit another cigarette.

Thirteen

As Em monitored the door of the security room, she thought about her father. He'd always been a positive influence in her life. When Em came home in tears because of other kids' taunting and teasing, her father would scoop her up in his big gorilla arms and say "There, there, now just give me their names and I'll take care of it" with a finger drawn across his throat.

They had played video games together, selections pulled from his collection of old consoles. Every afternoon, Em returned home from school to find her father camped out on the living room floor, a big square controller in his hands, Atari-green images flashing on the television screen. Em's father stayed at home.

How dare she call him a deadbeat without a proper job, Em had thought once after one of her parents' many fights. *He's a domestic executive.* Or, at least, he used to be.

What was he doing now, in his post-fugue state life? Had he bought into the business world, living in a high-rise in Manhattan and crunching numbers with other corporate drones while wearing a clean, pressed three-piece suit? Was he married again? Gay? Em worried about her father, but she didn't begrudge him his freedom. So many times she too had wanted to take that highway out of town and never look back. If there had only been one sign: a letter, an email, a phone call, she knew she could let him go for good, and revel in her knowledge that she had a vagabond father somewhere out there, hearty and hale, even if he never came home.

But she'd know what had happened to him soon enough, if Escodex kept his promise, and she was willing to take the little interdimensional bugger at his word. After watching the security guard sneak off for a smoke break, Em jimmied her state ID into the doorjamb, once again grateful for the combined experience of her fellow mental patients.

Dozens of security monitors lined the walls, each displaying a grainy black-and-white view of the store. A long wooden shelf on the opposite wall of the room held rows of DVDs, each labeled with a date and a location. Em scooped a pile of the discs and stuck them in the waistband of her pants. As she turned to leave, she peeked at the active monitors. One of them was pointed at the Sports and Outdoors section, at the place where Doug had shot himself. Not a trace remained of the suicidal employee or his scattered brains.

Em shook her head, smoothed down her shirt, and scuttled out of the room, locking the door behind her. After stashing the DVDs in her bag, she went to the sales floor to finish out her shift. It was three in the afternoon, so the store wasn't very busy, mostly retirees and stay-at-home mothers released from captivity to snap up bargains before their screaming brats came home.

Mrs. Nguyen was there, unloading a box of Creamsicles. "You ready for the practice this Saturday?"

"What practice?"

"Bowling practice. For the tournament. It's in three weeks."

"Yeah, I decided not to do that after all." Em slid her box cutter across the top of a case of frozen peas.

"But you promised! Don't think I'm going to go soft on you because of your condition." Mrs. Nguyen waved her box cutter around bossily, nearly slicing Em's cheek open.

"You could go soft on me. I wouldn't mind." Em was beginning to like the older woman in spite of herself. "Mrs. Nguyen, do you ever think about leaving Savertown USA? Getting a job somewhere else?"

"Where else would I work?"

"Your English is really good. You could work anywhere you wanted."

"I was born in Toledo, Em. Of course my English is good."

"Oh," Em said, fiddling with her box cutter. "Well, it's still true. You could work anywhere. Why do you work here?"

"I don't know." Mrs. Nguyen sighed, and swiveled her eyes to the fluorescent lighting. "I started working here in high school and I just never stopped. My parents couldn't afford to send all five of us kids to college, and I was the stupid one. Now they're dead. Too late to change anything."

"They should make you a manager then. You're smart enough."

"You trying to suck up?" Mrs. Nguyen asked. "I wouldn't want to do that anyway. It's not my place. I am happy where I am. We all are. You will be too, given time. You haven't settled in yet, but give it a few more months, you'll catch on."

Em wondered if that was true. Certainly, all the employees seemed to be happy, as if they were tuned in to some wavelength that she just couldn't pick up. Maybe with enough time she could learn to be content here, settle into the warm bath that was Savertown USA.

"What time is bowling practice, Mrs. Nguyen?" Em asked.

"Three o'clock," her supervisor said with a smile, wrinkles appearing at the corners of her brown eyes. "Bring shoe money."

"I'll be there." Em smiled back, pulled another case of ice cream from the pallet, and submitted to the systematic calm of the stocking process. *Boxes on the shelf, good mental health.*

Em parked her bike, then checked her bag. All of the security DVDs were there, just waiting for her to transmit them to Escodex. *This better work,* she thought. *I won't get so lucky again.*

When she went inside, Jackie was there with a half dozen of her friends. The boys wore plain white shirts and ties, and the girls wore dowdy beige dresses and wooden crosses around their necks. They were all linked in a circle, hands joined.

"The hell?" Em said.

Jackie's eyes fluttered open and she broke out of the circle. The boy on her left and girl on her right locked their hands together without missing a beat. "Please don't interrupt us. We're praying."

"Hey, I'm just trying to get to my room without witnessing any public displays of piety."

Jackie's hands shook. "Please leave."

"Fine," Em said, moving the heavy bag to her left hand. "But I think your friends should all know how terribly you're treating your only sister, a little lamb who strayed from the path and only needs a little nudging to get back on. Also, she's a paranoid schizophrenic with depressive tendencies. I don't think Jesus would approve of this."

A blond-haired, cherub-faced boy opened his eyes. "Would you like to join our prayer circle?"

"Get bent." Em went to her room and dumped the discs on the bed. They would be returned to the store tomorrow, after she downloaded the information onto a memory card to feed to Escodex. She sat on the floor and put on her oversized headphones.

Everything had been so simple once. Em longed to return to the days of her childhood, when things had been easy and had made sense. Em's awareness of the hidden meaning lurking behind the façade of society nagged at her like a splinter. Maybe this feeling was similar to what the kids downstairs went through when they thought about the Big J. A ghost who lives in everyone and everything, always watching over your shoulder, carrying you when you're too tired and leaving his wet footprints on the bathroom carpet. Em wondered if all that separated her paranoia from their faith was the fact that their delusion was endorsed by over half the members of Congress.

Downstairs, Jackie and her friends belted into song, drowning out Em's music. Em groaned, pressed her head between two pillows, and put a DVD in the laptop.

Em held the memory stick up to the box of frozen fruit cups. "Got it?"

"Perfect, Em. Job well done. Now, for your next assignment I'd like you to —"

"Hold on." Em scanned the aisles, but they were clear. "Okay."

"I'd like you to closely monitor the regional manager's meeting. Find some way to record him —"

I can't. Pendleton will take my phone for good if he catches me.

Escodex went on. "I don't care how you do it, just see that it gets done. I need to know if the invasion is localized or if it's spreading, because if it's spreading we're going to have to work faster than ever. More agents will be sent over. We can't allow this thing to establish additional nexus points."

I'll do it, Em thought-spoke. *Somehow.*

"What's the matter, Em? Your emotional reading is troubled."

Why won't you let me see you, Escodex?

"How could you see me? I don't exist in your dimension. I'm just a voice."

You could beam a picture of yourself into my brain. You can do it with sound, why not with sight?

"That's … not a good idea."

Em played with her fingernails. *Why not?*

"Why does it matter what I look like?"

I'd just like to know. Most people know what their boss looks like, and you're kind of like a boss. Except you don't pay me.

"I live on a higher dimensional plane than you. You take that as a value judgment, and perhaps in your world it is, but it shouldn't be. But we do live in a world more highly textured than yours. We have different senses, owing to our partial control of the fourth dimension."

That doesn't explain why I can't see you.

"Because of our utilization of the fourth dimension as well as the far different global differences separating our Earth from yours, we have a physical appearance that you would consider freakish. If you were to look at one of us, you would surely go mad."

More so, Em added. *So you're a monster. Do we look like monsters to you?*

"No. You look rather plain, actually. It's a little hard to tell individuals of your kind apart."

"Gee, thanks," she said aloud.

Escodex sighed, the artificial noise sounding clinical in Em's ears. "There you go making value judgments again."

"Blame my dimension." Em broke communication.

FOURTEEN

"Today I'd like to talk about goals."

Em's eyes wandered to the trapezoidal windows above Slazinger's head. "Goals?"

"Where do you see yourself in a year, Em? What steps are you taking to lead a more independent life? Let's talk about it."

"Okay," Em said. "You want to know my goal? To stop coming here twice a week. When I never have to look at your smug face again, that will be the happiest day of my life."

"You're feeling rage. That's good. It means you're feeling something."

"Oh, believe me, doc, it ain't easy. Not with all the pills you have me on." Em picked lint from her fluffy black sweater and let it dance in the reflected light of the window.

Slazinger fussed in his chair like a toddler awaiting a haircut. "Let's discuss that for a bit, the medical phase of your journey of healing. Do you feel the treatment is excessive?"

"I take twelve pills a day. Yeah, I think that's a little excessive."

"What would you have us do, Em? You've already had several relapses since I first saw you. Do you think the pills do nothing?"

"Oh, I know what you're doing, Dr. Slazinger." Em grinned in what she hoped was a maniacal way, a way that would make her therapist cower in fear. It didn't succeed.

"What am I doing." Statement, not question.

"You're trying to silence me. You're trying to silence the truth." Before her eyes, Slazinger became a troll standing in front of an iron gate, a wall separating her from the world and the world from the truth.

"I see. What's the truth? Can you tell me what the truth is?"

"I don't know," Em said, her breath catching in her throat. In Em's mind's eye, the doctor snarled with ivory teeth, emitting odors of swamp gas and farts. With his curved sword he countered Em, sparring with her until at last she gave in, to lie on the muck outside the gate.

"Do you want me to tell your psychiatrist to decrease your medication? Is that what you want?" Slazinger's eyebrows knotted together and he began to tap his pen against the yellow-paged notebook he always held.

"I don't know what I want," Em said. "I just know I don't want this. I don't want to spend my life drugged up on your little pills. I sure as hell don't want to spend two hours a week talking to you. Basically, I don't want to be crazy anymore. That's what I want."

Slazinger sighed and scribbled in his notebook. "I understand where you're coming from —"

"No, you *don't*." Em turned to the window again, hoping to glimpse more happy, normal people walking out of the dentist's office, but the parking lot was deserted. "And you should be glad for that. Fucking *glad*."

Slazinger continued as if he hadn't heard the interruption. "But, Em, this condition isn't your fault. You couldn't have planned for this. Why do you feel the need to compare yourself with others? That's not a very healthy attitude to have."

"It doesn't seem like anything I do is very healthy, right, Dr. Slazinger?"

"I didn't say that."

"But you're thinking it." Em turned back to him and rested her chin in her hands. It had been a long life, and it was only going to keep going. For now.

Em's mother dropped her off at bowling practice at three on the dot. Exhausted from a sleepless night, Em stumbled into the alley. She rented a pair of size eight shoes and picked out a ball.

"Em!" Mrs. Nguyen said, waving a hand. "Over here."

Time to get this over with, Em thought, lamenting her ill-planned deal. She trudged over to her team and put on the smelly, threadbare shoes. They were even more poorly constructed than hospital slippers, which had often been held together with little more than dental floss and wishes.

"It's time for you to take advantage of my effervescent youth so you can better compete in meaningless rivalry and further the clannish Savertown USA spirit," she said to Mrs. Nguyen.

"Go team," her supervisor replied with a smirk, as she took a hot pink ball from the rack.

For the next hour, Em rolled balls with the rest of the grocery-side workers, picking up tips from the seasoned players who showed up at the alley every week even when there wasn't a tournament on.

"One thirty-three," Peter, a stocker in the cereal aisle, said. "That's pretty good."

"It's *really* good," Mrs. Nguyen said, "if this is Em's first time. I bet we can get her score up to one-seventy before the big game."

"You know, I'm right here," Em said, watching her toe move in the worn shoe. "You can talk to me." *I should throw the game*, she thought, *to teach them not to ignore me like this.* It wasn't the first time she had been ignored. For Em's first month in the hospital, neither the doctors nor the staff had ever posed her a direct question. She'd cut her hand on a rusty nail out in the courtyard, and it had taken five days before they'd look at it, and she'd earned an undeserved "self-injurious" note in her chart.

But still, those bright numbers on the scoreboard left her with a strange sense of … pride? No, that couldn't be it. Em didn't care about bowling or her "team." She couldn't deny, though, that her score gave her a kind of boost. She couldn't pretend that she didn't feel just a bit lighter when her fellow players slapped her on the back and pumped their fists in the air. Especially when Mrs. Nguyen did it.

Just then the general merchandise workers walked into the alley. Mrs. Nguyen and the others booed and hissed.

"You're going down, losers!" Peter said.

"We'll see you in hell," someone from the other team yelled back.

Looking up, Em scanned the general merchandise workers. She didn't know them well. They took their lunch at a different time than her side, and were fewer in number. The grocery workers derided them as slackers because they never had as many pallets to unload and they didn't have to worry about weeding out expired goods or be overly scrupulous about cleanliness. As Em looked at her own tribe, with their sweat-soaked armpits and rotting teeth, she realized that the Savertown USA definition of "scrupulously clean" was highly relative.

"Oh God," Mrs. Nguyen said, sidling up to Em. "They've got Agnes Walker on their team. I didn't think she was playing this season. We're done for."

"Who's that?"

Mrs. Nguyen pulled a face that made Em feel like the village idiot. "Don't you read the newsletter? She's been the employee of the month four times in the past year. Lady is hardcore. Always the first to punch in, last to punch out. We all hate her." *And you should too,* her supervisor's follow-up glance seemed to say.

"That doesn't mean she's good at bowling." Across the room, the general merchandise workers cheered as Agnes threw a strike. "Okay, maybe it does."

"We're finished. We'll never win now."

"So can I quit?"

"Please," Mrs. Nguyen said. "You may turn out to be our secret weapon. You were phenomenal, and you're only going to get better." She left to take her turn.

Em studied the face of the frequent employee of the month. Agnes seemed a hard woman, her features gone to granite by many years of tireless devotion to her job. Her green eyes were deep-set and dull. Em looked away before the celebrated worker could notice her stare, but she didn't look away fast enough.

"What you looking at?" Agnes said. She held a brown bowling ball in her hand.

"Nothing."

"Bullshit. You're looking at me. Stop it." Agnes rolled her ball, taking down seven pins.

"I'm sorry." Em pretended to be interested in the fiber of the carpet.

Agnes felled the rest of the pins and strode over to Em. "I know about you. You're crazy. Don't go messing with our side of the store. We do good work. We are good people. Leave us alone." She jabbed an index finger into Em's chest. As the finger touched her, Em's brain felt like it was melting. A burst of cold radiated outwards from her chest, freezing her extremities, like tentacles working their way into her body. She looked into the woman's eyes. *Something else* lay behind them.

"Em, you're up!" Peter said.

She backed away from Agnes, keeping her face to the woman but her eyes averted. She picked up her own ball, the cold tentacles reaching with her. Whatever was inside Agnes was inside her now, like a second mind, a ghost hanging on her bones. The ball was warm to the touch, compared to the frigid temperature of her fingers. She threw it.

Gutterball.

"Where did she touch you?"

"Right here," Em said, touching her chest. "It hurt for two hours."

"We're definitely dealing with something big here. I'd like you to gather some information on this Agnes woman. How long has she worked here?"

"Seven years."

"Well, that's strange. I've never heard of her, not even in the memories of the shirker." That was what Escodex called Roger. "You say everyone knows her?"

"Apparently, she's won employee of the month four times in one year," Em said. "Aren't you supposed to be up on everything that happens in this store?"

"I am limited by not only what others remember," Escodex said, "but also how open their minds are. You read like an open book, but others are more secretive, their mental processes more circuitous. And if this sensation you felt has something to do with the entity, then there's no telling how it can rearrange memories and minds to elude capture."

Em heard customers pass by in the next aisle, and switched to thought-based communication. *So you want more pictures and stuff?*

"Yes, all you can find. Use your new camera." Em had bought a lapel camera from an online retailer a few days ago to record the regional manager's meeting that was scheduled in two weeks. It recorded both visuals and sound, and had cost her an entire paycheck. She hoped against hope that it wouldn't be swiped by a manager.

Escodex, when I looked into her eyes, she didn't even seem human. They were so … flat. Like a doll's eyes. I know I'm not the best at objective evidence, and maybe this whole "cold" thing is just a hallucination —

"No, you're on to something. This could be the missing piece of the puzzle. If the entity is taking human form to subvert the rest of the workers, we're in for a lot more trouble than we bargained for."

FIFTEEN

Em and Kevin walked hand in hand along the banks of the Monongahela River. Above their heads, the sky was gun-metal gray. Ice and rock salt crunched beneath their feet.

"Sometimes I wish I didn't love you," Kevin said.

"What the hell is that supposed to mean?" Em dug her fingernails into Kevin's palm and sucked on her cigarette.

"Just that it adds a lot of extra tension. Having to go behind my sister's back, covering up things with Slazinger. It's just a lot of work —"

Em gave him a look.

"Not that it's not worth it or anything, honey. But what with my parents coming back and all —"

"You don't want me to meet your parents."

"I want to ease them into it slowly. I'm supposed to be focusing on other things, like not killing myself."

"Well, you haven't killed yourself yet." Em let go of Kevin's hand and stared out at the stark gray river. The ice was about a half-foot thick, but wide cracks appeared in its surface. The winter had been harsh this year, but she had the feeling it was about to lift.

"But I *do* love you. And that's not going to change. So I guess I have to put up with a complicated life."

"Everyone's life is complicated," Em said.

"Not the lives of those hicks you work with."

"Don't call them hicks." Em's cigarette had burned down to a nub. She dropped it to the ground and stubbed it out with the tip of one winter boot.

"*You* call them that all the time."

"Well, I was wrong. They're still people. Maybe they don't bathe as often as we do, but they still deserve our respect and love."

"What a compliment."

"I'm in a complimenting mood." She put her arm around Kevin's waist and they walked away from the river. When they reached Kevin's car, they lay down in the backseat, heater flaring, Clear Falls' only halfway decent radio station on the stereo.

Nothing ever changes here, she thought as she removed her shirt, again dreaming of the day she would be allowed to cast off this place. She would take Kevin and together the two of them would steal his sister's car and drive off into the sunset. Where would they end up? Not Pittsburgh. They had to think bigger. One of the coasts, at the very least. Though she'd stay far away from New York City.

In the periphery of Em's vision loomed the red, white, and blue face of Savertown USA. Above the store, large clouds hung suspended in the sky. The clouds reached down with funnels like fingers, and there was almost the palpable smell of electricity in the air. The cloud lived.

Hallucinations, Em said, shaking her head, returning to the present moment. The happy place.

When Em went into work the next morning, the entire workforce was abuzz. It was the day of the regional manager's visit. Pendleton, in a fit of what Em diagnosed as manic excitement, made everyone wash the walls, wax the floors, and do other maintenance tasks designed to make his brown-nosing that much easier.

"What's the point?" Em asked. "The customers will just mess it up anyway."

"Then you fix it," Pendleton said. "Now get going, *Miss Kalberg*."

"This is stupid. I'm not cleaning up something that's going to be destroyed in five minutes."

"If you like your paycheck you will."

Em rolled her eyes and went off to polish the handles on the freezer doors.

The store was decked out like a party hall. Bunting lined all of the doors, even the doors to the bathrooms. The store's loose theme of a cozy fifties-esque neighborhood market had been ramped up with even more green street signs and fake gas lamps. *They're bringing it up to code*, Em thought. *There was a distinct lack of bunting in this place. Not up to snuff.*

The regional manager would arrive in fifteen minutes, enough time for Em to take a quick smoke break before joining the rest of the workers in front of his platform. She finished polishing the last of the handles and went out back, cutting through the employee lounge. On the way, she ran into Roger.

"Let me through," she said to the hulk of the man who stood in the doorway blocking her path.

"I thought it over. I want to help you."

"Too late now."

"No, it isn't. I know Escodex wants you to tape the meeting. That's why you're wearing that." He pointed to the camera pinned to her vest, which she'd thought below notice. "It used to ask me to tape things."

"You'll sabotage him. You think he's a killer."

"Not anymore." Roger's sweat flowed a little more profusely than usual, leaving dark ripe splotches under his armpits. "There's lots of things I can do to help. It has to be lonely, being the only person who communicates with him. Aren't you scared, Em?"

Em shook her head, but only a little. "I'll bring it up with him. Keep your mind open." She strode off toward the parking lot.

When she returned, fifty workers and a few dozen customers

huddled around the platform where the regional manager stood in his three-piece suit and Savertown USA vest. Em fought through the ranks and secured a position in the front row. She pointed the left side of her chest at the manager. *So what if he thinks I'm flirting?*

"Hello, valued members of the Savertown USA family. I am here to present a special award to this store. I've been to over three hundred Savertown USA stores all across the Ohio Valley region, and I can say without a doubt that Clear Falls is home to the cleanest, most friendly store I've seen. You've really got something special here, folks."

Yes, infiltration by an evil entity will do that for you, Em thought.

"Now, your store manager Lars Pendleton wants me to do the great honor of passing out this month's Employee of the Month award, so before I get on with other business, I'd like to do that. Mrs. Agnes Walker, would you mind coming up here a moment?"

"Her again," Mrs. Nguyen said, her brown eyes rolling to the back of her head. "Fucking goody-two-shoes."

"When the revolution comes, you will be spared," Em said under her breath.

"Huh?" But her supervisor's attention snapped back to the podium, where the Savertown USA jingle emitted from a plastic boombox. They took Agnes's picture with a Polaroid camera, gave her an engraved plaque, and awarded her a one-hundred-dollar gift certificate to Savertown USA.

Agnes beamed. "My favorite store."

"And remember, Agnes, you *can* spend it all in one place. Because at Savertown USA, America's favorite one-stop-shop for groceries, home supplies, entertainment, and clothing, you can do all your shopping in one convenient location, without all the hassle of bargain hunting!" The regional manager's spiel continued as Agnes was herded off the stage.

Em looked over at Agnes. The woman's talons gripped the gift certificate and plaque. She practically drooled with delight. But when Em stared into her green eyes, she felt that same revulsion, the same sense of seeing a primal, animal force buried underneath aging, desiccated flesh. Agnes Walker was a pit of evil wrapped in a very boring shell.

Agnes caught her gaze. The corners of her mouth quirked up, showing a short row of pointed brown teeth. A foul odor emitted from the lips, a line of chartreuse gas heading straight for Em. The gas blew into her face, and a voice began to speak.

You think you're on to me, but you're not. I am capable of feats far beyond what you or the little friend in your ear have seen. I can manipulate your mind in a thousand different directions. It is time for me to move on to higher dimensions. Your little friend doesn't like that. He wants me to fester here, to waste my gifts. He thinks I aspire to become a god. But soon he'll realize, and so will you — I'm already there.

Why do you have to disrupt these people's lives? Em thought. She was surprised to find that communication with the entity was just as easy as communication with Escodex. *Why here, at some stupid store in Shitsville, Pennsylvania?*

This place is a nexus. It's one of only a few weak points in our dimension where I can move to the next level. The universe is finite, Em, and this is the only nexus that has life. It's a bad coincidence for you, I know.

The gas came out thicker now, almost blocking her vision. She couldn't believe nobody else saw it. But they just sat there grinning, occasionally clapping when the regional manager made some witty remark. *I know about your little deal with Escodex. He's not going to tell you where your father is. Once he gets the information he wants he's going to leave you behind. Why should he care what happens to you? The beings in this dimension are like worms to them. But I could tell you.*

You're lying, Em thought.

Get off the case, and I'll tell you about your father, what happened that day he went to the store and never came back. I pity you, Em. We're quite alike, you and I. Think about it. The foul gas dissipated.

It's just scared, Em thought. *It knows Escodex is on to it. That just proves we're closing in.* She pocketed her camera and broke for the employee lounge, where complimentary pizza and pop awaited.

Em secured her bike after the long ride home from work — there'd been less snow today than yesterday — and let herself in the house. Her mother was on the couch, one hand in a Cheetos bag while the other clutched a remote. A Wes Summersby DVD played on the television. When she noticed Em, the lines around her mouth deepened.

"Em, we need to talk."

"Is it about that institution?"

"You upset your sister terribly the other day, embarrassing her in front of her friends."

"So punish me. Good mothers ground their daughters when they misbehave, or hit them. They don't cart them off to the loony bin."

Her mother set aside the remote, but kept one hand in the Cheetos bag. "I just want what's best for you. I can sense you slipping away. You spend so much time in your room. That's not good for you, to be so isolated. Dr. Slazinger called me —"

"So much for doctor-patient confidentiality."

"— and he said the same thing. You're heading into a negative thought spiral. He said you acted very strangely at your last session."

"That smacks of subjective value judgment."

"Well, that's what he said." Em's mom patted the space next to her. "Honey, you know you can talk about anything with me. I won't judge you. Why do you spend so much time in your room?"

Because I'm decoding secret messages in your favorite television program, Em thought. *Is that what you want to hear?* "I'm just thinking. Reading. I have to keep my mind in shape if I want to go back to school."

"There's more than one way to keep your mind in shape, Em." Her mother sighed. "Where did I go wrong?"

"See, again it's all about you. You, you, you. Maybe you should go talk to Slazinger if you're feeling so bad about yourself." Em could tell by her mother's face that she was hurt, but she didn't care.

Her mother's eyes returned to the television screen. "Please just think about what I'm saying. I won't bring it up again."

"At least not for the rest of today," Em muttered as she stomped upstairs to her room.

As hellish as home could be, it didn't compare to the hospital. As hazy as her memory could be, she remembered the other patients with perfect clarity. Her roommate Amber, who had spent most of her time crying. Trevor the Jesus Freak, her partner in crime if not in politics. The frequent flier Dinah, who cut herself and wrote hundreds of pages of poetry about the patterns in the blood. And then there was Melinda, a catatonic schizophrenic who lay in bed all hours of the day, except when she was turned and washed by nurses. Em liked Melinda best.

While in the hospital, she never had a single moment of privacy. Every waking second was spent with other people, whether it was in her room, at group therapy, or on one of the weekly field trips to the park or the candy store. If she sat alone on a couch for five minutes, she'd be accosted by an orderly "asking" her to join in a game of cards. The television was under lock and key, and they could only watch programs by consensus, which could always be vetoed by a member of the staff if they proved to have "upsetting content," by which they meant any content at all.

Her only privacy was on Friday afternoons, when Amber and Dinah were at the eating disorder breakout session. Em would sit on Melinda's bed and brush her long blonde hair, speaking to her in a calm, low voice.

"You don't know how lucky you are," she would say. "Spending all day in bed, without a care in the world." Of course, that wasn't true. Melinda was schizophrenic, and she experienced the same inward-turning hallucinatory episodes Em did. She'd just fallen so far into them that she'd never found her way out the other side.

Em spent many long hospital afternoons wondering what Melinda thought about during her sleep. When Melinda strained at her restraints, Em imagined her chased by phantoms through a twisted wood. When Melinda smiled and opened her eyes, Em thought of her stretched out on a gleaming golden beach. Melinda was an older woman with an earthy sort of beauty, so unlike her other two roommates, scar-crossed and heavily made up with cosmetics they bought at the dollar store on the trips into town.

What had happened to Melinda? And what had happened to Em? She went to four group therapy sessions a week, during which time Dr. Atchison asked her to talk about her break, while he held an open file containing exact details on his lap.

"I don't remember," she would say.

"But what do you *think* happened?"

"Why don't you tell me what happened? You have my file."

"You wouldn't be learning very much if I did that, would you?"

"Actually, I would. Because then I would know." But Atchison would just shake his head and move on to Dinah or Amber. They were always eager to show off their latest poems.

Three times a day, the patients lined up for medication, which they chased with Dixie cups full of water. At first, Em had lashed out against the nurses, demanding to know exactly what she was taking and in what dosages. After a few spells in the "quiet room," however, she learned to keep her mouth shut and literally take her medicine.

Em's mother had never called her in the hospital, though she sent a card on Em's birthday. She felt a mix of envy and revulsion as she heard her roommates take calls from their parents. She hated the way they talked with blissful abandon about the conditions of the hospital, and gloat how they'd be a shoo-in for some fancy creative writing program because of their "dramatic life experience." They were both so mad at their parents for putting them in here, and by the way, could they get some money? Em knew Amber and Dinah would both wind up here, again and again. She was determined not to let it happen to her. Once was enough for a lifetime.

Her best friends at the hospital were the other psychotics: Trevor the Jesus Freak, whose Bible spoke to him in flaming letters, and of course Melinda.

One night, she woke to find Melinda gone, spirited away by people or forces she couldn't comprehend. Nobody ever answered her inquiries into the fate of the catatonic, and the other girls didn't seem to mind. Em learned not to mind, either. Two weeks after Melinda's disappearance, Em was sprung by her stern-faced mother.

And now, here she was, on the floor of her bedroom ready to decode secret messages in the speech pattern of America's Favorite Self-Help Guru, all rights reserved. The people at the hospital would imprison her again for sure if they knew what she was doing. But then, they also thought *Murder, She Wrote* was inappropriate viewing material.

"Come on, Wes, tell me what you *really* think."

Em listened. Buried in the high end — treble was turned all the way up — came that same alien squeak, each phrase separated by five-second bursts of atypical static which Em surmised were themselves pregnant with information.

"Follow me … give me all your money … cast aside your family … I am the one …"

She wrote it all down. Every last word.

Sixteen

Mrs. Nguyen stuck a tray of cheese fries under Em's nose. "Special treat for our secret weapon!"

Em took a fry coated with what looked like orange toxic sludge. "Thanks."

"Your average is one-seventy, Em! Aren't you paying attention to your score?"

"Uh, no. Is that good?"

"It's *great*. Those general merchandise jerks won't know what hit them. Agnes's average is only one-sixty or so. And they have no team spirit. Typical GM."

"Can you tell me more about Agnes?"

"What about her? She's a suck-up."

"Have you ever seen her do anything strange? Besides the sucking up."

"No, she's just a regular old lady. Widowed. Has a couple cats. Not much of a life outside the store."

"What does she do when she's there after hours?"

Mrs. Nguyen shrugged. "Helps Pendleton out, I guess. Cleans out the back room. She's always been a volunteer, organizes the sign-up drive every year to get people to do the big yearly inventory. Normally she's in Fashion Alley, but she pitches in wherever help is needed on that side." Her supervisor sighed. "Sometimes I think I should be more like her. My aisle looks like crap compared to hers. And I can't ever stay and do inventory; I got two kids at home."

"You do good work, Mrs. Nguyen. Don't let her shame you."

"Now *you're* sucking up." The woman put her bowling shoes back on. Another round was scheduled to start. "Anyway, she's all right, just a little boring. Most of us are just pissed because of those hundred-dollar gift certificates. That's a lot of money."

"Don't I know it." She pushed the cheese fries toward Peter. "So are those slackers showing up for practice today?"

"Yeah, probably. They won't turn down a chance to make us look bad." As if on cue, the door to the alley swung open and the general merchandise workers, led by Agnes, marched in.

"Well, well, look what the cat dragged in," Peter said. He was the next best bowler on the team after Em.

Agnes, who wore a T-shirt emblazoned with the words "Employee of the Month — January," grinned widely, showing off a gold-capped incisor. "You ready for a fight?"

Em chose a ball. As she glided down the floor, arcing her right hand in back of her to throw the ball, she felt something tug at her mind. Vertigo. Confused, she spun around, the ball flying from her fingers into the crowd.

"What the *fuck*?" yelled one of the GM workers as she dived out of the way.

The other grocery workers groaned, but Mrs. Nguyen gave her a pat on the shoulder. "That's okay, Em. It happens. Don't let them psych you out."

Em flicked her gaze over to Agnes. A puff of brown smoke exited the woman's thin lips. "I'll be okay."

She lined up for her second throw. She felt the same tug, but prepared for it. Three pins fell to the ground.

"Some secret weapon," one of the women on the general merchandise side said, snickering. Peter went to take his turn.

Em slumped down on the molded orange chairs that flanked the lanes. She reached her thoughts out, searching for the entity.

See? I told you I could manipulate your mind. If you don't want more of that, you'd better give up.

I won't.

I can give you everything, Em. I can make you bowl a perfect three hundred. I can make your mother and sister respect you as an equal member of the family. I could even cure that little mental disorder that plagues you.

No, you couldn't do that.

How do you know? Trust me. I may surprise you.

Em shook her head and looked away, breaking contact. It was her turn. She took a ball and headed for the lane.

"Bombs away!" yelled Agnes-the-person. The general merchandise workers covered their heads in mockery.

Em gritted her teeth and strode forward. The ball hit the pins like an explosion. Strike.

Was that you?

The entity did not respond.

After transmitting the regional manager's speech to Escodex, Em told him about her conversation with the entity. *Agnes is definitely the nerve center. It spoke to me through her. I saw its smoke.*

"That's impossible. It can't communicate with regular humans, just the host."

Do you think I'm lying?

"No, not lying … well, you are a pretty unreliable witness, Em." Escodex paused. "I sense you feel hurt by that."

Escodex, do you have mental illness in your dimension?

"No, we are all born physically and psychically perfect. I do not know if it was always this way or if we perfected ourselves. Personally, I think that we were made that way, due to the properties of our parallel big bang, which created all the stars in the sky and a better version of Earth."

She made a face. "Wow."

"Yes, I'm aware it's impressive."

Em took a deep breath and thought-spoke some more. *If you had the power to cure me, would you do it?*

"I'm not allowed. We are only to intervene in a crisis that directly affects us, like this one."

So you can do it, Em said, *but you choose not to. Some friend you are.*

"If I cured you, Em, what would stop me from curing everybody with schizophrenia? And then it would be cancer. How about I solve world hunger?"

I do all this for you, risk getting fired or thrown back in the crazy house, and you won't cross a couple of neurons for me? A tear slicked down Em's cheek.

"I already told you I'd tell you about your father. I thought that was what you wanted more than anything else in the world."

I can want more than one thing. The beings in this dimension are capable of that, you know.

"If the entity told you that it would fix you, it's lying. Why would you trust a thing like that? That would be crazy."

At least it was willing to make that kind of promise. A janitor walked past. Em hunkered down and hid the frozen pot pie under her hair.

"I appreciate all the work you've been doing for me. I have a new assignment —"

"Not right now." Em cut communication and went to the deli. She pushed her lapel camera into Roger's palm. "Here. You do it. I'm done with him."

"Did Escodex say I could help? It hasn't opened up to me yet."

"I don't care. I'm through. This is your job now." She stalked off toward the parking lot.

"Em, wait!" Roger's hand clasped her shoulder. "Is something wrong? Did you guys fight?"

"You could say that."

"Come here," he said, turning Em toward him. "Tell me what's wrong."

She buried her face in Roger's flab. Tears flowed out, staining his blue sweatshirt a deep royal. "I'm just so damn sick of being crazy."

He rubbed a calloused thumb against the back of her neck. It felt like sandpaper. "I know, I know." He hung a card reading "back in five minutes" on his counter. "Let's go outside." They pushed past the heavy double doors to the parking lot. The snow fell in a light drizzle, blanketing them with a thin sheen like baby's breath.

After work, Em went straight from her mother's car to her sister's room. Jackie was bent over her desk, lost in a book.

"I want to apologize for the way I acted the other day. It wasn't right of me to embarrass you in front of your friends like that."

Jackie's eyes were ringed with exhaustion. "Did Mom make you say that?"

"I'm saying it because I mean it. It was wrong. Will you forgive me?"

"I suppose I have to. Turn the other cheek and all."

"I don't care what Jesus would do. I want to know if *you* forgive me."

"Yes, Em, I forgive you." Jackie sighed. "Oh, I wish you could see yourself the way other people see you. Don't you know how much we care about you? How much we want you to get better?"

"Now who's stealing lines from Mom?"

"You're going to laugh at me, but I want you to come to one of my healing circles next week." Jackie handed her a brochure. Em wondered if she had a whole box of them under her bed or something, one for every occasion. "It's at the New Life Covenant Church on Pine Street."

"Have I seen this brochure before?"

"We've been passing them out all month, here and in Connellsville and Uniontown. It's our big annual icebreaker meeting."

"Oh, now I remember." The canary yellow fliers had been strewn all about the Savertown USA parking lot, clogging the drains with fluorescent abandon.

"So will you come? I know you don't believe in anything, but if that's true, then what can it hurt? Mom would be pleased."

"New Life Covenant is a cult church."

Jackie frowned and turned back to her reading. "Whatever."

Mom *would* be pleased if Em went, and maybe that was reason enough for her to go. She wouldn't dare ship Em off to the nuthatch after she'd made strides toward recovery with The Lord in hand. He was practically as good as Wes Summersby. And Jackie was right, it wouldn't hurt anything. She might even get a few laughs out of it. "Okay, Jackie. I'll go to your meeting."

Jackie looked up. "You sure took a long time to think about it. Are you planning something?"

"No, just spending some quality time with my sister."

"You better not embarrass me."

"Jesus tells me to tell you to give me the benefit of the doubt."

Jackie got up from her desk and wrapped her arms around Em. "Thank you. I just know it will do you some good. We're not a cult.

We're just a bunch of like-minded people getting together to talk about God."

That would be great, Em thought, *if you didn't conflate God with a narrow slate of morals and call anyone who disagrees an infidel, or worse, legally insane.* "Sounds like fun, Sis."

Jackie frowned. "Thursday at seven. Don't forget."

"I won't." Em pulled free of Jackie and walked down the hall to her own room.

It was the day of the big bowling tournament. Em got up at eight in the morning, showered, dressed in her brand-new bowling shirt with the Savertown USA logo across the back, and rode her bike to the bowling alley right outside the old downtown shell. Her wheels slipped on the thin ice carpeting the road, so she went slowly, riding her brakes all the while.

Damn these early risers, Em thought as she blinked crust from her eyes. People weren't meant to get up this early on their day off. It was unnatural.

The parking lot was crowded with cars, mostly family sedans and pickup trucks with bumper stickers advertising Republican candidates up for election four years ago. Em locked her bike to a lamppost and went inside, where she spotted Mrs. Nguyen and Peter. "Sorry I'm late."

"You're out of breath," her supervisor said. "Did you bike here? Why'd you do that? I could have given you a ride."

"Didn't think of it." A lie. Em didn't like being beholden to anyone.

"Well, you better not be too tired to play. We start in a couple of minutes."

Em laced up her rented shoes with the big purple eight on the back and entered her initials into the electronic scorecard. She tried not to look over to the general merchandise lane, where Agnes and her vocalizing halitosis were no doubt lying in wait. She took a bright pink and blue ball off the rack and started stretching.

She ignored Agnes, but Agnes didn't ignore her. "Ready for the big game, crazy girl?"

Mrs. Nguyen bared her teeth, an angry lioness defending her cub.

"Fuck off, Agnes. Don't let her into your head, Em."

Em watched a puff of the brown smoke exit Agnes's lips and head straight for her like an arrow. *Remember our little conversation.*

She was the first to bowl. Lining up at the mark, she flew down the alley floor, releasing the ball in a perfect arc. A strike. *Guess he was bluffing.* Smiling, she dropped into a hard plastic chair.

As the other workers took their turns, she watched them, studying their faces and interactions with one another. Peter took the red ball engraved with his name off the rack and carried it to the lane. Every move of his was graceful, serene. Em could almost see the individual muscles contract and expand in his arms and legs and neck. It was like he was walking through water.

Sound slowed down along with movement. The cheers of "her" side and the catcalls of the other side stretched out along the full length of the audible spectrum. Em could hear every tone and nuance in their voices, each with their own personal and sinister meaning. Whole conversations were embedded in a single phrase.

Em groaned and put her head between her knees. She was panicking, or hallucinating, or something. A reaction to one of the twelve daily pills? She wasn't sure. Em fumbled for her bag, where she kept the vial of blue pills used to stave off panic attacks. She choked one down, stealing a bit of Mrs. Nguyen's Coke as a chaser.

But still, the slowness remained. Em had to stay sharp. She watched Mrs. Nguyen line up her ball. As she started to stride forward, a tendril of brown smoke languidly snaked across the waxed floor.

"Watch out, Mrs. Nguyen!" Em yelled.

The ball slotted into the gutter, and her supervisor pulled a face. "What is it, Em?" she hissed.

But Em's attention was still on the brown smoke. It fully covered the floor now, at least a quarter of an inch thick, a bubbling stew of sinister motivation made tangible. At least to her.

Em didn't see Mrs. Nguyen's second throw. But she did see the ugly shoes wade through the soupy mix on the older woman's way back to her. The shoes beat out a code. The code warned of microscopic surveillance bots sent out by Savertown USA to monitor the work drones off-hours. The bots were in her jawbone.

"Your turn again," Mrs. Nguyen said. "Come on, get up."

What she means is: get up, Em, so that I can use you like a piece of farm equipment. You are being activated by your friendly supervisor-slash-puppeteer, who turns the key in your back when she needs you and lets you rust in the corner when she doesn't, the brown smoke whispered.

Em looked around at the other workers, all smiling and waiting for her to act. *I may or may not be right,* Em thought, *but other people will always be right.* Therefore, it is logical to follow them. She rose from the bright orange plastic chair — the color cut into her like a military slogan — and took a random ball from the rack. It was too heavy, but things always felt heavy when she was drugged.

Em threw the ball in the general direction of the lane. Her eyes zeroed in on Agnes. *It's you, isn't it? You're doing this.*

The ball clicked into the gutter.

Stop it.

But the acrid gas did not emit from Agnes's lips. Em wanted to scream. *Open your mouth! Let it out!* Instead, she went back to the orange chair, the white noise in her head drowning out Peter's exhortations to get back to the lane, bowl her second frame.

You know it's completely insane to believe that you're talking to a poisonous gas that lives inside a person's body, right? But it was equally insane to listen to the voice that had just told her that, so where the fuck did that leave her? Em put her arms around her knees and closed her eyes to the screaming orange of the chair.

Left, right, left, right. Stomping soldiers entered her field of vision, their bayonets piercing the sky, their boots marking the streets with blood. *Kill the traitor.*

That would be Em.

Two loud pops rang in Em's ear. "Snap out of it!"

Em opened her eyes. It was Mrs. Nguyen, her lips white around the edges.

"Come on, get up there. If you don't take your second frame we'll have to forfeit! Not that you're doing us very much good."

"I can do lots of good." Hadn't she taken ten thousand bayonets to the shin just now, all for the good of her team? *Lousy ingrates.*

"Forget it, Judy, she ain't gonna play," Agnes said.

"*Please*, Em. We've been training all this time." Mrs. Nguyen worked Em's fingers into the holes of a ball. "Just walk over there and let this ball go. You might even hit something."

"I don't want to hit anything. I'm a pacifist."

"That's it," a man from the other side said. "It's been six minutes. The rulebook says you forfeit after five. We win!"

All at once, Em's head cleared. The hallucinations turned off like someone had pressed a light switch. The brown substance that had coated the floor, been controlling them all, receded within moments. She took a deep breath.

"You blew it, Em." Mrs. Nguyen's face was hard.

"But Mrs. Nguyen, I —"

"I don't want to look at you right now. Please leave."

It was you, Em thought. *You made me do this, and there will be more of it if I don't do what you say.* Up to and including permanent insanity.

All the way to the lamppost, she burned with righteous indignation. She had been taken advantage of, manipulated by evil. *I'm a fool, a pawn. I'll show you. You won round one, but I'll take round two.* Rage carried her to her room, it helped her slam the door, then transported her to the bed, where despair took over.

Em pulled the sheets over her head and cried herself into an early-afternoon nap.

Em pressed a container of ice cream to her head, wincing only slightly when the frosty surface touched her ear cartilage. *Give me my next assignment.*

"So the silent treatment is over?"

Cut the crap. I want to kill it.

"Good to see you haven't turned traitor. I was worried there for a little bit."

Traitor. Bloody footprints lined the aisles. A sheen of red. *What do I have to do?*

"We have to attack the nerve center. Once it is disabled, the entity will lose its eyes and ears. Then it will be as blind as me, only able to communicate through indirect means. It will take a while for it to commandeer another body, and in that interval, it can be captured, then disposed of."

Whatever. I'm ready for anything. Let's go.

"You realize that means we have to kill Agnes Walker."

Em did know that, knew it ever since she had first laid eyes on Agnes and felt the entity in her. She just hadn't wanted to admit it. The entity crossed the line when it messed with Em's tenuous grip on sanity. "Fine."

"I thought you said you didn't want to kill anyone."

She's not human, right? She's the entity. The entity has to die.

"If you say so." Escodex paused. "I need you to introduce a line of code — it's something we've cooked up here in my dimension — into Agnes's brain. It will be enough to temporarily dislodge the entity until I can figure out what comes next."

Which means it can come back.

"Yes, it's only a stopgap measure. If you only destroy the nerve center without preparing a suitable vessel for the entity, it will jump into the nearest host. Maybe even you."

Em thought it over, her skin prickling as she imagined the brown smoke inserting itself into her mind, infecting every synapse and neuron. She shuddered. *Okay. Give me the code, tell me how to get it into her. This shit's gone on long enough.*

"Contact me again before the end of your shift. The code should be ready by then."

"I will." She peered up. Mrs. Nguyen was advancing on her. *Three o'clock.*

"Oh, and keep an eye on Roger. He may not be what he seems." Escodex broke the connection.

"You're getting moved to a different department," Mrs. Nguyen said as she towered over Em's hunched body. "I don't want to deal with you anymore."

Any time before yesterday Em would have been overjoyed to get out of the freezer section. Her hands were permanently chapped and her chest hurt from inhaling the frigid air laced with food smells. But now that she knew how disappointed — no, enraged was more like it — her supervisor was, she balked at the change. "Please, Mrs. Nguyen, no. I'm really sorry about the tournament. *Really —*"

"Go see Pendleton." Mrs. Nguyen snapped her head away, closing off any further appeals. Putting the ice cream into the freezer, Em trudged off to Pendleton's office. As she walked down the brightly lit center aisle, she heard a susurration all around her, the other workers at games of gossip.

Paranoia? Yes, but it was based in reality this time. They were all talking about her. And why shouldn't they? She'd fucked up. Let them all down. Proven herself crazy in practice as well as in theory. Em put her head down and walked a little faster. *At least when I get to Pendleton's office, that's just one set of accusing eyes I have to deal with.*

She was wrong. Tony the night manager was there too, along with the counselor who had talked with her after Paula's suicide, and Roger. "What are *you* doing here?"

"Em, Roger believes that you may be in trouble. We want to hear both sides of the story."

"You're going to fire me." It was clear now. Roger was going to tell them about Escodex, and his story would be corroborated by Mrs. Nguyen, who had seen her crouching with a box in her hand enough times to know that something weird was up, even if she didn't know what the weird thing was. They were all against her, making her fight for a stupid job that she didn't even want — except that she did.

"Nobody's talking about firing you. We're just ... trying to get to the bottom of things."

You want the truth? The whole sordid details? Okay, let's have at it. Your store is at the nexus of a dimension-hopping point, and you're being invaded by an evil entity ensconced in the body of your Employee of the Month. Your employees are being killed off one by one as the entity drains their energy, along with their will to live. Does this sound a little crazy? Well, brace yourselves boys, this ride's just beginning. "Please don't take my job away. It's all I have."

"Em, what exactly went on at the bowling alley yesterday? Judy's already told us her version of events, now let's hear yours."

"I freaked out, okay? I couldn't take the pressure and I cracked. It won't happen again."

"Tell him about Escodex," Roger said.

Worlds collided. Em's head swam, and her mouth was dry. She felt as if she was going to faint. But she had to keep cool. "I don't know what you're talking about."

"It's this little alien she thinks she talks to through the merchandise," Roger said to the managers and the counselor. "I swear to God, she told me all about it!"

"Whatever, Roger," Pendleton said. "Em, we're going to put you in women's clothing until we get to the bottom of this. We'd also like you to talk a little with Dr. Michaels once a week in the break room. At Savertown USA's expense, of course."

Em stole a glance at the bland-faced Dr. Michaels. "I already have a therapist."

"Ours is better." Pendleton waved his hand. "You may go now. Roger, you stay."

They're so scared of having another suicide on their hands, Em thought, *but they're using the wrong tactic to uncover them. They're looking for obvious cases, but Jimmy, Paula, and Doug weren't obvious. Roger and me, now that would make sense. Either the entity can't use our energy because we're crazy, or it has some other reason for keeping us alive.*

Em got up and left the room. She mouthed the word "traitor" at Roger as she passed him, but she knew he didn't see it. He was going to have problems of his own to deal with, very shortly.

As she sauntered down Savings Lane — store code for the main aisle — to her new post, a cold shiver crept up her back, into her brain, staying there until all at once she made a horrifying connection.

Fashion Alley. Agnes Walker's department. The entity.

Oh, shit.

Eighteen

"**M**y parents called," Kevin said. He turned away from Em, toward her bedroom window latticed with frost from an early-February cold snap. "They're coming back on the eleventh."

"That's four days from now."

"I can do the math." Kevin flopped back over. He looked miserable.

"Sorry. I'm a little distracted." Escodex had programmed the stalling code into her phone at the end of her last shift. Now she had to figure out how to get the code into Agnes. Escodex had been a little vague on that point.

Maybe in his dimension, they have outlets in the backs of their heads, so you can stick machines in and feed them information that way. A society of living machines.

"Are you even listening to me?" Kevin asked.

"Of course. You have my full attention."

"I don't know how I'm going to face them. I won't be able to lie. Margery will tell them that I tried to kill myself and had to go to the hospital."

"Tell them she's lying."

"I can't. I'm no good at it."

"Come here," Em said, twining her fingers in his hair and pulling him toward her. "You know I'll be there for you. No matter what happens."

Kevin buried his face into Em's shoulder. Hot tears leaked through her thin blue sweater. "I know."

"What time are they coming home?"

"Two," he said, cupping Em's breast with his palm.

"Then call me at three. Or text or whatever. We'll get through this." She kissed him. "What are your parents like, Kevin? They must be pretty bad if you're this scared of them."

"They're old. In their sixties. Kind of traditional. Always wanted me to buck up, be a man. They could tell pretty quick I wasn't going to ever be an athlete, so then they wanted me to succeed in school. Become a doctor or lawyer, get a wife, a family. American dream, right?" He unlocked himself from Em's shoulder and wiped the back of his hand across his face. "They just put a lot of faith in me, and I couldn't live up to it. *Can't* live up to it."

"They don't control you anymore. You're an adult. You don't have to live up to their expectations, you just have to live with yourself."

"Easier said than done, Em."

"I know." *Don't I know.*

Kevin unzipped his jeans and took off his shirt. Em pulled the light cord over her bed. The light from Em's bedroom windows fell across them in stripes, dust motes clinging to the air before them.

That night at dinner, things were more relaxed than they'd been in months. Em chalked it up to her agreement to attend the healing circle at the church on Pine Street. Her mother had even put away the brochures from the group home. They'd littered the dining room table for weeks.

"How's school going, dear?"

"Fine," Jackie said.

"And what about work?" Directed at Em.

"Okay. Getting a lot of shipments in. I may be picking up an extra day sometime soon." Em decided not to tell her about the transfer to another department, or the freak-out at the bowling alley. No use worrying her mother and upsetting the delicate counterbalance she'd worked so hard to achieve.

"Well, that's great." Mom took a bite of meatloaf. "Your Uncle Steve may be coming to spend a few days here at the end of the month."

"May as in *may*? Or may as in definitely coming for sure?" Em said.

"As in definitely coming for sure."

Em groaned. She hadn't seen her uncle in five years, but she hadn't cared for him even then. He was a hotshot heart surgeon from Chicago who drove a Turbo Porsche and had been married three times. He made any excuse to distance himself from his Pennsyltucky upbringing, which is why he only called on Christmas and never wrote. "Why does he want to come here? I thought he hated us."

"Nobody hates us, Em," her mother said in her best you're-just-being-paranoid-stop-it-please voice. "He said he has some big news and wants to share it with us in person. It was too important to talk about over the phone."

"Oh, who cares. He's probably just getting married again."

"Don't be so flip. His girlfriend's coming too, so I expect you to be nice to her."

"Will do." Em scooped more mashed potatoes onto her plate.

"And you too," her mom said, pointing a fork at Jackie. "His girlfriend's Catholic."

"I will be a perfect example of tolerance and empathy." Jackie bowed her head.

Em and her mother exchanged glances, then broke into hysterics.

Working under Agnes was a lot like taking orders from a mentally deficient, micromanaging ape.

"These are red hangers. *Red*. They're for pants and pants *only*. Do you understand me?"

"I know my colors, Agnes," Em said. She might have been crazy, but she wasn't stupid, and that was something Pendleton and Agnes Walker didn't get. Judy Nguyen had got it. But now Mrs. Nguyen hated her, along with everyone on the other side of the store. The general merchandise workers didn't think any more highly of Em, even if she'd won the big game for them.

"Hrumph," the old woman said, shaking her head. "Acted pretty strange at that game the other day, girlie. Like a terrorist. You a terrorist?"

"*No.*"

Agnes clucked her tongue as she heaved a sheaf of blouses onto a table and began folding. "You wouldn't tell me if you were one."

Em sighed, and tugged at the code-laden memory card worn around her neck on a string.

"How do I get it into her?" she'd asked Escodex.

"It can either be viewed or heard. Plug it into a computer and it should open automatically."

"But how will I get her to watch it? We don't, like, hang around outside of work or anything."

"You can figure that out. I have faith in you."

Bad idea, Esky, she thought as she turned the memory card around and around in her hand. How do you convince an entity-infested old woman into sitting at a computer for five minutes, and where would she even find one here? There were display units in Electronics Terrace, but they were locked behind steel cages so customers couldn't fiddle with the drives. They could only play solitaire and poke at a trial version of a money management program.

The loudspeaker, she thought. *That might work.* It was as good an idea as any.

After work, Em biked straight home and set up shop in front of her laptop. She knew from her snooping that the loudspeaker, which Pendleton spoke into often to spout chipper messages to workers or remind customers that there was fifty cents off premium toilet paper in the next half hour, was tuned sensitive enough that it could pick up her boss's breathing or the rustling of papers. It did not have to be loud to be effective, Escodex had said. She would make it as soft as possible, so that it might stay undetected by most of the people in the store yet audible to her intended audience of one.

She loaded the signal onto her old portable digital recorder, the one she'd gotten for her seventh birthday. As she put the hot pink device into her bag, she thought about her dad. He'd given it to her.

"You can use it to record conversations," he had said. "So much of interpersonal communication is lost on initial hearing. We can only know people's true intentions on a second or third go-around." Her father had never talked to her like she was a little girl, which was one of the reasons she loved him.

That recorder caused friction the night she used it to record and study her parents' lovemaking while crouched outside their bedroom door. Em's mom had heard her daughter replaying the machine, listening for the coded messages. Dad had told her everything contained coded messages.

"You told her to do *that*?!" her mom had screamed. She'd tensed, as if to throw Em's gift against the wood-paneled wall, but let it drop at the last moment into Em's waiting hands. Safe.

"No! That was very wrong, Emmeline." He gave Em a stern look, but she could see the wink inside it.

"You're teaching her to be crazy. Like *you*." Em's mom had spun on her heel and locked the door behind her. Three months later Em's father ran out of cigarettes and ice cream, and was seen no more.

"Guess I'm in the doghouse now, kiddo," he'd said in his nasal voice that sounded out of place even to a seven-year-old. "You really shouldn't have taped us, Em. Sex is a private thing for adults."

"I'm learning to listen, like you do."

And now she was a fucking expert.

The next morning, Em came in early. She clocked in and swiftly left the break room before the pep talk began. The loudspeaker squatted on Pendleton's desk like a poisonous toadstool. She switched on the recorder, letting the barely-there auditory code drift through the wires that led to the speaker boxes bracketed to the four corners of Savertown USA. She couldn't hear it at all, but she knew it was playing. She let the code run its full thirty-second length and went back into the employee lounge, hiding the player under her vest.

She stole a glance at Agnes as the workers launched into the jingle. Em sensed a change already, a feeling of something ripped from existence that had been there only moments before, like a dull backache suddenly spirited away. Em peered into Agnes's green eyes. They were blank, but a *human* blank.

Em had bought some time. She smiled at Agnes, human being to human being. Her chest ached when Agnes returned it.

NINETEEN

Em wrote down all the messages heard in her mother's Wes Summersby DVDs on one handy notepad. The hidden messages now filled up forty-five pages. A lot of it was repetitive bullshit, but there were multiple key phrases too, picked out in pink highlighter. Every page of the notebook was headed with the name of the DVD or television broadcast, its original air or release date, and a general outline of what old Wes was flapping his gums about that day in his fake Texas accent.

You're sure crafty, Summersby, Em thought. *It takes a real sharp listener to pick up all this stuff.*

Unhappy with the sounds she could hear from her laptop speakers, she'd bought an amplifier from a skinny music nerd at Savertown USA named Chris, who'd talked up its specs until he was out of breath. "You really get the full range of tones. Treble, bass —"

"I'll take it." She'd set up the equipment on her desk. To her mom and sister, it just looked like she'd treated herself to a new stereo system. They weren't aware of its true purpose.

Well, she thought as she popped a CD into the drive, *it plays music too.*

So many of the true messages were buried beneath layers of backscatter, but she determined that the messages divided themselves into two general categories: ones meant to incite death or suicide among listeners, and others meant to inspire belief in Wes Summersby as some sort of prophet or mystic.

"What have you gotten yourself *into*, Mom?" Em muttered as she recopied an illegible notation. Her next step would be to get her mother away from Wes's mind-controlling messages. She wouldn't be able to live with herself if Mom died.

No matter where you go, she thought, there are people trying to get you to kill yourself. First the entity, now Wes. And of course, all those people at the hospital, they'd tried too. Oh, they'd tried to make her think that they were trying to make her better, make her a functional member of society, but they knew as well as Em did that she'd be better off dead. Her mother would be in debt for years with all the hospital bills Em had incurred, not to mention all those prescriptions. And Em would have no way to pay her back. She'd never get a job good enough to even support her own sorry ass. One life was not worth all that money, or all this attention.

"With surgical focus, she stared at me and said, 'I'm going to reach out, get into your head …'" the voice on the stereo sang.

Em ejected the CD. Guided by Voices. She put a less apt band on and let her mind drift away, where not even Wes Summersby could go.

Things had improved at the store over the past week. Agnes, temporarily rid of the evil entity, remained passive. Almost friendly, even. The routine in general merchandise remained the same as the motions Em performed in the frozen food section, except her hands weren't chapped and bleeding from sub-zero temperatures. It would be a win if she could stop thinking about Mrs. Nguyen's disappointed face.

She was arranging a stack of marked-down post-Valentine's Day red sweaters festooned with pink hearts on a rack when the fabric began to ripple and shimmer.

Em put the security tag to her ear. *You know I don't like you doing that.*

"I need to confer with you."

Em sighed. *Shoot, little dude.*

"We must schedule a time to meet tomorrow. I've arranged a meeting with some top agents and I want to patch you in."

I can't, Em thought-said. *Kevin's parents are coming back tomorrow.*

"Yes, let's put off saving the world so your whiny boyfriend can have a shoulder to cry on."

Em's mouth flew open. "Oh, fuck you."

"I'm just repeating what's in your mind. It's not my fault if you don't know it consciously."

I can't do it and that's final. I have a life outside of you and this store.

"Fine. I'll reschedule." If Em could see his little higher-dimensional eyes, she was sure they'd be rolling in their sockets. Or whatever body part people on Escodex's Earth kept their eyes in.

Escodex, do you have love in your dimension?

"Of course we do. Do you think because we don't use pleasantries we don't know what love is?"

But you're always so cold and logical.

"I'm transmitting messages from another dimension into a completely different language. I'm surprised I'm doing as well as this."

I love Kevin. And tomorrow is going to be very stressful for him.

"You do not care for this person as much as you think you do."

That's a terrible thing to say.

"It's none of my concern. I'll check in with the agents and get back to you. Don't make any more appointments without consulting me."

Ten-four.

He paused, the sign that he was consulting her memory to riddle out an idiom, then disconnected. Em hung the last of the sweaters on the rack and slunk away to the parking lot for a smoke.

Em sat cross-legged on her bedroom floor, cell phone in her lap.

They must be just getting home, she thought, checking the time. Again. *He'll be calling me any moment, asking me to come over. And I will go over. I'll comfort him and make him forget, and let him cry on my shoulder with those big brown eyes of his.*

She just had to wait.

Maybe they got lost, she thought, *or there's heavy traffic. Heavy traffic on a Wednesday afternoon, that could happen. Or they got hit by a car and now they're dead.* Em knew the chances of that happening were slim. Too bad for Kevin.

She could call him. She *should* call him. But Em wasn't that kind of girlfriend. She'd seen girls like that in the hospital, some with restraining orders filed against them. It was pathetic.

Em slumped down on the floor again, her back flush to the wall. She closed her eyes and retreated into the happy place.

In the happy place, Kevin had never gone crazy either. He greeted his parents' return with a clear mind and an open heart. He introduced them to her — Em and Kevin had met through some other cosmic fluke, since Slazinger was not involved in this fantasy — and they had all gotten along great, had talked and laughed the entire night through.

Em meditated like this, legs crossed and back pressed to the wall, for a long time. When she opened her eyes, it was four o'clock. *Dammit! Why hasn't he called?* She stood up and drove her fist into her pillow.

Maybe they'd killed him. Could they be so ashamed that they'd do that, put their suicidal son out of his misery? It couldn't be. *But maybe —*

Em was about to bolt out of the house in Kevin's defense when she felt the steel manacles of doubt clamp onto her mind. *That doesn't make a whole lot of sense*, she thought. *They're not going to kill him. You're being crazy.*

But what else could explain it?

At five-thirty, Em's mother called her for dinner. She tucked her phone into her pocket.

That night, after dinner, Em rode her bike the half hour to Kevin's house. Flurries whipped at her cheeks even through her heavy scarf. Ice patches glinted on the road like canker sores.

Kevin's in pain, she thought. She knew it without even talking to him. He needed her.

At last, she arrived at his house. The Collinses lived in a decent-sized split-level almost twice the size of Em's house. Small trees and rows of cube-shaped topiaries garnished the front lawn. An RV squatted on the circular driveway.

Em parked her bike in the back of one of the cube bushes and peered inside. The lights were on. Silhouetted against the curtains were four figures. They were sitting close to one another on the long living room couch, possibly watching television.

Nobody's throwing anything or yelling. They're just sitting there. Strange. She watched the family through the bushes a few minutes more before turning her bike around and beginning the long trek back home.

TWENTY

"You're not getting out of this," Escodex said.

I'm not trying to get out of anything. Em grunted as she marked down a stack of bright green Christmas yoga pants. It was getting harder to hide her connection to Escodex. Sooner or later Agnes was going to realize the jewelry pinned to Em's ear was a plastic RFID tag, not something from Hot Topic.

"You're troubled."

No, I'm just giving in. I'm trading my own wants and needs for yours. No doubts, no worries, not as long as I listen to that little voice in my head. Your voice, Escodex.

"Do you want to talk about it?"

Why should I talk and risk getting fired? You can scan my memory for anything you want to know.

"It's about that male, isn't it?"

He's not a male, Em said. *He's a man. A human man. He's going to call me.*

"You don't want to know what I think."

You're right, she thought. *I don't want to know.*

"Beginning of your shift tomorrow. Don't be late."

I can't be late. I have to be here in time to sing the jingle.

"I know the jingle well. I don't envy you."

"Nobody envies me." Em fiddled with the tag. *Listen, I've got to break. Old Lady Walker's really been on my case. I'm not up to quota.*

"I understand. We'll speak tomorrow."

Em took the chip from her ear. She turned to find Agnes at her side.

"Were you just talking about me? Who were you talking to, anyway?"

"Nobody. I'm going to go put these pants on the rack now. They're a hot item." She turned away before Agnes could reply.

After work, Em walked — too slippery for bikes today — to Kevin's house. She hesitated as she walked up the polished stone walkway to the front door.

It's so much nicer than our house, she thought. The Collins' doorbell was housed inside a brass dragon's mouth. It shone like the most precious of metals.

Calm down, she told herself, *it's not a competition*. Kevin's house still made her feel like shit. How could Kevin break down, when he had two parents that were together and a big house like this? Em at least had an excuse for being so fucked up.

She took a deep breath and rang the doorbell. It played some classical song that Em supposed she should have known, but didn't. The doorbell at Em's house emitted only a low, broken squawk.

A slightly plump blonde woman with nice teeth answered the door. Em had never felt compelled to notice someone's teeth before, but this woman's were truly spectacular — perfectly straight and that just slightly off-white color that let Em know that while she took care of them on a regular basis, she wasn't a fanatic. She thought about Kevin's lips. *Guess nice mouths run in the family.* "I'm looking for Kevin. Is he here?"

"He's in the den. Who are you?" Again, her smile.

"I'm his, um, friend. Emmeline." She ran her tongue across her own crooked, way-past-eggshell teeth. "Are you his mom?"

"Why, yes, I am. Would you like to come in? We have cookies."

"Okay." Em stepped inside. "You have a very nice house, Mrs. Collins."

"Thank you, dear. You know, I don't think Kevin's ever mentioned you."

"We've only met recently."

"Oh." The woman set a tray of Oreos on the coffee table. "Well, I'll go get Kevin. Make yourself at home."

Em gingerly sat on the ornate flower-printed couch with gilt arms. She nibbled at a cookie from the tray. *These aren't even generic*, she thought. *La-di-da.*

"Em," Kevin said. "You came over."

"I wanted to make sure you were okay. You didn't call … you said you'd call."

"I'm okay," he said. "Listen, you can't stay here."

"Why not? Your mom seemed to like me."

"Oh, God, you didn't tell her you're my girlfriend, did you?"

"No." She put the cookie back on the tray. "*Am* I still your girlfriend, Kevin?"

"I had a really long talk with them last night. About the suicide attempt, about Slazinger, about everything. Everything except you. They want to send me to a place in Vermont where I can get better. And I sort of want to go."

"They're going to put you in the hospital? But you're doing just fine!"

"No, I'm not. And it's not a hospital. It's out in the country, with all these trees and things. It's in Vermont. I'll be staying in a cabin with five other guys and a counselor. They do some really intense therapy there, and survivalist classes."

"Survivalist classes."

"How to survive in the woods, how to shoot, how to build fires." Kevin shrugged. "It's useful."

"And you want to stay in this place. You're not objecting."

"They have an eighty percent success rate, Em." He took her by the hand. "That's high."

"How long are you going to be staying at this high-class asylum? One week? Two?"

"A month. But that brings me to my other point —"

"Which is?"

"I was about to say it. I can't see you anymore." Kevin let go of her hand and walked across the room. "We're poison to each other. I need to be with someone less intense, less —"

"Someone sane."

"I'm just as wrong for you as you are for me."

No, you're not. You're the only stable thing in my life. I need you, Kevin. Em couldn't say any of that. "Well, fuck you too."

"I won't forget about you."

"Enjoy your vacation," she said. "Send me a postcard written in squirrel shit."

Kevin's mom burst into the room. "What's all this racket? Is there a problem?"

Em spun to face the pleasant-looking woman. "I was just leaving. By the way, I fucked your son." She slammed the heavy oak — *real* oak — door behind her as she stomped from the house. The bitter wind teased the tears on her face, chilling her, forming ice crystals on her cheeks and under her chin.

Em called the next few days off work, not realizing until after the fact that she'd be blowing off the rescheduled meeting with Escodex's superior officers. *Screw that*, she thought. *I've got a life of my own. I can't be putting everything off just to cater to the whims of some voice that might not even really exist. That's just crazy.*

Right now, "everything" meant lounging around the house in sweatpants, eating ice cream out of the carton, and watching reruns on daytime television for hours on end. Em had heard this was what you did when you went through a break-up. She couldn't understand why it didn't make her feel better.

"Honey, we need to talk."

Em craned her head around her mother's body. "I'm missing *Pawn Stars.*"

Mom picked up the remote and shut off the set. "Is this a relapse? Do you need me to call Dr. Slazinger?"

This must be serious, Em thought. *She never turns off the television.* "It's not a relapse. Kevin broke up with me."

"That nice blond boy who came over a couple of times? That's too bad, Em." Em couldn't avoid her mother's bear hug, and elected to go limp. "Maybe we should call him anyway. Breakups are hard."

"I'm *fine*," Em said, pulling away. "Don't baby me." She went out to the carport to smoke, something that was guaranteed to keep her mother far at hand.

This pain would subside. It always did. As she sucked smoke into her lungs, she could already feel her anger burn down into a small cinder, something to sweep under the carpet and then forget about, almost as if it had never existed at all. *Kevin* wasn't the problem here. The problem was Wes Summersby.

When her mother left for the afternoon shift, Em took the seven Wes Summersby DVDs from her room and added another three from her mother's recent haul. After stuffing the discs into a garbage bag and tucking them into her own bag, Em stalked out to the carport and got her bike. The street still seethed with icy sores, but it wasn't as bad as it had been.

She rode to the bridge above the Monongahela River, taking the long way so as to avoid the Arroways' house. She hoisted the bag from her shoulder, leaned over the balcony, and chucked the bag of DVDs into the river.

See you in hell, Wes. She wiped her hands as if removing imaginary dirt and rode back home, stopping for a few moments at a convenience store to read the day's headlines.

FOURTH SUICIDE AT DISCOUNT STORE IN THREE MONTHS
Families Look For Answers

Shit, Em thought. *Here we go again.*

"You broke your promise," Escodex said.

"I had important stuff to take care of." Em turned on the faucet to hide her voice from any nebby customers waiting to take a dump.

"Like watching TV and eating junk food," he said. "That's right, I'm scanning your memory, kid. I am very disappointed in you."

His voice sounded even more emotionless and clipped than usual. "I'm sorry. I've got a lot on my plate, Escodex. Kevin broke up with me. I'm sick from a disease that you could easily fix but choose not to, and by the way, I still hate you for that. You make me run around and do all this stuff for you, and it's going to get me fired. They'll put me back in the hospital because of you. So don't give me your shit. I'm goddamn tired of it."

"You must not care very much about knowing where your father is."

"And you're holding that information hostage. That's another reason I hate you."

Escodex paused, but his voice didn't become any softer. "You inconvenienced us, Em."

"And all of this doesn't inconvenience me?" There were voices at the bathroom door, so Em switched to thought talk. *I'm supposed to be getting my head together. I didn't even want to be involved in this. You're slowing down my recovery and wrecking my life. You think I'm your servant. You think everyone in this dimension is worthless, but we're people. And people can only take so much, and I can take less than most.*

Escodex paused. "Are you finished?"

Em sighed. "What did they say? The agents."

"We have decided to move forward. In three weeks we will issue the final blow to the entity. We're going to kill the monster once and for all, before it has a chance to ascend into our realm or suck more life energy from your dimension. And you, Emmeline Kalberg, will play a key role in this fight."

"Do I have a choice?"

"Not really."

"Well, why change things now?" She ducked behind a carton of belts and stoically received her instructions.

Em worked in the toy section of Savertown USA, covering for an absence. She fronted a row of puzzles, making sure the edges of the boxes ran flush with the edge of the shelf. *Like a well-oiled machine,* she thought, Pendleton's fake-homey voice in her mind. Em wiped a speck of dust off the cheek of one of the blonde-haired children on the box. *Perfect.*

Suddenly, the ground began to shake. The cracks between the large tiles in the floor widened, and boxes clattered from the shelves. *An earthquake? In Pennsylvania?* Em held onto the shelves, bracing herself like the victims she'd always seen in disaster movies set in San Francisco.

She pressed a puzzle box to her ear. "Escodex! Help me!" Silence.

Em realized for the first time that the store was deserted. No customers or employees were rushing past her, and the only screams in the store were her own. "Escodex!"

Still gripping the shelves, Em crept toward the emergency exit. She was able to hang on to shelves and displays most of the way there, but the last stretch was a mad dash across a dozen feet of shuddering tile. She staggered through the fallen merchandise like it was an obstacle course and pushed through the emergency door, cringing at the squalling security alarm.

The ground outside was still and stable under her tired feet. The sun had fallen far past the horizon. No cars waited on the black-topped lot, no people were to be seen for miles. Em, annoyed by the scream of the alarm, walked off toward the stand of trees at the edge of the lot.

God, I wish I had a cigarette, she thought, but her bag was back in her locker in the crumbling megastore. She drew her arms around her thin worker's vest and trudged on. She saw something back in the brush, some kind of large animal or person, its movement flashing between the interlocking branches of the grubby trees.

The tiny "woods" opened up into a forest. Em gasped as she walked underneath the giant boughs with their piles of snow. Squirrels scurried around her feet.

This isn't real, she thought.

Up ahead she saw a thinning of the greenery indicating a clearing. Em ducked underneath a pair of low-hanging branches and went inside. In the middle of the clearing, crouching on a rotted log, sat her father.

"Hey there, kiddo."

"Hey, yourself."

"You don't seem too surprised to see me."

"It's as likely a thing as anything else, considering the circumstances."

"Come here," he said, patting the log. She sat down beside him. "Haven't you missed me?"

"Well, yeah. But you aren't *you*. I'm having a psychotic episode."

Em's father tilted his head back and laughed. "You're right, in a way. This is a socially acceptable psychotic episode. Otherwise known as a dream."

Em crossed her arms. "Isn't this a little too logical for a dream?"

"Yeah, maybe. But I don't make the rules here. It's your dream."

Em studied her father's kind, smiling face, with its warm brown eyes and stick-out ears. He hadn't aged a day from the moment when she watched him get into the car from her bedroom window. "What happened to you, anyway? Where did you go?"

"I can't tell you that, honey."

"Then what's the point of you showing up in my dream? Do you have something important to tell me?"

"Just that I love you, and I'm very proud of you."

"Well, now I know you're just a dream. No parent would ever be proud of a kid like me."

Em's father put his arm around her, and pointed upwards. "Look at that, Em. Concentrate."

"The moon?" It hung fat and heavy over the tree-boughs, bright as a spotlight.

"The answers are all around you if you look for them."

"Answers to what? The answer to where you are?"

"Pay attention, Em. Like I always taught you. Deep listening, deep sight."

"I already know how to do that, Dad. Too well."

Her father stood up. "I have to go now."

"No, don't go." But Em knew this had to end eventually. Dreams were a time-dependent psychosis.

"I love you, Em. Stay strong. And keep watching."

"I will." Em gazed around, trying her hardest to capture the scene in memory. As she looked — looked *deep* — the world began to melt and she found herself back in her bed.

He's alive, she thought, *and he's speaking to me.* She knew she couldn't back down now, even if it meant killing Agnes. She buried her face in the pillow. *He's alive and he's waiting for me to find him.* And she would.

Twenty-One

Jackie's church was located in the basement of an abandoned consignment shop. Em locked her bike on a telephone pole next to a hand-lettered cross-shaped cardboard sign reading New Life Covenant Church. A hastily scribbled arrow pointing downward was etched below the letters.

"Here goes everything," Em muttered as she prepared to embrace the healing power of organized religion.

Jackie had already arrived. Em slid into the next seat, a hot pink one with a cracked back. "How did you get here so fast?"

"Jeff drove me here after school." She indicated a nervous-looking boy wearing a dress shirt sans tie. The buttons were fastened all the way up to his Adam's apple. *Thou shalt not display uncovered necks, for it is sinful.* "And you can't sit here. I mean, you *can*, but you're supposed to sit in the front. Since you're going to be healed."

Rituals, Em thought. She inwardly rolled her eyes. "Well then, I'll just mosey on over."

Before sitting down in her assigned seat — she now saw that the three chairs at the head of the room were labeled — Em strode to a card table at the end of the room to get some cookies and milk.

"Hello there, Sister." A twenty-something man with a shock of black hair and piercing green eyes interposed himself between Em and the table of food.

She reached a hand around him. "Just getting some food. I'm *starving.*"

"Yes, we're all hungry for the Word."

"Actually, I'm hungry for some cookies."

"*Em!*" Jackie grabbed at Em's arm. "You'll have to excuse my sister, Reverend. She doesn't know what she's saying."

"Of course I know what I'm saying, *Sister.*" Em pried Jackie's fingers from her arm. "You're the reverend? So this is that new, hip Christianity all the kids are talking about."

"Yes, I received the call young. I believe my youth has really helped to bring a fresh voice to the church. We're doing a lot of very exciting things down here at New Life Covenant."

"Uh-huh. So can I have some food?"

"The body must be sated before the mind can be healed." He moved aside and spread his arm out like a model on a game show. She collected a napkinful of stale gingersnaps and a plastic cup of milk and went to her seat.

Another of the healees-to-be sat in the chair to her left. The woman, dressed in a red blouse with a beaded rose on the shoulder, hacked into a stained handkerchief which she held in one claw-like hand topped with inch-long acrylic fingernails.

"Oh, don't worry, dear, I'm not contagious."

"Neither am I."

"Name's Loretta," the woman said, extending her hand. Em shook it with three quick pumps, then discreetly wiped the woman's filthy residue onto her jeans. "I'm here because the good Lord saw fit to strike me with emphysema, and I've come to ask Him to restore my health, if that is His will."

"I'm here because I'm a paranoid schizophrenic with depressive tendencies."

"The Lord works in mysterious ways."

"Yes, I'm sure it was the Lord who got you hooked on smoking. You had no personal choice in the matter at all."

Loretta the coughing woman narrowed her eyes. "How did you know I smoke?"

"Your fingers are all yellow. Like mine. See?" Em held a hand in Loretta's face.

"I don't think I like you very much." Loretta turned away, a frown on her brown, wrinkled face. "Reverend Freddy's gonna fix you up good."

Let's bring out the stake and burn up some witches, Em thought. *Reverend Freddy's coming to town!* "Well, I certainly hope so. I'd hate to think I came down here for nothing except these crappy cookies." She ate the last of her rock-hard gingersnaps.

"Attention, brothers and sisters! I would like to begin the service." Reverend Freddy stood at the head of the room, his arms outstretched. "We're going to spend tonight participating in the healing of these three poor souls, who have come here to be touched by the light of the Lord."

"Amen," the congregation said in unison.

Em looked to her right, where a middle-aged man had slipped into the last empty seat at the front of the makeshift chapel. She couldn't determine his ailment, but she decided to keep a wide berth, just to be safe.

"Before we commence with the healing, I'd like to take a few minutes and rap about God." Reverend Freddy put one foot up on an empty chair.

Please, no, Em thought.

"We have three people here today who have asked to be healed. Some might say that the Lord gave these people the short end of the stick. But we of The Faith —" he said with audible capitals, "— know that there is no such thing as misfortune. There are only varied blessings, meted out by the whims of the Lord. Tonight, we ask Him to relieve the suffering of these people because of their God-given gifts. We do not seek to question the mind of God, of course —"

"*Of course,*" Em muttered under her breath.

"— merely to open the lines of divine communication. The cure is in God's hands, and it is up to Him to dispense it. Let us pray."

Em bowed her head with the rest of the congregation, but did not mouth their prayers. She cleared her mind of all weighty thought. She thought about pancakes.

"Heavenly Father, we ask you to watch over us as we come together this night to praise your name and ask you for guidance. Grant us strength as we seek to do your bidding on the physical plane. Grant us the serenity to accept your sacred plans with dignity. Amen."

"Amen," the congregation said.

Reverend Freddy put his hand atop the head of the slim, mustachioed man to Em's right. "Lord, first we ask you to reconsider the case of this man, your humble servant Thomas. You have chosen to bestow stomach cancer upon this man, and while we do not doubt your decision —"

A great wave of energy like a silent hum washed forth from the gathered worshipers in their plastic chairs. They were praying. Em crossed her arms around her chest and tried to become smaller. Her eyes flipped shut.

Jackie's energy was clear in the throng. *Don't screw this up,* she seemed to be projecting, *please don't screw this up, Em.* Em tried to open her eyes to look at her sister, but it was as if they were glued together. This energy was more powerful than any she had experienced before. There was no telling what might happen if she were to open her eyes. Maybe blindness. Maybe death.

"— heavenly Lord, take this child into your arms —"

And then she saw it. The flash of the machine. Her machine. She had created it. She had built it with her own two hands, through the power of instant revelation. Some kind of transceiver, that was what it was, two-way communication just like that shared between Em and Escodex through the channel of the microchips buried in the merchandise. She was turning the dials, homing in on a signal —

Can you hear me? Are you out there? Can you hear me?

— while suspended under a massive framework that scraped the ceiling. *This is big*, Em thought. *With this machine I can change everything. I can bring solace to the suffering, alms to the poor, hope to the downtrodden. I can do anything.*

"What's wrong with me?" the memory-voice said. "If you're out there and are listening, tell me that, at least. Why are you making me do these things?"

"Have faith. All will be revealed in time."

"I bet you say that to all your prophets."

"Pay attention. Listen for the signs." It was her father's message, but not his voice.

"But I'm failing all my classes. People turn away from me in the halls. Something is wrong."

"That's not going to matter. The world is dying. Its spark is going out."

"And I can save it?"

"No. Nobody can save it. What I need you to do is destroy it, destroy it so that the others will not keep the empty world going after it has died, in the gray zone of purgatorial reality. Trust in me, Emmeline Kalberg, and I will repay you eleven-fold."

"But why *me*?"

"Why not you?" And when the flat yet loving voice said this, it made perfect sense. All questions flew out of her head as she gripped the brass handles on the underside of the machine and felt the rattling in her bones sync up with the proclamations in her mind.

It had been a full-body divine experience. And it had *really happened.*

Em's vision disintegrated. She was back in the cult church on Pine Street, gripping the undersides of the chair with her fingernails so hard her cuticles ached. Sweat poured down her face. Before she could stop it, a low whine escaped her mouth, drawing the attention of Reverend Freddy.

"I'm pleased you are getting something out of this, Sister Emmeline, but it's not time for your healing yet. Thomas is first. Please wait your turn."

Em tore herself from the seat and staggered through the gaping faces of the congregation. A hand, maybe Jackie's, reached for her, but she pushed it away on her sprint up the steps and through the glass double doors. She inserted her key into her bike lock with trembling fingers. A loud bang sounded behind her.

"Em, are you okay?" Jackie.

"I'm sorry, Jackie. I'm sorry for everything. I'm sorry I wasn't a better student." *Or prophet.* "I'm sorry I embarrassed you in front of all your friends. I shouldn't have come here."

"I'm not mad at you."

Em took the handlebars of her bike and steered it down the sidewalk. Jackie followed close at her heels. Em kicked her away as gently as she was able to. "Best take off, Sister. I bring bad news."

"You shouldn't go home by yourself. Just come back inside and we can call Mom."

But Em didn't listen. She swung herself onto her bike and merged onto the road, the echoes of memory shaking the tiny bone chips in her ears and obscuring the street before her eyes. She had to get home. She had to get home *right away*.

To redraw the plans for the machine. To rebuild. To issue the final proclamation to a dying world. The proclamation of total destruction.

In her bedroom, Em crouched over a sketchpad. A rough sketch of a machine — the machine, her machine — sprawled beneath her.

The machine was the rough shape of an octopus. The operator would lie underneath a wooden central column supported on short legs. His or her hands grasped onto the brass handles at the sides of the bottom of the column. The handles sloped upwards to become thick, rigid ropes like violin strings that were attached to the eight corners of the machine. Wooden framework held up the brass strings, keeping them aloft. An array of dials and switches spread across the underside of the column, where it could be manipulated by the operator. These controls were detailed further in an inset in the corner of the paper.

As she studied her sketch, Em felt an inescapable desire that the machine should exist. It was more than a desire, it was an *ache*. She could feel its eight extensors twitching in their fitful nonexistence, waiting to be born.

I made it before and I can make it again.

The world was dying. Anyone could see that. When the world finally died, it would be replaced by a Potemkin Village that looked exactly like the true world. Only by issuing the final proclamation of the machine could Em destroy the world completely and stop the false world from coming into existence.

Buying time. The phrase had tickled her brain once before, but now she knew what it really meant. The powers in charge wanted to keep the world going even after its spark died so they could cash in lock, stock, and barrel on time itself, in a capitalistic system even more pure than that which reigned at Savertown USA. The people in control would be trading on the future like it was a resource.

Only utter destruction would keep this from happening, and only the voice in this machine could offer the keys to total destruction.

And this, she thought, *this is the entity. It is them, taking over the dead world so they can use it as a commodity. It's all coming together. Escodex is a prophet like me, a prophet in a reality whose spark hasn't gone out. He wants to stop it from escaping into his reality because he knows this reality is doomed.*

The signs were all here. Unexplained suicides, life-sapping television therapists, missing fathers … it all came together and it all fit. The machine would be the key.

And the machine would live again. Studying her sketch, her nose almost to the rough-grained surface, Em calculated the amount of raw materials she would need to birth the machine. Her mind worked like lightning, the equations being solved almost before she could think of them, almost as if they were being guided by an external computer jacked directly into Em's brain.

What was she saying, *almost?*

TWENTY-TWO

As Em walked into the bathroom the next morning, she felt like she swam in gelatin. Everything looked flat, like she watched the world through a distorted Instagram filter.

It's these damn pills, she thought as she opened the medicine cabinet for her morning doses. *They're dampening my senses.* As she shook out one of the red pills, two of them slipped into the sink and slid down the drain.

Shit. Mom would kill her. Em's pills were expensive, and she only had enough to keep her going until her next appointment with Slazinger, and who knew if she was ever going back there? She'd missed her last two appointments. Work stuff. Escodex stuff. *Life* stuff.

Well, she could skip a few doses. That way, if her mom did come in here and count the pills, she would think Em was on schedule, and Em wouldn't have to admit her clumsiness. What could missing two little red pills do? Nothing. Em took the other two pills, the green antidepressant and the blue anti-anxiety drug, and put all three bottles back in the cabinet.

She padded downstairs to the kitchen, where her mother ate a breakfast of eggs and bacon. "I made you a plate," her mother said, gesturing.

"No time. I have to get to work."

"There's always time to eat." Mom stared at her until Em sat down. She picked up her fork and started eating. "Don't forget, Uncle Steve will be here tomorrow afternoon. Four o'clock."

"Do I have to be here?"

"Of course you have to be here. He's *family*."

"Family that hates us."

"We'll be going out to dinner at the Grille. You like that place, don't you?"

"Not really. Their food is lousy."

Mom rolled her eyes. "I'm so sorry, Your Highness. I didn't know."

"What you wouldn't know could fill a warehouse." She'd meant it to sound funny and light, but her mother's expression showed that it had been anything but.

"Just don't embarrass me."

Em waited until her mother left the room, then scraped the rest of her eggs into the trash. Food would only slow her down; the rumble in her belly would make her focused, alert. She took a few deep breaths, then pushed her way outside into a somewhat clearer world.

At the store, Em held a discounted linen skirt printed with grape vines to her ear. She didn't even bother with the thought-speech. "What's up, Esky?"

"I have the plans," Escodex said. "Let me beam them to you now." A series of blueprints, similar to the one she had drawn for the machine, flooded her mind. "Don't worry about remembering them right now. These plans are time-released. They will come back to you gradually, as you need them, when your mind is clear."

"What if I can't find the materials to build them?"

"They can all be found here, within my communication limit. This store has furnished the materials for its own salvation."

"Salvation," Em said, turning the word over in her mind. Then she took a look at the plans, which had lodged in her mind in the form of a perfectly encoded memory. "What the hell, Escodex, there are *guns* in these plans. I'm not carrying a gun."

"Those are energy-redirection guns. They drive the entity out of anyone it infests. You'll be saving lives with those guns."

"Except for Agnes." Em's spine suddenly went cold. She didn't want to kill the old woman, but it had to be done, right? For the good of everyone, it had to be done.

"Em, are you feeling well? Your mind feels turbulent today. I checked your memory. You didn't take your red pill this morning, the one that prevents paranoid thoughts."

"It fell down the sink."

"You really should take your medication. If your mind is not clear, you won't be able to remember the plans."

"I can see them *now*."

"You have to take care of yourself. My dimension depends on it."

"Great, now even my delusions are nagging me about my mental health." Em draped the skirt over her head as she arranged a rack of belts by their length, width, and buckle color. "Nobody would believe I lost it. They don't have access to my memory. And it's only two doses."

"I *need* you to be sharp, Em."

The red blouses stacked neatly on the table before her glowed with an almost ethereal light. Every grain of wood on the table stood out sharp and distinct. The world was alive again.

"I'll remember the plans, Escodex. I'll help you defeat the entity and turn back the entropic forces."

"And you will know where your father is. That's the real prize, isn't it?"

But it wasn't, not anymore. The disappearance of one man paled in comparison to the greater issues very near at hand. Em now knew her father's leave-taking was just a sign, just like the suicides of the employees or Jackie's church or, well, everything. Everything was meaningful, nothing was wasted. In the land of metaphysics, where all was connected, where one thing always led to another, her father's disappearance helped to form a chain of events that could be no more avoided or explained than the genesis of life itself. With every breath she took, Em witnessed the cosmic cycle.

On her shoulder fell the rough hand of Agnes Walker. "Pick up the pace, Kalberg." Her voice was toneless, hard, and clipped. Her touch was graceless, thick, and angry. And in her eyes burned the fire of the entity, returned from its brief slumber.

The next night, Em and what passed for her entire extended family took a trip to the only three-star family-style restaurant in Clear Falls. Jackie called shotgun, which left Em in the back seat next to Uncle Steve. Next to him, in the other window seat, sat his new-ish girlfriend, Lydia.

"My, but this car is quaint," Lydia said, wrinkling her nose at the rusted two-door sedan.

"Where's the Porche?" Em asked.

"We flew," Uncle Steve said. "Took a taxi down from Pittsburgh."

Just like always, Em thought. *Pissing away money on a flight that would take eight hours to drive at most, then bragging about it.*

"I could have picked you up at the airport, Steve," her mom said. "You didn't have to take a taxi."

"Eh, don't worry about it. The heart business is booming this year. Lots of fat people out there. It's a good time to be a thoracic surgeon."

"How heart-warming," Em said. Jackie giggled, which was almost worth the fierce look Mom gave both of them. Em stared out the window until the sedan pulled into the dinky, trash-cluttered parking lot.

Sal's Hometown Grille was a restaurant that had spent its previous life as a slaughterhouse. The batwing doors led into a room lined with paneling and the black-and-yellow regalia of the Pittsburgh organized sports machine. Fake buffalo heads wearing sunglasses and pompadours lined the walls. The whole production made Em feel vaguely ill.

A waitress wearing cowboy boots and a bolo tie seated them at a cow-shaped table. She passed out menus die-cut to look like pigs. The dessert listing was in the snout.

"I have an announcement to make," Uncle Steve said.

He's getting married, Em thought. *Again.*

"In three months, Lydia and I are getting married. We'd like to fly you all out to Chicago for the ceremony."

"Well, isn't that *lovely*," Em's mom said.

"We're having the ceremony at Holy Name Cathedral. It's been my dream to get married there, ever since I was a little girl." Lydia flushed.

"Yeah, it's going to be a big event," Steve said. "Catered dinner, a string quartet, the works. Nothing's too good for my special lady." He gave Lydia's shoulder a squeeze.

"How many people are attending?" Em's mom asked.

"Oh, around two hundred. Lydia's family, a bunch of people from Lutheran General, some of our friends from the country club. We'd love to have Em and Jackie there too, as bridesmaids."

Em and Jackie exchanged glances. *Catholic church*, Jackie seemed to be saying. *Paranoid schizophrenia with depressive tendencies*, Em fired back.

"We'll think about it," Em's mom said.

The waitress arrived with their drinks and took their orders. "It's on me," Steve said. Em flipped to the page with the steaks.

"Your mom tells me that you're making excellent grades in school," Lydia said to Jackie. "Have you been looking into colleges?"

"I want to apply to the Academy of the Light, but Mom says it's too far away." The Academy of the Light was a Christian liberal arts school in Cheyenne, Wyoming. It was the only institute of higher learning endorsed by New Life Covenant Church.

"It's not even accredited, sweetie," Mom said. They'd had this conversation so many times before that Em could have recited it from memory by now.

"They're working on that," Jackie said, turning away.

"And what about you, Em? What are you studying? I don't think your uncle told me."

"I don't go to school. I'm a stocker at Savertown USA. It's that big-ass building you pass right as you come into town. Can't miss it."

Lydia's face instantly fell. "Well, I suppose everyone goes through life at their own pace. You are planning on going to college eventually though, right?"

"I don't think so. It doesn't really matter." *Because the world is dying,* Em thought. *The spark of the world is going out and you don't even know it.*

"You ought to be studying medicine," Steve said, pointing the tip of his straw at her. "There's a world of opportunity in medicine right now. People are lazier than ever, and that means there's lots of call for doctors."

"I don't think I want to be a doctor."

"Or a nurse. There's call for nurses, too. Or a physician's assistant, that's wide open, too. I've got a few friends at Penn State, I can get you into a great program." He took a sip of pop. "You'll be making sixty grand a year right out of the gate."

"I don't want to do that, either. And I failed biology twice in high school."

"Oh, that's just because you weren't motivated. That's the trouble with kids today, no motivation. They're content to get some crappy job and live with their parents forever, so they don't have to take initiative for anything. They just want to coast. You're better than that, Em."

"What exactly are you basing that on?" Em said. She felt her mother's long-nailed hand dig into her side.

"Em will go to college when she's ready. Lord knows I'd like to have her out of the house. We're looking at next fall."

Liar, Em thought. *Slazinger said I can't even start thinking about school until a year from now. But then, you can't possibly tell your accomplished brother about Slazinger, because then you'd have to admit that you have a fucked-up kid.* She reached under the table and pinched her mother back.

"Well, give me a call when you do want to get off your ass and go. It would be quite an achievement to have two doctors in the family."

"I don't want to be a doctor," Em repeated. Her mother started to shush her again when the food arrived. She picked at her bleeding steak, death on a plate.

If they only knew, she thought, *all I'm trying to do for them. They'd think it was a delusion but they'd be wrong. Those suicides actually happened. That's physical evidence you can take to the bank.*

"Don't pick at your food, Em. Eat it."

"Oh, don't encourage her," Uncle Steve said to Em's mother. "She's beginning to look a little sloppy. She's going to have to slim down if she wants to get into one of Lydia's bridesmaid dresses. A girl should keep a trim figure."

"I'm not fat," Em said, self-consciously looking down at her body. "I was too thin before."

Uncle Steve snorted. "Whatever."

"Oh, shut your dick mouth," Em snapped.

"Emmeline," her mother said, pounding her fist on the table hard enough to make the forks clatter.

"No, I'm sick of it. He comes over here after five years of barely speaking to us, throws his money around like he's a king, then insults us. If I said this kind of stuff you'd kick my ass, but because he's a rich doctor he can say whatever he wants."

"You will respect your uncle and his fiancée."

"Or what, you'll throw me out of the house? Fat chance of that. You know what would happen if you did. I'd be living on the street in a cardboard box. Just imagine the shame." She turned to Steve. "For your information, I'm fat because of a side effect from medication. I was going to college, but I got kicked out when I had a psychotic break. I've been working at the store because I *want* to get my head together, I *want* to be normal, but it's getting harder every day. Maybe you should consider that before you pass judgment on me."

Mom's teeth ground. Jackie stared downward. Lydia fiddled with her napkin. "Oh God," her uncle said, rolling his eyes. "Not that old excuse."

"What." Statement, not question.

"Mental illness is the oldest excuse in the book. Your mom *should* kick you out of the house. That would make you grow up mighty fast."

"No, it would make me a homeless person living on the street."

"This meal is over," Em's mom said, raising a finger. "Can we get some boxes over here?"

"Psychiatry is a whole industry created just to keep people from taking responsibility for their lives. They give you a bunch of sugar pills, make you see a therapist so you can blame all your problems on other people, and for what? You just need a swift kick in the pants, girl."

"They have some pretty big side effects for sugar pills," Em said.

"Boxes! Please!"

"Just leave it, Bea. Remember, it's on me." Steve stood up and dashed his napkin onto the table. The five of them swung through the batwing doors back to the parking lot.

In quiet fury, they rode the fifteen minutes back to the family home. As Mom went downstairs to prepare the den for the visitors, Jackie gave Em a hug.

"I'm really proud of you for standing up to that guy." Jackie shook her head. "I don't like him."

"I thought you had to love everyone."

"You're really going to get it when Mom comes back. You know that, right?"

"I think you're wrong," Em said. "Mom thinks he's a blowhard, too." Em gave her sister a final squeeze and headed toward her bedroom.

The next morning, Em shook one red pill out of the vial in the cabinet. After skipping the last two doses, it was time to get back on track.

Goodbye, color, she thought. *Goodbye, sound.* She poured a glass of water and held the pill to her lips.

But what if Uncle Steve is right? Em hadn't taken her pill in two days, and she felt a lot less crazy the last two days than she had in the days immediately following the revelation, when she had been medicated. Her responses were all screwed up. Maybe the pills *were* placebos.

Even if they were, what could it hurt to take them? Well, there were the side effects — weight gain, dulled senses, lack of motivation. And they cost an awful lot of money.

She could try it. She could try being without the pills for a little while. She could keep it all under control, and start right back up if she had to. These colors were just so nice, and this sense of purpose was just so fulfilling.

But I promised to take them —

But the world is dying —

She bit down hard on her lip as she slipped the pill down the drain.

Twenty-Three

The problem with conducting your own reality testing, Em thought, *is that sometimes the people you're surrounded with are not all right in the head, either.* Such was the case with Agnes Walker. For the past few days, her supervisor had become more ruthless, more distant, less *human*. Her green eyes grew ever-sharper in the pudgy mass of her face. Bit by bit, the entity had retaken Agnes's mind.

"Stop dallying," Agnes said when she caught Em crouching against the floor in communication with Escodex. "There's work to be done."

Oh, there's work to be done, but not what you think. I have to defeat the evil force inside you. I have to destroy the world completely. The spark is dead, and you are a symptom.

The guns still bothered her. Escodex tried to convince her that the guns weren't lethal to any being except the entity, but she didn't see how the entity could be extricated from Agnes without hurting her. They were as finely enmeshed as a chemical compound.

"Maybe she won't die," he had said. "She might just be a vegetable for the rest of her life."

"I wouldn't call that living."

"You know it has to be done. Otherwise, the employees will keep dying. And then your whole universe will be destroyed as the entity takes all available energy for its push into my dimension."

It's going to be destroyed anyway. Might already be.

"You haven't been taking your pills."

This was true. She'd been off the red pills for a week, and had stopped taking the others soon after. "That's none of your business. I'm doing what you're asking me to."

"It is if you can't interpret those plans."

"Everything's going to be *fine*," she said. "You'll see." She broke communication and continued folding rayon blouses.

At home, Em skirted Uncle Steve and Aunt-to-Be Lydia. She ate all meals in her room, picked up extra shifts at the store, and took the back door — the one that did not cut through the den — into the house. It was a fairly effective quarantine, though she caught sight of his judging face once or twice.

He's right, you know. It really is all a lack of initiative. I feel like I could do anything now, if the world wasn't dying.

Em bent over the God-machine blueprints scattered on the taupe carpet of her bedroom. She clutched a pencil and waited for inspiration to hit when the door rattled in its frame. She hesitated, but answered it anyway.

Jackie tiptoed in and eyed Em's blueprints. "What are you doing?"

Em stuffed her sketches of the transceiver underneath her bed. "Nothing. Well, I was drawing, but that's nothing."

"I hate that guy."

"I think everyone hates that guy. Even his fiancée. Even *Mom*."

"I'm not going to that wedding."

"I don't think I'm even invited anymore. I haven't got the initiative to walk down an aisle."

"You look really good, Em. Did you lose some weight?"

"A little, I think. My clothes are looser."

"And you seem a lot less depressed. Those pills must be working."

Well, it's kind of a funny story, Em wanted to say. *It turns out the pills were keeping me from realizing my full potential as the one who will save the world by destroying it. But I figured it out. That's why I'm okay.*

"Yeah, guess so."

"Em, what do you do when you figure out you like a guy?"

Em raised her eyebrows. "Does Jackie have a boyfriend?"

Jackie smiled. "It's that guy Jeff from church. The one who drove me."

"Oh, I remember. Mister I-button-my-shirt-*all*-the-way-up."

"After you left, he came outside. We held hands, and I really wanted to kiss him, but … Reverend Freddy kind of doesn't like that. He made us swear we wouldn't kiss anyone until we signed a promise agreement."

"Well, you don't have to listen to Reverend Freddy. If you feel like kissing him, you go right ahead and kiss him."

"How long did you wait?"

Wait? Em felt like laughing. Even though she'd been a morose, unpopular teenager, she'd dated a fair amount of people in the tri-county area and was for a time considered an easy lay. She didn't care about any of the people she slept with. She just liked sex. That wasn't the right path for Jackie, though. "Don't worry about what I did. Every relationship is different. When it's the right time to kiss Jeff, you'll know. You'll just feel it. But if you decide to sleep with him, tell me about it. I'll help you get some protection."

"Oh, no," Jackie swung her head so fast her long ponytail banged against the sides of her face. "That's expressly forbidden. Not until marriage."

"If that's what you want," Em said, and she meant it.

On the seventh day of their Pennsyltucky vacation, Steve and Lydia left, declining Mom's offer of a ride back to Pittsburgh. Em watched him go from her bedroom window, as she had watched her father leave over a decade ago. As the taxi sped away, Em had to admit that

Uncle Steve's visit had been something of a turning point. He was an asshole, sure, a man who didn't really love his would-be wife and flaunted his money and reacted with knee-jerk bigotry toward anything he didn't understand. But it was his bigotry that had inspired her to throw off the chemical straight-jacket of the medication. Because of that, she would be able to approach the final destruction of everything with a clear mind.

Em went into the bathroom and shook three more pills into the sink.

The next day, Em and Jackie shoveled the front walkway. It was the first week of March, but the heavy snowfall this year meant that there was still a layer of sludge on the ground. Em dug in, feeling the scrape of the metal shovel on the concrete walk, the way the vibration of the shovel traveled through her body like an electric shock.

In her headphones, the jangle of Neutral Milk Hotel was replaced by the breathy tones of Elliott Smith. Em hummed along, moving the shovel in time with the music.

A series of sharp honks pulled her out of her trance. Em yanked off her headphones and sidled up to the maroon car with the gouge on its side. The window rolled down. "Got a minute?" Roger's blue eyes squinted against the bright sun.

Em scowled. "What do *you* want?"

Roger eased himself out of the car. "Follow me."

Em made a time-out sign to Jackie and reluctantly followed the fat man. He swept the snow off of her mom's parking chair and lit up a cigarette, offering one to Em.

"Em, I'm worried about you."

"You came all the way here to tell me that?"

"I didn't think you'd talk to me at work."

Em released a puff of smoke. "Probably not."

"You may not believe it, but there's a lot of people back at that store who care about you. I know Judy's awfully concerned, and Mr. Pendleton —"

"— thinks that I lack the proper Savertown USA spirit."

"That doesn't mean he can't care about you as a person. Even the boss has a heart, Em. I've seen it."

Em shrugged her shoulders. She didn't believe him about Pendleton, but Mrs. Nguyen had always been straight-up with her. Her heart tore as she thought about how she had disappointed her old supervisor at the bowling tournament. "So what? I don't have a future there anyway. I'm almost washed up."

"Yeah, you're probably right about that. But you're too smart for that place. So is Judy, so am I. The difference is that you're young. You can get out of that place if you want to. Don't let yourself lose yourself."

She turned to him. "What?"

"I know you haven't been taking your medication."

Em snorted and made sure her sister wasn't listening. "How would you know that? It's not true. And even if it was true, who could you tell? Nobody will believe you."

"You'll tell them soon enough with your actions." Roger shook his head. "I've been where you are, though. You're not going to listen to me. You have to experience it yourself, get down to the very bottom before you can start pulling your way back up. Maybe you'll even go through this two, three times before it sinks in. I hope not." Roger's jaw worked as if he had something more to say, but couldn't place it.

"If you don't think I'm going to listen to you, then why did you come over?"

"I don't know. Just … don't give up hope. I know it's tough. I wasted ten years of my life on this shit. I was in and out of the hospital all the time, living on the street until the cops picked me up and the whole cycle started over again. I thought that would always be my life. Until I figured out a way to succeed."

"You're a deli boy at Savertown USA. I wouldn't call that success." Em ground out her cigarette under her boot.

"It's better than living in a hospital. It's better than what I was ten years ago." Roger shook his head. "And things are so much better for you, Em, with the new pills and all the support systems I never got. You're much smarter than me. You won't be working at Savertown USA for the rest of your life."

"I don't *have* a support system," Em said. She thought about Slazinger with his little black notebook and blasé expression. "I don't have *anything.*"

Roger stood up. "Well, I've said my piece. It's all up to you now." Roger hefted himself back into his ugly car. The muffler growled as the car lumbered away.

Jackie looked up from her shoveling. "Who was that?"

"Nobody important," Em said, as she watched Roger's car recede down the horizon. "Just some crazy man."

Twenty-Four

Em's first session with Dr. Michaels took place in the employee lounge, while everyone else toiled away on the sales floor. As she waited for the company psychologist to arrive, she gazed at the poster-plastered walls of the lounge. The inspirational office art and notices of Savertown USA potlucks and baby announcements burst at the seams with symbolic meaning.

Em didn't know what to think about this appointment, which had already been rescheduled several times. *On the one hand*, she thought, *I have to see this company shill, who is going to be even less competent than Slazinger. On the other, I get out of work for an hour.*

The door swung open and Dr. Michaels entered. Unlike Slazinger, he wore a three-piece suit. Not a cheap suit, either. A Savertown USA employee badge dangled from his breast pocket. "Hello there, Miss, ah —" He checked his files, apparently forgetting her name though they'd met twice before. "Kalberg. Can I call you Emmeline?"

"No, you may not."

The corner of the doctor's mouth twitched, but he took a deep breath and sat down opposite her. "Your manager, Lars, asked me to come down and speak with you today. Now, I don't normally do this type of thing, but I decided to make an exception in your case. Lars is a very good friend of mine."

"Larsss," Em said, letting the s trail off.

"Miss Kalberg, have you been under a lot of work-related stress lately?"

"Not any more than usual."

"How are things with your family?"

"I think I should save the good stuff for my regular therapist."

"According to your employee record, you've been displaying bizarre, erratic behaviors in line with a self-reported pre-existing psychiatric condition. Tell me, Miss Kalberg, are you on any sort of medication for this condition?"

"Yes," Em lied.

"Now, I don't have any authority over your course of treatment, I can't make you do anything, but perhaps it might be prudent to make an appointment with your regular doctor to, um, discuss this situation."

"If you'll permit me to get a word in edgewise, Dr. Michaels, may I ask which of my behaviors are quote-unquote 'bizarre and erratic'?"

He consulted his notes. "According to your old supervisor, Judy Nguyen —" he pronounced it *engine-yen*, "you had a little meltdown at the company bowling championship."

"That's not *at work*. That was an extracurricular activity. I can't be faulted for freaking out on my own time, can I, doctor?" She looked him square in his dull hazel eyes.

"Some employees, and more importantly *customers*, have witnessed you kneeling on the sales floor holding merchandise to your head, and appearing to either talk to or concentrate very hard on it." He tapped his fingers on the card table. "On *store time*," he added snarkily.

"I just get tired sometimes. I have to sit down. I haven't damaged anything."

"You have to admit that it's a little confusing to our valued customers."

"So is subtraction."

Dr. Michaels gave a heavy sigh. "Miss Kalberg, I get the feeling that you don't like working for Savertown USA very much."

"No, I like it. If it wasn't for my coworkers and the customers, this would be heaven."

"Come on now, Emmeline. Every person in this store works extra hard to bring a little bit of convenience and quality to the lives of average Americans. The last thing they need is to be put down by some know-it-all teenager doing this job for pocket change."

"Well, if these people need the money so badly, maybe you shouldn't pay them nothing but pocket change. They might work a little harder that way."

Dr. Michaels raised his eyebrows. "I don't control the wages."

"No, you just try to convince people that they don't suck."

Dr. Michaels made a note in Em's permanent record. "Like I said, I can't control what you do. I'm not your doctor. But I think you're heading down a very dangerous slope, and maybe you should think about letting your coworkers help you through it." He leaned back. "Even though we're all stupid and evil."

"Suggestion noted." Em looked at the door. "Can I go now?" *See what you've done?* Em thought. *You're making me want to go back to work. That's pretty evil.*

"Yes, Miss Kalberg, you can go. But can you try to do just one little thing? Try to enjoy the simple pleasures in life. Maybe if you were a little more cheery, you'd see that life can be a wonderful thing, and you wouldn't be so depressed all the time."

Don't you see, Dr. Michaels? If it wasn't for me and my "bizarre, eccentric" behaviors, there wouldn't be any simple pleasures, because there wouldn't be anything at all. You may not like me, but you need me. All of you. "Okay," she mumbled, as she went back out to the sales floor.

Agnes wasn't around, so Em dug into the box of spring-themed ponchos, fresh off the truck from a Honduran sweatshop. She hadn't even finished re-organizing the display when Agnes appeared at her side. "Back from your psycho appointment already?"

"Takes one to know one," Em said, *you unearthly evil entity.*

Agnes face reddened. "Ungrateful child."

"Agnes, how long have you been working here?"

"I've worked here since the store opened." She cocked her head. "I reckon about seven years now."

"And before that?"

"Cashier at the Clear Falls Drugstore. Worked there about thirty years before it closed. Why do *you* care?"

It is fitting that her conscious mind will die with this store, Em thought. *Her life as she knew it ended when the drugstore closed. That was not only the end of independent business in Clear Falls, but of this town's overall independence. What is left for her if she survives? A life of ponchos and holiday sweaters, a life of patriotic vests and company jingles. That may be a life, but I wouldn't call it living.*

And yes, Dr. Michaels was right, Em *was* elitist. She didn't want that kind of life for herself or the people she cared for. People like Mrs. Nguyen, Mr. Pendleton, and even Agnes deserved better. They deserved to live in a society where they could build their own businesses, forge their own dreams, not kowtow to a company line dictated from up above by multi-billionaires. Dr. Michaels was wrong. Em *did* see the small beauties in life, the preciousness of every living thing. And she knew that even the lowest humans of them all deserved better than this.

"No reason. Hey, are these supposed to be marked seventy-five percent off? Looks like a mistake to me." Em looked up at her supervisor. For a split second, she could see the way the entity lurked inside Agnes like the writhing of a wasps' nest. Agnes, the paper shell, was hollowed out completely until only one emotion remained: fear.

Even through it all, Agnes Walker lived. And she was *scared*.

"They're Christmas sweaters. We'll never sell them now. Might as well just give them away."

"Agnes, I'm sorry you have to work with me."

Just for a moment, Em could see Agnes's humanity. She could tell that Agnes wanted to cry out, tell Em what was happening. Then the entity came back, flickering in those green-brown eyes like St. Elmo's Fire.

"You're right, it's not easy working with a nut. Now get those security tags on that box of pants. We ain't got all day."

Em nodded, and returned to her work.

That night, Em dreamed of flight. Held by straps against a narrow seat, she watched the slow progression of clouds like transparent glaciers against the night sky.

"This is your captain speaking. We are experiencing slight turbulence —"

The plane bucked. Em's fingernails scraped the leather armrests. She looked around to discover that she was the only person on the plane. She closed her eyes and took deep breaths.

Happy place.

An in-flight magazine peeked out of the pocket of the seat in front of her. She turned to the centerfold. Printed there, as big as life, was a picture of the octopus-shaped transceiver.

Someone passed by her in the aisle. It was Reverend Freddy, dressed in his button-up dress shirt and cardboard collar.

"What are you doing here?" Em said.

"You never got your healing."

"You can't heal me. Nobody can."

"God loves you, Emmeline Kalberg." Reverend Freddy leaned over her and gave her a kiss. His lips were sandpaper.

"Let me up," Em said. "I have to see the pilot." She wrested Reverend Freddy away and stumbled to the cockpit.

The plane bucked again. Oxygen masks tumbled from the ceiling. Em ran toward the front of the plane, only to be halted by a hand which reached out from the bathroom and pulled her inside.

"Don't go in there," Dr. Slazinger said. "That way lies madness."

"Well, what have I got going for me now?"

"You won't like it."

"I don't like you."

"And yet," he said, his eyebrow arcedm "if you go in there, I will be forced to put an 'against medical advice' notation on your chart. And I'll tell your mother."

"The world is dying. Its spark has gone out." She pulled away. "I don't care about my mother."

The cockpit was locked. Em beat at the handle with her fists and screamed. *I have to save this plane. If this plane crashes, then I've failed. Why are they making me fail? Why are they doing this to me?!* Suddenly, the confident voice of Trevor the Jesus Freak spoke in her mind.

"The edges are strong, sister, but the center cannot hold."

She punched the door so hard a small bone in her hand snapped, but the door popped open. Em said a silent prayer of thanks to the prophet and walked over to the pilot. It was Agnes Walker, staring straight ahead at the distant formless clouds.

"Back to work, Kalberg."

"Let me see your eyes."

She turned and Em looked. *Deep* looked. It was not the entity that burned in Agnes's eyes this time. It was Escodex.

"Don't crash this plane!"

"What else can be done?" Escodex said with Agnes's mouth. "You can't remember the plans. You're the one crashing this plane."

She looked at the control panel. In place of real controls sat a strip of cardboard crayoned with bright colorful shapes. "I'm trying."

"No, you're not. You're wasting your time on delusions. You've got no available mental energy."

"How do I know *you're* not a delusion?"

"Please," Escodex said. "You saw headless Doug on the camp chair. You spoke with Roger."

Em sank into the co-captain's chair. "I'm just so confused."

"You need to take your medication. You need to get your head together. You need to save my world and yours."

She gazed into the window above the ersatz control panel. The plane spiraled into a gaping vortex. As the plane dipped in, blackness spread throughout the cockpit. It nipped at her toes and froze them like liquid nitrogen. Em tapped her legs. They shattered.

The plane dove straight into the heart of the entity.

It was all her fault.

Another work day. Em stocked with a fevered intensity she hadn't felt in months, ripping the tape off the boxes of imported sweatshop-ware with gusto. The creases of the table-stocked blouses approached fine art in their perfection. She'd even sung the loyalty song that morning, belting it out at the top of her lungs like she led an army.

She'd seen Pendleton shake his head and leave the break room when she started to sing. Em pitied him for his lack of enthusiasm. He needed to try harder.

"This top," Em said, holding a flower-pattered blouse against the body of a middle-aged woman with a bad perm. "It was *made* for you. By slaves."

The woman grunted. "I don't like it."

"You should trust me. I know what I'm doing." She tossed the blouse into the woman's cart, then turned to the next customer, a teenager.

The girl's face glowed with a fierce inner light. Struck by her beauty, Em almost couldn't speak. She plucked a teal poly-cotton sweatshirt from the rack and held it between herself and the teenager, like a screen.

"This color would look really great on you."

"You think so?" The teen snapped her gum, which Em only heard instead of saw, because of the screen.

She swallowed, concentrating hard on her words. "It's on sale. Only $9.99. That's nine-nine-nine. I bet you have that much."

"I'm just here to buy some socks."

"*No!*" Em pulled down the screen. "You have to *trust* me. Socks are out. *This* is in." The sweatshirt drifted to the tile floor. "I'm a professional."

"Girl," Agnes said. Her boxy foot stepped on the teal shirt. It wouldn't be of use to anyone anymore, especially not this radiant young woman. "What you doing? You're freaking out the customers."

"You're just jealous because I'm better at selling than you are." Em turned back to the beautiful teenager, but she was already gone.

"Take fifteen." Agnes picked up the shirt and put it back on the rack, even though she'd already tainted it with her touch. "Go on, *get.*"

Em wanted to fight Agnes. *She* knew what was best for these people, *not* the entity. Instead, she flipped two double middle fingers at her supervisor and went to her locker to get her pack of cigarettes.

On the way back from her locker, Em spotted Mrs. Nguyen, deep in the process of training a fresh young mind in the ways of buying and selling. "Hi!" Em said, waving her hand at her old supervisor.

Mrs. Nguyen's eyes opened wide, and she took a few steps back.

"That's okay, Mrs. Nguyen. I love you anyway!" She wasn't needed in this department anymore, her work here was done. Em skipped toward the exit.

Outside, the Monongahela River snaked in the distance like a blue ribbon. *That's funny, I shouldn't be able to see the river from here.* There it was, though, boldly flowing before her eyes. A pale pink flier skittered across the asphalt in the wind. Em scooped it up. It was the tract from Jackie's church.

The world is shrinking, she thought. *That's why I'm able to see the river. It actually has gotten closer.* Her cigarette sputtered like the sparklers Mom bought every year for the Fourth of July.

She held the tag stolen from a pair of pants to her ear, but Escodex wasn't answering. It didn't matter. There were other things to attend to. She had to see if the river was shrinking.

It was. Em could ford it with one step. This was bad news. The entropic forces expanded faster than she could fight them. If this kept happening, the final confrontation between Em and the entity would be no match at all. She still didn't remember any of Escodex's plans. A normal-sized cigarette butt floated upon the river.

So only the natural features of the world are shrinking. The rivers, the trees, the land. All manmade structures are stable.

"You know what this means. You can never be outside again."

I know what it means.

"Will you warn the others?"

Of course she would warn the others. That went without saying. But she needed allies, backup. "You!" she shouted at a passing man. "Come over here."

"Hey, lady. What are you doing?"

"The river. It's shrinking." She held out a hand. "Help me."

"That's a *storm drain*, lady."

Em shook her head. "You're wrong. It's the Mon River."

"You're gonna get your foot caught."

Em looked down. It *was* a storm drain. The man in the parking lot had changed it with his mind. So he was an ally all along. "Thank you. You've saved us all."

The man shook his head and went into the store. Em shrugged and followed him inside. It felt like she'd been outside for hours.

Before she'd even stepped ten paces, Pendleton grabbed her by the collar. "Come with me, Miss Kalberg." He led her off toward his walled domain. He'd dealt her many hard blows there.

"Mr. Pendleton, did you know the river is *shrinking*?"

He shook his head. "Em, you know what I have to do."

"You're going to … drain it? That doesn't make a whole lot of sense."

He pushed a piece of paper across the table. "Sign this."

TWENTY-FIVE

Em balled her pink slip in her fist and jammed it in the pocket of her coat. Swinging onto her bike, she pedaled the three miles back home.

Peer pressure, that's what did it. The other employees joined together to force me out, because they were scared of my performance, worried about how I'd make them look. She knew her reality testing was sound. This wasn't her fault.

It still hurt like hell.

Rejected.

She rode down to the river, the *real* Mon River, the place where she had thrown her mother's Wes Summersby DVDs to a watery grave. The riverbed thawed at a rapid pace in the early-March heat, and the first shoots of green burst from the concrete of the bridge above the flowing water.

Em leaned over the overhanging ledge of the bridge and stared at the blue — really, more like gray — depths. *It would be so easy*, she thought, *to throw myself in. No more voices, no more visions. Just an eternity in the depths of the water, as the current carries my body north to Pittsburgh, to be nibbled by fish and frozen by ice.*

Em squinted. Out in the river she spotted a lump. A very familiar lump.

It can't be. They had to have floated away by now, right? It was the bag of DVDs filled with their encrypted messages. Still here in town. Still trying to poison Em, her mom, and anyone else who might come in contact with them.

Em screamed. She needed a weapon, something to ward off the

mystical forces that sought to invade her family structure. Looking around for an object that could possibly deal with these threats, her gaze landed on her bike, the mint-green Huffy with the rusted chain and plastic handlebars. It would have to do.

Goodbye, old friend. She hoisted the bike over her shoulder and heaved it at the lump. It sank into the river, its handlebars disappearing with a small ripple. She felt a pang of regret but swallowed it away.

"It's good that I did that," she said. "It's *good.*" A necessary sacrifice for the town and her family. Not a senseless waste of her only form of transportation. A *good* thing.

The black bag remained. She threw smooth river-caressed stones at it, but none connected. She threw every stone she could find, but it was no use. Em left the bridge, slid down to the stone-less riverbank and buried her head in her arms.

She hadn't managed to destroy the evil DVDs. She couldn't remember the plans Escodex had given her, not a single one. And now she had no bike. She'd have to walk home.

Em raised her head from her arms and walked down the gravel-lined road. No sidewalk. Not in Clear Falls.

The sky darkened. Em walked faster, her ankles damp and freezing. She slipped on the gravel, catching her fall with a mile marker. It dug into her hand. In the dying light, her blood looked black.

Like evil, she thought, *like the entity. Maybe it's inside me now, maybe I'm finally infected.* What had Escodex, the little voice in her head that never talked to her anymore, said?

It's recruiting. Taking up forces. For the final destruction of all things in your world.

She moved onto the road. At least it was mostly flat but for potholes. Some cars slowed, but none stopped. Not for her. Not for the waste of human life that was Emmeline Kalberg. A red convertible, so like Uncle Steve's car, loomed up ahead.

I should have done this long ago, before I built the machine, before I heard the voices, when I was just a scared, sad teenager. I could have avoided all of this. Mom and Jackie would have been spared. I can't turn back the clock. At least I can make it kind of right.

She was kidding herself. Things would never be right. But she wouldn't have to be here to see them.

Kill yourself, the voice of the horn said, and it was the voice of Wes Summersby.

Em spread her arms wide and greeted the oncoming vehicle. It ripped through her like water vapor.

Kill yourself, the voice of the driver said, and it was the voice of her father.

Shows what you know, she thought. *I'm already dead.*

"Em?"

Em unsealed her eyes, which felt like they'd been taped together. "Mom?"

"Shh. Stay down." The shadowy figure at Em's side brushed back her hair and thrust a cup full of something liquid into her hand.

Em gazed around, blinking. Her mother, dressed in her wrinkled bank teller's uniform, stood over the bed. Jackie lingered in the doorway, her attention buried in her phone. "Where am I?" All at once, realization dawned. "I'm in the loony bin again, aren't I?"

"No, Em. This is the Clear Falls hospital."

She looked at the paneled walls and ratty curtains. This was Clear Falls, all right. "What happened?"

"You were hit by a car. They couldn't find your bike. Someone must have taken it." Mom took the glass of water back and placed it on the night-stand. "I told you not to ride that thing around here. This isn't the city."

Em drew in her breath sharply and kicked off the sheets. She flexed her fingers and toes. Everything was still there, still intact. A thin layer of gauze was plastered to her side, which pounded like a bass drum. "Where are my clothes?"

"In the trash. They were filthy."

There was something different in the air, something Em couldn't quite put her finger on. She tried to go over the events of the past few hours. *Had* someone taken her bike? Why had she been so upset? Then she remembered.

Oh, shit, she thought. *Pendleton fired me.*

She froze in place for a few moments, distantly aware that Mom and Jackie were both staring at her. *Shouldn't I be more upset about this?* She felt at her side again. It was raw and tender with road rash.

Mom laid a hand on her arm. "Em, I know you stopped taking your pills."

The dam burst. Hot tears ran down Em's cheeks and she couldn't even lift her hands to catch them. Her mother's face grew distorted be-hind the tears, like something out of a monster movie. "How did you know?"

"I've been suspecting it for a while, but you admitted it when that driver brought you in. You begged the emergency room to call me. You begged for your medication." Mom sniffed and ran the back of her hand across her eyes. "I suppose you don't remember any of this."

Em shook her head no. She looked over at her sister, who was still focused on her phone, the light reflecting off her fishbelly-pale face. Jackie's eyes met Em's briefly. She covered her phone with her hand and left the room.

"Will I be here long?"

"Not unless you want to be. We can go home now." Mom's voice quavered.

"But you don't want me back there." Em's eyes welled up again.

"I didn't *say* that." Mom grabbed a corner of Em's bed sheet and twisted it around in her hands. "You know I love you, right?"

Em shrugged. "I guess."

"I don't always show it." Mom released the double handful of sheet. "I think I was afraid to show it, especially after your father left us. You just reminded me so much of him, and it hurt."

"Because I'm crazy."

"Not just that." She pushed a strand of hair from Em's forehead. "I was afraid you'd leave, too. That I'd drive you away, just like I did him."

"You didn't drive Dad away."

"I didn't *help* him." Mom dropped back down into the folding chair on the other side of the room while Em swung her legs over the side of the bed. "I tried to help you. When you almost got kicked out of school in the ninth grade, I talked them into letting you stay. Do you remember that?"

"A little," Em said. She barely remembered being in high school. That was another world, locked away behind smoked glass.

"I thought about sending you to a doctor, but you know, I couldn't really get off work that much, and our health insurance didn't cover anything. I checked. I could have done more. A lot more."

"You did what you could," Em said, letting the cliché go dead in her mouth. "It's *my* life. I'm the one who's responsible."

"Em, why did you stop taking your pills?"

Em shrugged. "I don't know."

"That's not good enough. Were there side effects? That doctor back in Ohio said there might be side effects." Mom shook her head. "I should have asked you about them."

Em wondered if hallucinating a tiny person who lived in frozen food and yelled at you for not taking your medication was a common side effect. She probably shouldn't mention it. "Things just weren't as fun anymore. And I was getting fat. I don't want to be some gross Saver-town USA lifer. Like Paula. Like Roger."

Mom quirked an eyebrow. "Who's Roger?"

"Some jerk at work." Em slid to her feet, wobbling slightly. "I want to go home now. If that's okay."

Her mom sighed. "It's okay. Please promise me you'll take the pills, Em. We can work on the side effects. You may not care if you live or die, but I care. I care a lot." She sniffed. "I love you, baby."

Em looked over at the doorway. "Where did Jackie go?"

"Out to the car, I think. She's been really worried about you."

Bullshit, Em thought. She forced a smile. "I'll take the pills, Mom. I promise. But I need you to promise me something. Promise you won't send me away."

"That wasn't supposed to be a punishment, Em. It was ..." Mom paused. "I promise I won't bring it up again."

"Good." Em groaned as the pain from her road rash-covered side shot through her ribcage and down into her thigh. She didn't want to think about what she looked like under the gauze. "I love you, too."

She bundled herself into her jacket and went out to the car while Mom finished up the paperwork. Jackie was still on the damn phone. Standing in the parking lot, Em clutched her side with one hand and tapped on the window with the other.

"Jackie? Can we talk?" Em blew a stream of freezing air past her lips. "I didn't know the 'Ask Jesus Anything' subreddit was so popular."

Jackie rolled down her window and stuck her phone in Em's face. "Who's Escodex?"

Twenty-Six

"You don't have to do that," Jackie said.

"Preventative measures," Em said as she propped the oversized road atlas against the window of the private reading room of the Clear Falls Library. She'd already stuck a chair underneath the doorknob and stuffed a hoodie beneath the door itself.

Jackie turned the phone around and around in her hands. Her brow furrowed. "So who *is* Escodex? You know, Em, we didn't need to come all the way over here for you to answer the question. I'm missing Bible study for this."

"Spoiler alert: Jesus dies." Em winced as she settled into the chair opposite Jackie. She'd had a hard time convincing her mom that she was well enough to have a little "girl time" the day after being struck by a car. It had been even harder to convince Jackie to drive them here. Eventually, though, the constant streams of texts from Escodex coming through on Jackie's phone had gotten the better of her.

"You're such an asshole." Jackie pulled a face when the swear left her lips.

Em smiled. "Let me see your phone."

Jackie frowned, but passed the phone over. It was a cheap pay-as-you-go flip model from Savertown USA. Em's phone, which she rarely used, was similar. Em opened the phone and scanned through the list of recent texts. There were seven from Escodex in the past twenty-four hours, all of them asking about Em.

He's real, Em thought with a start. *Escodex wasn't a hallucination. Maybe nothing else that's happened to me is real, not the machine or Wes Summersby's secret messages, but he is, and so were all those deaths.* She looked up at Jackie. Would this be enough proof for her?

"Jackie, do you remember the people who died at Savertown USA?"

"Of course I remember them. It made the national news." Jackie picked at a thread on her sweater. "Those poor people."

"They weren't suicides," Em said. She almost found herself blurting out *aliens!*, but bit her tongue. "What would be the odds of four unrelated people, three of them without any previous mental problems, suddenly offing themselves? It didn't make any sense then, and it doesn't make any sense now."

Jackie frowned. "What does this have to do with the texts on my phone?"

"I'm getting to that. Look, I know I'm crazy. I know that. You don't have any reason to believe what I'm about to tell you, and once I tell you this you'd be perfectly within your rights to call up Mom and have her send me back to the nut house." Em spun the phone around on the chipped table.

"You shouldn't talk about yourself that way."

"Only sane people care about terminology."

Jackie rolled her eyes. "Get to the point, Em."

"Escodex is ... not from here."

Jackie squinted. "He's a foreigner?"

"Very much so. Unbelievably so." Em sighed and slid the phone back across the table to her sister. "He's from another dimension and recruited me for help. The thing that's causing the deaths, this entity that's making all those workers kill themselves, is also not from here. I don't think either Escodex or the entity is really good, for the record."

She paused. Jackie let out a breath. "Okay."

"You *believe* me?"

Jackie shrugged. "I don't know. Like you said, you're crazy." Her voice wavered on the last word. "But you seem sane now. You've been very lucid this whole time."

"Thanks, I guess."

She opened the phone again. "But why is Escodex contacting *me*?"

"He probably got worried when he didn't hear from me. He knows I have a sister." She pointed. "And your phone is from Savertown USA. He communicates with me through the products they sell."

"Why didn't you come to us before?"

Em laughed. "Crazy girl tells family that beings from another dimension are murdering her coworkers and communicating with her through RFID chips in merchandise. Come on, Jackie."

Jackie looked out the window. The road atlas had fallen from its perch, which slightly concerned Em, but not enough for her to put it back. "Would he talk to me?"

"There's only one way to find out."

They didn't speak during the drive to Savertown USA. Em cinched her hood tight around her face, hoping it would be enough to keep her ex-coworkers from identifying her. As soon as they entered the store, though, a familiar short woman with severely tied-back black hair ran up to them.

"*You*," Judy Nguyen said. "I don't think you should be here, girl. Not after what happened."

Em looked around. It felt like all eyes were on her, closing her off, boxing her in. When she started to shake, she felt Jackie's hand slip into hers. "We're customers," Jackie said. "Maybe you can stop people from entering stores in North Korea, but you can't stop us. It would be un-American."

"Don't let Pendleton see you," her old supervisor said, ignoring Jackie. "I'm glad you're alive, Em." She patted Em on the shoulder with one of her insulated mitts.

"We'll be quick," Em said. She didn't look at Mrs. Nguyen.

Em led Jackie to the back of the store where the storage bins and organizers were located. It was the least-trafficked part of the store. "Here," she said, holding a plastic sewing box out to Jackie.

She took it. "What do I do?"

Oh, right. "Just place it close to the side of your head. Left side. Then think at him."

"What do I think about?"

Em shrugged. "Whatever you want. If he's been sending you messages, maybe he'll be expecting you."

Jackie swallowed audibly and held the plastic container against her head. She bit her lip. Her forehead wrinkled. Finally, she pulled the container away. "Nothing."

Em glared at the sewing box. "*Really*, Escodex?"

"But that doesn't mean I don't believe you. I do! Or at least, I might. There have been a lot of weird things going on in this store, Em. I don't think you're making them *all* up."

"Thank you?"

Jackie put the sewing box back to her temple. Suddenly, there was a low beep in her pocket. She pulled her cell phone from the pocket of her long Pilgrim-style skirt and held it up to Em.

"TELL EM TO OPEN THE CHANNEL."

Tell yourself to turn off the caps lock, Em thought. She took the sewing box from Jackie. "You."

"Where have you been?"

"None of your business." Em knew he was pulling the information from her anyway. She could feel the memories of the past three days unwind from her mind like a spool of thread before he gently snapped them back into place. "This is all your fault anyway."

Escodex continued as if she hadn't even spoken. "Now that your mind is clear of troubling interference, I really need you to concentrate on the images I sent to you. We're running out of time, Em."

"We have exactly enough time." Em looked over at Jackie, who was watching her with eyes big as saucers. She switched to thought-speak. *Why won't you talk to my sister? If you'd speak to her, she'd have to believe in you!*

"I do not care if she believes in me or not."

Em groaned. *What do you mean, out of time?*

"While you were gone — and I won't go into how foolish and reckless you were — the entity claimed another victim."

"Someone else died?"

Jackie's head jerked up.

"Not dead. Something else. It's my belief that the entity placed a certain code in your regional manager during his last visit. He will be returning to the nexus point shortly, at which point the code will be detonated. The death toll could be immeasurable, and every death on your plane makes the entity that much stronger."

How many people are we talking here, really? Five? Ten?

"Don't be crass."

Em peeked around the side of the storage container section to make sure Pendleton wasn't listening in on the one-sided conversation. *At least with Jackie here I look kind of normal,* she thought. *Just two sisters out on a shopping trip, placing plastic containers on the sides of their heads to make sure they ... work?*

"Excuse me," Jackie said as she tapped Em on the shoulder. "What's going on?"

"Private conversation," Em spat.

"With, um, Escodex?"

"Right," Em said. She put the box back up to her head. *If you've tapped my memory, then you know what happened. I can't tolerate you in my head anymore. It's too confusing.*

"This isn't about you, Em. It never was. You need to look outside yourself. People are dying. My world is being affected."

"Your precious *world*." Em sat down on a pile of plastic containers that had been placed upside-down on the slick floor with its cobblestone pattern. *The regional manager. Where is he now?*

"Out of my range. But I know he's coming back. The entity can't travel outside the nexus point any better than I can."

And Agnes?

"Still here. Still dangerous. I need your help, Em."

Em closed her eyes. She didn't want to be here. At this moment, she'd have even preferred the stifling sameness of the hospital to this bright-lit retail paradise with its sinister secrets. But here she was. *I can't do it alone. I need my sister. And I need Roger.*

"I cannot speak to your sister. And as for him …" Escodex made an untranslatable sound.

Roger's the only other person who can hear you, even if he is the shirker. I need Jackie to know I'm not crazy. Or at least, not that crazy.

Pause. "After all this, are you afraid I don't exist?"

"No," Em said. "Well, maybe."

A shadow fell over them, then. Em gazed up. Jackie. "Sis, I don't want to interrupt your conversation, but there's something happening in the aisle."

Em peeked out. Agnes was staring down one of the newer workers, a bleach-blonde cashier on her way to the break room. Em sensed the intensity of her beady green eyes from ten yards away.

"What is she doing?" Jackie said. "Your workplace is *weird*, Em."

"It's not my workplace anymore."

As Em watched and waited, the brown gas emanated from Agnes's lips and seeped into the body of the blonde. Em slipped her hands over her ears and clamped her mouth shut. *Like that will do anything*, she thought. If the entity wanted her, nothing would stop it.

The entity did not come to Em. It circled around the blonde, who wavered on her feet, nearly dropping over. Agnes reached out a hand to steady the woman. Together, they walked hand-in-hand toward the break room. Em felt the presence of the entity trailing after them like a scent cloud.

It's recruiting, Em thought. "Jackie, how much of that did you see?"

"It looked like she was going to faint but the old woman caught her."

Em shook her head. "That isn't what happened." She looked back at the plastic sewing kit lying on its side in the middle of the sparsely populated container section. Escodex could wait. She needed to get the plans out. She needed to talk to Roger. "Come on," she said, taking a fistful of Jackie's coat and guiding her toward the exit.

"Where are we going, Em?" Jackie whined. She pried Em's fingers from her drab gray coat.

"I don't know." Em hadn't seen Roger since they arrived, which probably meant he wasn't anywhere in the store. He had a way of finding her out, and vice versa. Crazy attracting crazy. She looked at the place where Agnes had recruited the cashier, still tainted with wisps of rusty brown energy. "But we can't stay here."

Jackie dropped her head, then slowly trudged behind Em, out of the store into the frigid snowy world beyond.

TWENTY-SEVEN

R oger found her the next day, as she was filling out an application at the local Burger King.

"You're actually pissing around with this when the whole world is in danger?" he said, pulling on the sleeve of her hoodie hard enough to make her pen slip. "Where have you *been*, Em?"

"You know, you shouldn't sneak up behind me unless you want to get your ass kicked," she said, ignoring his question. She slid the application to the other end of the table. "Where have *you* been?"

"Working," he said, "and trying to communicate with it."

"With Escodex?"

"With *anyone*. Things are getting worse, Em. Whatever's causing all these problems, it's spreading. The smell is unbelievable." He wrinkled his piggish nose.

She looked up sharply. "Smell?"

"It's like something's rotting in there. Lots of weird smoke, too. Pendleton says it's something in the HVAC. Business is way down."

"Fuck the business," Em said. "Can you come to my house this afternoon? Five o'clock? It could be sooner, but I have an appointment."

"Yes, but what is this about?"

"Escodex. The entity. All of it." Em tore the application in half. She'd promised her mother she'd fill out one application a week. There was no requirement she turn the things in. "You can get us access to the store."

"Us?"

"My sister." She sucked down the last of her Diet Sprite and tossed the empty cup into a garbage can.

"You told her about this?"

"Escodex revealed himself to her." She shrugged. "I was unavailable."

"You're not going to tell me what happened."

"You're crazy, too," she tossed back. "Figure it out."

After Roger left, Em walked to Slazinger's office. She ducked her head against the cold snap and buried her gloved hands inside the thick pockets of her down jacket. She let her mind go blank. It was the only way to deal with the cold and the feel of wet snow against her calves. Cars whizzed past, lightly spraying her with street muck. She thought of her bike, degrading away in the depths of the Mon.

No use crying about it, she thought. *I did that before, and this is after. It's a whole new world now.*

Em had time to kill. She wound her way to the strip mall across from Slazinger's office, on one side of a four-lane mini-highway plated with a sheet of ice. She pushed her way into the comic book store that flanked one side of the strip. The male employees behind the desk didn't even look up.

She hadn't expected to find Kevin here, of course. He was probably still in Vermont, in that not-a-hospital that was still a prison. She picked up the latest issue of *The Hardened Criminals* from the shelf and immediately put it back down. Too many painful associations. Instead, she walked to the coffee shop next door.

Em felt the wrong inside before she even opened the door.

The blonde cashier that Em had seen in Savertown was sitting at one of the tables, crying into her latte. The waves of the entity's power drifted off her like action lines in a comic book. After ordering, Em tiptoed over to the cashier, not sure what to say. *I don't even know her name*, she thought.

"What do you want?" the blonde said, her mouth puckering sourly.

"I …" Em paused. If this were Agnes, she'd have a plan, which may or may not include bashing her over the head with one of the coffee shop's chairs. "Do you work at Savertown USA?"

"Yes," the blonde said. Her eyes were unfocused, glassy. She clearly didn't recognize Em from Em's stint in the store. She dabbed at the corner of her eyes with a napkin. "I'm sorry, I don't know what came over me."

"Don't apologize," Em said, although she didn't know why she should be trying to make this person — this *creature*, if what she'd seen in the store yesterday had actually happened the way she thought it did — feel better. "What's wrong?"

"I need to get back to work," she said, rising. When she stood, something like a second outline moved with her, brown tones wavering and shimmering in the dingy winter sunlight. "He will be upset."

"Mr. Pendleton?" Em asked, only realizing too late that she shouldn't have said his name. This woman didn't know she used to work at the store, and she wanted to keep it that way.

But the blonde cashier didn't even seem to register Em's words. She cleared her cup robotically, face like stone. Em realized what it reminded her of: the night shift workers, toiling zombielike throughout the wee hours of the night, their souls drained by the entity for its evil uses.

Definitely recruiting.

"You don't have to go back there," Em said lamely. Of course, though, the cashier did. What could Em possibly do to dissuade her from walking away from her only source of income? Nothing. There was nothing else in Clear Falls for this woman, nothing for any of them. And in only a few years' time, Em would be subject to the same fate if she stayed here, forced to work in a minimum wage job managed by jerks. Even if there were no space aliens or intergalactic sleuths in the picture, the economic landscape of Clear Falls, Pennsylvania was a dystopia.

Even if Roger and I save it all, Em thought, *we're still fucked.*

She slurped the rest of her coffee, then prepared to dart to the medical plaza on the other side of the road. It was always a challenge to cross that street without a light, but she hadn't been hit yet.

"I don't know if I should see you anymore," Dr. Slazinger said. This was Em's first appointment with the good doctor since she'd walked headlong into that car. "I think your treatment needs may be beyond my abilities."

"I'm fine *now*," she said, shrugging.

"Your mother told me what happened. Were you *trying* to kill yourself, Em?"

Em looked away. "No."

"Because that's what it sounds like to me."

"So you're going to trust your opinion over my actual words? That's a way to really build trust between us."

Slazinger made a few notes on his pad. "I heard from Kevin Collins today."

Em made her voice sound as even as possible. "How is he?"

"Doing better. A lot better. He'll be coming home next week."

"What does that have to do with me?"

"I just thought you'd like to know. *Kevin* isn't afraid of letting other people help him through life."

Em rolled her eyes. How much longer would she have to go through this sham? Until the entire population of Clear Falls was recruited by the entity? "I'm not afraid. I just don't think anyone can help me."

"I've been trying to help you for the past four months, Em." He folded his hands on top of his pad, the same annoying gesture that had always irked her. "Why isn't it sinking in that nobody is out to get you?"

But they are, Em thought. *The entity's foot soldiers are out to get me. Jackie saw it too, even if she didn't see all of it.* Of course, she wasn't going to bring *that* up, not when she was so close to achieving her goals. "I have no idea."

Slazinger sighed and ran his hand through his over-coiffed hair. "Tell me what happened that last day of work."

Em thought back. It seemed so long ago, although of course, it had only been two days since she'd hoisted her bicycle into the Monongahela River and woken up in the emergency room. "They fired me and I was really upset. I don't know why I was upset. I didn't like working there anyway." She lapsed into silence, hoping that would be enough conversation.

He made another note. What the hell was he always writing in there? "Your mother said you stopped taking your medication. Why?"

"Do I need a reason?" Em punched the arm of the chair. "I didn't like the way it made me feel. Too slow. Slow and dumb, like a person who was going to work at Savertown USA forever."

"You hated the store that much?"

"I did when I was there." Em looked out the window again, even though it was the same stupid parking lot that it had always been. "Not anymore."

Slazinger sighed, lacing his bony fingers across the back of his skull. "I need to know you won't do this again, Em. Would you consider checking yourself back into the hospital?"

"No." *Not until this is over. Not until I know the planet is safe.*

"Well, I can't force you. I'm not some evil entity out to ruin your life. I'm just a doctor."

Em looked up sharply. "I never said you were an evil entity. If any-one knows what an evil entity is, it's me."

Slazinger quirked an eyebrow, but for once didn't write anything down.

Roger pounded on the front door at five-oh-three that afternoon. Em crossed her arms about her chest and glared at him.

"You're late."

"Traffic signals."

"Traffic signals, my ass. I *walked* home and still made it." Em looked around, then hurried Roger up to her room. *I really should have cleaned up a little*, she thought.

As Em pulled the blinds, Roger stood awkwardly in the middle of Em's room, a caged gorilla. He squinted at her Sleater-Kinney poster and collection of ironic mugs.

"What's the matter, Roger, haven't you ever been in a girl's room before?"

"Not in ten years."

"It shows." She spread the blueprints out over scattered 45s and scribbled-in notebooks. "These are the designs Escodex beamed to me. I need supplies. And I need to know how to read a blueprint. Not that you'd know anything about that."

Roger traced his finger along the lines of the bell-shaped weapons. "You know, Em, I used to be an engineer. Maybe I can help you with this."

"Like a train engineer?"

He rolled his eyes. "No, an electrical engineer. I studied at Caltech before, well, you know."

"Before you broke down."

Roger hunched over the blueprints, his forehead wrinkling with the strain. "This is a combination suction and energy conversion device. The parts should be simple enough to get. We could buy them at the store."

"No," Em said. "I don't want to go back there right now."

"Then we'll have to get over to that specialty electronics place in Connellsville. It's a short drive." He ran a finger along the creased paper. "What are you going to use for the casing?"

Em shrugged. "I guess I didn't think that far ahead."

Roger shook his head and handed the blueprint back over to her. "I'm free the day after tomorrow. We'll go to Connellsville then."

The door creaked on its hinges. Em looked up to see Jackie standing before them. "What's this strange man doing in our house?"

Em rolled up the blueprint. "Do you remember what we talked about yesterday? Escodex? When we were at the store?" Jackie's face remained blank. "Any of this ring a bell?"

"You weren't serious about that, were you, Em?"

"Oh, *come on*," Em said, tossing the roll of paper across the room.

Roger stuck out his hand. "Roger Cermak. I used to work with your sister. We're figuring out some … technical things."

Jackie didn't take it. "Have *you* heard that voice?"

Roger nodded. "She's telling the truth."

Jackie crossed her arms and looked over at the corner where the blueprint lay over a stack of tattered vinyl records. "So there is an alien, and it's communicating through RFID chips …"

"Not an alien," Em said.

"Close enough," Roger said.

Before Em could stop her, Jackie crossed the room and picked up the blueprint. She smoothed it out on the bed. Her eyes widened. "Em, this looks like a *gun*."

"It's a combination suction and energy conversion device. Not a gun."

"There's a trigger."

"Okay, it's a gun."

"What your sister means to say," Roger said, "is that this is private business. It doesn't concern you, and you should probably stay out of it."

Nice, Em thought as she ticked her esteem of Roger up a notch.

"If she's planning on killing a bunch of people, then it does concern me. I'm not going to let my sister turn into a mass murderer."

"Not a mass murderer," Em said, rolling her eyes. "Just one murder, and they're not even *human*." She looked to Roger for support, but apparently he'd tapped out.

Jackie stepped away from the blueprints. She picked up a stained coffee mug from Em's dresser and passed it back and forth in her hands. "Who are you going to kill?"

"You don't know them."

She set the mug down with a thunk. "*Who*, Em?"

Em sighed. "Agnes Walker. She used to be my supervisor at Savertown USA. Now she's the human avatar of an evil alien entity who's trying to recruit dozens of other workers to bring about the end of this world." She paused. "Yeah, I know how it sounds."

Jackie spun on Roger. "And you … *agree* with this? With killing someone?"

"The entity within Agnes has killed at least four people so far. Maybe more." Roger shook his head. "I don't see what else we can do."

"Besides, it might not kill her. It might just, like, suck the entity out and leave an old miserable woman behind to rue another day." *Fat chance.* "You're the one that said Savertown USA is weird."

"Not *alien weird*," Jackie said. "I just … I don't know what to think."

"You don't have to think about it," Em said. "Just don't tell anyone. This is all going to be over very soon."

"Because you're going to kill someone."

Em flopped down on her bed, put her hands over her eyes, and groaned. Across the room, Roger shifted around awkwardly, waiting for his cue to exit. Em wasn't about to give it to him. "Jackie, why do you believe in God?"

"That is *not* the same thing and you know it."

"You believe because it, like, explains things. Well, this is the best explanation for what's going on at Savertown. I know it and Roger knows it. And if you stop us from carrying out our plan, you'll be as responsible for what happens next as the entity."

Roger grunted. "No, she isn't."

"Shut up, Roger."

"If you need to tell," he continued, "then go ahead and tell. I told on Em. It made sense at the time. Now this makes sense. I wish it didn't. I wish Em was full of crap."

"She *is* full of crap." Jackie frowned at herself in Em's mirror, and tucked a stray strand of hair into her ponytail. "In more ways than one."

"At least I'm not the one who thinks shorts are a one-way ticket into Satan's army."

Roger's phone buzzed. Em noticed that it, too, was one of the cheap Savertown flip models. *Well, that's all we can afford*, she thought. "Yeah?" She watched as his face turned a variety of shades not found in nature.

Em sat up. "What is it?"

"I have to get over to the deli. Pendleton just stuck his hand in the slicer. For 'no reason.'"

"*Fuck.*" She slid the blueprints under the bed. "I'm coming with you."

Em looked over at Jackie. Her own hands were up near her mouth, pulling on her lower lip while her whole body trembled. "What do I do?"

"Pray, Sister. Just pray."

TWENTY-EIGHT

Pendleton wasn't dead yet. That was the best anyone could say.

Roger's arms waved toward the line of massive slicers. "How did this happen?! Were you even *watching* the machines?"

A meth-skinny woman with papery skin crossed her arms and glared at him. "He just started yelling at us, about the cleaning and that. A lot of folks crowded around him, like they was hanging on his every word." The deli worker made a motion with her hand. "Next thing you know, he's jammed his hand into the slicer."

Em covered her mouth with her hand. *The entity's recruits.* "These workers, what did they look like? Did they, uh, have kind of an *energy*?"

The woman looked Em over, but didn't seem to recognize her as a former employee. "Well, they weren't normal, I'll say that much. All on drugs or something, I don't know."

Em looked out at the ambulance, which was just pulling away. Perhaps the entity had been unable to recruit him. Or maybe it wanted him out of the picture for some other reason. "Roger, clock out. We're going to Connellsville *today*."

"I just got here, Em. I need to clean this up." Suddenly, he leaned over the sink and vomited into it. "Oh, God, I think I saw a fingertip."

"There's more than just a couple of fingertips at stake here."

He furrowed his brow. "That's easy for you to say. You don't have bills to pay." He sighed and turned to the woman, who was glued to her phone, oblivious to the damage. "Mandy, can you take care of this?"

"Sure," she said, not looking up.

"Mandy!" Roger gestured to the blood-spattered deli. "Clean this. Now. If you find any, uh, parts ..."

"Put them in milk," Em said. She could have sworn she saw that on television once.

Mandy frowned at Roger and slowly started to mop up the spatters, growling under her breath. Roger shook his head, then pointed toward the exit.

"Let's go."

Roger pulled the car into Em's driveway. Even though the blueprints for the energy weapons were still lodged in her mind, she wanted to have a physical copy to refer to once they were in the electronics store. As she passed through the carport on her way into the house, her heart sank. Mom was home, ahead of schedule.

Can't let her slow me down, she thought. *Can't let her see me.*

Em eased the door open slowly, hoping Mom was up in the bedroom napping, or otherwise occupied. No such luck.

"Where were you, Em?"

Em feigned puzzlement. "Shouldn't you be at work?"

"Jackie told me what happened at the store. I had some PTO coming to me." Mom patted the space next to her on the sofa. "Do you want to talk?"

Em froze. "What *exactly* did Jackie tell you?"

"That Mr. Pendleton cut his fingers off. They're saying there's some kind of … virus going around Savertown USA, or something. That's why there have been so many people hurting themselves there." Mom shook her head. "I'm so glad you're not working there anymore."

"Me, too," Em tossed off as she went up the stairs. *No time to waste.*

"Em!"

She gripped the banister and gritted her teeth. "Yeah?"

"I asked where you were. And who's that man parked out in our driveway?" Mom peered through the blinds, eyes narrowed.

I think I liked it better when she didn't care about me, Em thought. "Don't take this the wrong way, Mom, but I'm kind of busy."

Mom reached out and put a hand on Em's shoulder. She resisted the urge to shake it off. "Do you think you had any effects from this virus? Maybe you should go see Dr. Slazinger about this. Or we can take you to the ER. They're thinking about closing down the store, just temporarily."

After it's too late, she thought. "We can't afford that. And anyway, I'm fine. I'm the last person this ... thing is going to affect."

Mom crinkled her nose. "You're in a weird mood, Em."

Yeah, well, you would be too if some clueless person stood between you and the total destruction of everything. "Listen. I'll be back tonight. Don't worry about me. I know what I'm doing."

"Let's watch some TV."

"*No!*" Em said, shaking off her mother's hand. She took a deep breath. "I appreciate that you took some time off for me, but I didn't really need you to. The person in the car is a friend. We have plans."

"I don't think I'll ever understand you, Em." Mom sighed and started back down the stairs. "Promise me you won't go back to that store."

"I promise," Em lied. She vaulted the last few stairs to her room and rummaged underneath her mattress for the blueprint, then folded it neatly and stuck it in her back pocket.

When she crossed the living room, her mother was staring at a game show, as oblivious to her as any member of the entity's army. *A good daughter would stay here with her*, Em thought. *But I'm not a good daughter.*

She rapped on Roger's window. "Let's go."

Roger's stony silence extended throughout the drive to Connellsville. Em reached out to turn on the radio, anything to block out the voices that drifted into her mind despite the layers of muffling medication. The radio was dead.

"Doesn't it bother you?"

"Huh?" Roger took his eyes off the road for a second.

"The silence. I can't stand it." She cupped her hands around her ears. "It makes me hear things."

Roger shrugged. "You tune it out."

"I find that hard to believe." Even alone in her room, drifting off to sleep, Em always kept her music on low, a ward to keep the voices at bay.

"I've been living with this for almost as long as you've been alive, Em."

"Whatever." Em looked out at the rolling expanse of shit-brown Appalachian landscape littered with patches of melting snow. In the distance she could see the strip malls of Connellsville, like a doorway into Hell. "Why did you come here, Roger?"

"To help you save the world?"

"No," she said, sneering. "To Clear Falls. You said you went to Caltech. You're not from around here, I know it. Who the hell moves to Western Pennsylvania?"

"It was cheap. It was small. Not so many people. I couldn't *stand* people, then. Nobody I knew lived here." He eased onto an exit. "I was really worried about people knowing where I lived."

"Because you were paranoid?"

"Part of it was that. Part of it was shame. Everyone in California thought I was hot shit. Could have been the next Steve Jobs. After I cracked up ... I couldn't stay there. I couldn't let them see me like this, all fat and crazy."

Em could have comforted Roger, tell him that it wouldn't have been as bad as he thought. That his true friends wouldn't have abandoned him. But she'd already lied once today. "Still, though. This place sucks."

"It's not that bad."

"I'm not staying."

"No," Roger said. "You'll go off and find your own place to hide." He guided the car into the tiny parking lot of the store, which was nestled in between a sign shop and a local ambulance chaser whose commercials were all over channel 64. They went in.

Roger's brow wrinkled as he scrutinized the crumpled blueprint in the aisle of the cramped specialty electronics store. "What are we going to use in this place marked 'storage'?"

"I was thinking a memory card. I've used them to transmit information to Escodex before," she said.

"It's a shame about Agnes. She wasn't always this bad." Roger shook his head. "I must be crazy to go along with this."

"You *are* crazy, Roger. That's why we *can* do this."

Roger turned back to the blueprint. "About that casing. I think it'll have to be something we can take into the store in broad daylight, during Agnes's shift. It can't look like a weapon."

Em looked around the cramped store, with its numerous pegboards laden with hundreds of miniature components. They all looked the same to her, though probably not to Roger the ex-engineer. At the counter, the bored cashier scrutinized them. *He's probably wondering if he should call the cops*, she thought. She grabbed Roger's shoulder and pushed him into the next aisle, where they couldn't be seen.

"Do you have any ideas?"

"Maybe," Roger said. "Let me think about it."

"We're running out of *time*," Em replied. Or were they? She needed to get back into the store and reconvene with Escodex. She needed to gauge the advance of the army. "Are you working tomorrow? Do you think you can get me into the store?"

"Pendleton's not coming back. Nobody's going to kick you out."

Em swallowed. "What I mean to say is, will you *protect* me?"

Roger looked Em up and down, then scoffed. "You don't need anyone's protection. Don't be a baby."

"I'm serious. She's on to me. *They're* on to me."

"But you're immune, right? We both are."

That's what this is all banking on, Em thought. *That we're both too crazy to be recruited. Because if we're not, it's all over.*

Suddenly, the dark visage of the cashier loomed over them. "Are you two about finished here?"

"No," Roger said.

"Yeah, you are. Come on, I'll ring you up."

Roger sighed and spread his collection of parts out on the counter. "Don't worry," he told Em, "I have everything we need, except the casings."

Em nodded. "I'm gonna go outside." She lit a cigarette and squinted out at the gray sky. Sometime very soon, the regional manager would arrive, and the entity's army would make its move. She wondered how long it would take Roger to create those weapons that didn't look like guns, but totally were.

In the distance, Em could see the smear of color nestled in a bend of the Monongahela River that was Clear Falls. She imagined the sick energy of the entity pouring out of the town, snaking its way across the world. All because of the "code detonation" of the regional manager, something that would create so much damage that the entity would somehow break forth and lay ruin to the entire dimensional plane.

But not if we stop it first, she thought. *Not if we get the entity right in its nerve center.*

Roger came out, a tiny plastic bag in his fist. "I need to get back to the deli, make sure Mandy's actually cleaning."

"Are you sure it's safe?"

Roger shook his head. "No. But life goes on. Get some rest, Em. You'll need it."

TWENTY-NINE

Em had just taken her night-time meds when her cell phone buzzed. "What is it, Roger?"

"I figured it out! The casings. We'll use hair dryers, the Savertown USA generic model. Nobody will be able to tell they're weapons, and the diffusers will decentralize the energy beam so it's less focused." He paused. "Unless you think that would look weird."

"No, I'm sure that it won't look weird to carry souped-up hair dryers into the store and start jamming them in people's faces."

Roger sighed. "So when are we going to do this?"

"Escodex will let me know," Em said. "I have to get into the store to talk to him."

"I'll give you a lift. I have a shift tomorrow anyway. Be ready around ten." Roger hung up.

Em could already feel the pull of fabricated sleep towing her under. She forced herself out of bed, draping a blanket over her shoulders, and went to the bathroom. Squinting against the bright light, she peeled away the gauze on her side. A thin layer of dried blood glazed her skin.

Not as bad as what Pendleton's got, Em thought. She washed her wound in the sink, then stumbled back to her bed, the drugs making her limbs heavy. Her mom was already asleep, oblivious to the forces amassing only a few miles away. *She thinks it's a virus*, Em thought, *and I guess it is.*

But they wouldn't close the store. Nothing could close the store. The entire economic structure of Clear Falls did run on Savertown USA, after all.

Em just barely hit the bed before blacking out, one leg askew over the side.

"I can feel the evil all around me," Em said. She bunched her hoodie tighter over her face.

"Are you sure it's not just the usual level of evil?" Roger was already dressed in his patriotic vest, the plastic pricing unit in his hand.

Em sniffed. "Yeah, there's definitely more evil."

Roger left to clock in, while Em scouted out a vacant corner in the garden department. Not so many people buying garden equipment this time of year. She held a ceramic pot up to the side of her head. "Escodex?"

No reply.

I really need to talk to you.

Nothing. She shook the pot and reached for another. *Maybe that one didn't have an RFID chip in it,* she thought. After trying a half-dozen separate products she stopped calling out: Escodex was gone. Or at least temporarily disabled.

Em rocked back on her haunches and put her hands over her face. They'd still be going ahead with or without Escodex. But it sure would have been nice to have his guidance. How could he just abandon her like this?

"Em?"

She peeked out through her fingers. "Kevin?"

The red, white, and blue blazer hung awkwardly on his too-skinny frame. He held the pricing gun like he was afraid to touch it. "What are you doing?"

"What are *you* doing? Here. In that uniform." She quickly reorganized the ceramic pots. "I thought you were in Vermont."

Kevin ignored that. "Were you talking to the GrowGood Adobe Mini-Planters?"

"*No,*" Em said. "Listen, I think you need to get out of here. Haven't you heard? There's some kind of virus in the store. People are killing themselves. Pendleton cut off his fingers."

His eyes widened. "You were *so* talking to those planters."

"God, you're stupid." Em stood up. "I can't believe I fucked you."

Kevin's pale face turned red. "I work here now. This is my department, and I don't want you scaring off the real customers."

"I *am* a real customer." She picked up a sprinkler head and tossed it from one hand to the other. "Ring me up, boy. Chop chop."

He rolled his eyes. "This is so humiliating."

"Am I the one humiliating you? Or are you humiliated because a rich kid like you doesn't work in a place like this? I can't imagine you need the money."

"It's just for a little while, and they have a lot of openings."

"They have a lot of openings because everyone's been *dying*!" Em shoved the sprinkler head into her pocket and stepped toward Kevin. He stepped back. "I'm serious, Kevin. Some crazy shit's about to go down, and you don't want to be in this store when it does."

"What? Are you going to shoot up the place?" His mouth formed an O. "You *are* going to shoot up the place."

"It's not what you think."

Kevin turned and Em leapt onto his back. They collapsed on the slick linoleum floor in a tangle of limbs. Em pinned Kevin down, grinding her palms into his Savertown USA-branded shoulders.

"Get *off* me, you crazy bitch!"

"How can you not *see,* Kevin? How can none of you *see* that there's something wrong and evil going on in this store? You need to get out before it's too late!" Em didn't love Kevin anymore, but she'd be damned if someone else in this town died on her watch.

Coldness pricked her skin like a thousand tiny needles. She was surrounded by a ring of employees. The shit-brown mist that was the telltale sign of the entity's army wafted from them.

"I give up." She released Kevin from her grip. "Have fun with your new friends, Kevin. I hope it's worth seven-fifty an hour." The eyes of the entity's army followed her, tearing into her soul like tissue paper. Em had to look away.

"Well, arrest her or something! She's going to shoot up the store!"

"It's being handled," said an anonymous brunette Em didn't know. "Trust the management chain."

She didn't look back to see what happened to Kevin. She didn't care.

Em walked home from the store in shaking fear. Could they really call the police on her? Surely other customers — real customers — saw the altercation between Kevin and her. She could almost see the headline: "Mentally Ill Woman Threatens to Shoot Up Store, Warns of Silent Invasion from Beyond the Stars." She popped into the same comic book store where she'd failed to find joy in her favorite series.

"She returns."

Em stared at the greasy-faced man behind the counter. "Don't look at me."

The man held up his hands. "Okay, lady." He reburied his nose in an issue of *Spawn*.

She paced the store, thinking. Where could Escodex have gone? How could he have abandoned her in the final hours? She put her hand in her pocket and came out with the sprinkler head.

He'd been able to communicate with Jackie through her Savertown USA phone. What if he could extend his range with other products? Em placed the stolen sprinkler head against her temple. *Escodex?*

She heard a distant, low chatter. But then, she always did. She plugged up her other ear with a finger. *I really need to talk to you.*

There was a distant tapping like Morse Code through Styrofoam. Em frowned. There definitely seemed to be *something* on the line. She needed more input. Em dumped the contents of her bag on the floor and looked over to the clerk, still staring at his tattered comic book. *Good.*

She picked out the items that she knew had been purchased at Savertown USA. There wasn't much. She'd bought a discounted mp3 player a few weeks before she was fired. There was a small notebook she'd swiped from the stationery section for no reason at all. Finally, there was her employee badge itself, which Pendleton had neglected to take from her. She pulled out the hair tie holding up her ponytail and bound all four items together as well as she could. Em put the clump of items up to her head and thought-spoke as loud as she could.

Escodex, are you there? What's happened to you?

The reply was distant, words from another room, but she'd recognize the haughty voice anywhere. "There have been incidents. The entity made a play for the higher dimension. Its signal is … stronger, somehow. Have there been further unusual developments on your side?"

You have no idea.

Escodex paused, and Em felt the familiar tickle that meant he was scanning through her recent thoughts and memories. "You've built the weapons. With the shirker."

He's not shirking anymore. Roger is in this all the way. I can't built those weapons without him. He's doing all the work.

"You have to hurry up, Em. If the entity can be detected on my side of the divide, then it's already too late for your dimension. But you can still help us."

"It is *not* too late!"

Across the room, the greasy clerk looked up briefly. Em sneered at him.

"I may not have been able to talk to you, but I've still been watching. Are you aware that the entity has been amassing a force of workers under its control?"

Oh, I'm aware.

"We need to stop this now, before the regional manager returns to the store, and before the entity's ancillary forces become too much to control."

But Roger isn't finished yet!

"Right, he's still working there." Escodex made an impatient sound. "Where is your sister? It can't hurt to have another gun."

No, Em said. *I'm not bringing her into this. The entity will take her over.*

"It will take her over anyway if it wins. As well as everything and everyone in my dimension."

You know I don't really care about your dimension, right?

A plaintive whine emanated from the front of the store. "Hey, you know, if you're not going to buy anything, then maybe you should leave."

"I'm going." Em shoved the bound-together object into her bag along with the other items. She flipped the clerk off as she exited, and slammed the door behind her.

"You look ... different."

Jackie frowned and crossed her arms over her body as if by instinct. "What do you care?"

Em squinted. "Are those my jeans?"

Jackie turned and started going upstairs. "I knew this was a mistake."

"No, no," Em said, grabbing her sister by the arm. "Don't change. It suits you."

Jackie rubbed her palms on Em's jeans. "I feel naked."

In a plain T-shirt, hoodie, and pants, Jackie wasn't showing any more skin than she had been before. In fact, she might have been showing less. Em didn't think her sister would appreciate Em's bringing that up, though. "Is it Casual Tuesday at New Life Covenant?"

"It's Wednesday," Jackie said. She took a deep breath. "And *no*. Jeff broke up with me."

Mr. Button Shirt, Em thought. "Well, fuck that guy. He doesn't own you."

"He wouldn't sign a promise agreement. Then I caught him in the parking lot with Loretta."

"That old lady with emphysema?"

Jackie rolled her eyes. "Different Loretta."

Em sat on the couch and patted the space next to her, but Jackie wouldn't sit. "Jackie, you're sixteen. Why settle now? Settle when you're older, like Mom did."

A tear slicked down Jackie's cheek. "Jeff didn't ask Loretta to sign. Reverend Freddy said it was all right. He blessed their union."

"That's actually a little creepy, Sis."

Jackie swiped at her eyes with the cuff of the hoodie, which was also Em's. "You wouldn't understand."

"I do understand. You remember Kevin, right?" Or did she? Em and Kevin had mostly hung out far past the time when good Christian girls went to bed. "You have fun for a while, then you don't anymore and you find someone else. Or you're just alone. That's the way it's supposed to work."

"Not for us," Jackie said. "Not when you serve a higher calling."

Em gestured at Jackie's outfit. "So are you getting out? Ready to be a normal person again?"

"I don't have a choice. The reverend excommunicated me." Jackie's face reddened, and she slumped against the banister and buried her head in her elbow. "He said my energy was impure."

Em's stomach fell. "Is this because of how I acted at the, um, healing?"

"Not everything is about you, Em. This is all me. If you're not willing to give up *everything* for God, then don't even step on the path." She sniffled. "That's what he said."

"He's an asshole." Jackie looked up sharply. "Sorry, he is. What he said is bullshit. If these people were really your friends, they'd stand by you. They'd help you onto the path, not just reject you for some made-up reason." *The path that doesn't exist*, Em thought, but didn't say. "I'm sorry this happened to you, but you're better off."

"You don't know *anything*," Jackie said. She peered down at Em's clothes on her body and launched into a new storm of tears. "My spirit is damned now."

"Join the club." Em pushed past Jackie on her own way up the stairs. There were things to take care of before Roger's call: letters to write, goodbyes to be said. Tomorrow she could be dead, or thrown into a mental hospital or prison cell. Jackie caught her by the wrist.

"I didn't tell anyone."

Em extricated her arm. "I know you didn't."

Jackie sniffed. "When are you going to do it?"

"Tomorrow, I think. That's when the regional manager comes by for a visit. We need to stop Agnes before she detonates him."

"Detonates him?"

Em shrugged. "That's what Escodex called it. He said the entity laid some kind of code in him. It will kill *everyone* if it goes off. Everyone in Savertown. Maybe everyone in the world."

Jackie ran her finger up and down the chipped wooden banister. "I can go with you if you need me. I'm already damned, what's a little hooky going to do?"

"No. Stay away from the store. Go to school." Clear Falls High was several miles from the big-box nexus point. "We have it under control."

"That's what you said before."

Em sat down on the carpeted steps. "Before?"

"When you were in college. Mom knew there was something wrong. You told her everything was under control. But it *wasn't*."

Em looked down at her shoes. "This is different."

"Yeah, because it's even crazier."

Em swallowed. "It's different," she repeated. *When I built the machine,* she thought, *I built it for all the wrong reasons. Stupid reasons. Crazy reasons. Nobody was out to get me or anybody else. Now there is. And it's out to get all of us.*

"I guess Roger believes in this too, though. That makes it a little less crazy."

Em wasn't about to pull any of the skeletons out of Roger's closet. "I appreciate you keeping quiet about this. And I'm glad you're out of that cult. Even if you're not happy about it yet."

"Yeah," Jackie mumbled. She played with the sinful zipper pull on Em's worldly hoodie. "Be safe, Em."

"You too. I'll call you when it's over. If we win." *If we kill Agnes Walker.*

Jackie passed Em and opened the door to her room. "You'll win. Have some faith."

Gonna need more than faith to get through this one, Em thought. She smiled. "Thanks, Sis. Keep the clothes. They look better on your skinny ass anyway." Then she went into her own room to close things out. To finish whatever needed to be done before the salvation of all things.

THIRTY

On Thursday morning Em slipped into her father's old too-big jacket and descended the stairs. For once, she didn't need to sneak around..

She checked her phone. Roger's text had come through twenty minutes ago. *It's ready. Meet me @ the store.*

Em paused at the door of Jackie's room. Jackie would be at school now, far away from the scene shortly to erupt at Savertown USA. She hoped Jackie was smart enough to stay there.

Mom had left for work a half hour ago. No problem there. Em grabbed a slice of bread and shoved it into her mouth as she latched the screen door behind her.

The sky swam with red and orange wisps that streaked across and touched the farthest point of the horizon. Western Pennsylvania had struggled out of winter slowly and sluggishly, like a man barely escaping quicksand. Long cracks were just starting to break through on the river's thin ice sheet.

Not much longer now, she thought. *Time to make my peace with the world. I may not be in it for much longer.* She stopped on the overpass and leaned over it, looking at the exact spot on the Monongahela where she'd hurled her bicycle into a watery grave only a scant few weeks ago.

Clear Falls was, Em had to admit, a very pretty town. From the view on the overpass, she could see how the river cradled it like a catcher's mitt, nearly encircling the town on its twisted course through the craggy mountains. Below, the houses looked like patches on a quilt: an orange patch for the terracotta roofs of the small cluster of rich people who commuted to Pittsburgh every day, a gray slate patch for the shingled and aluminum-sided houses in Em's part of town, a shiny silver one for the trailer park at the town's far northern edge. Corporate insignia marred the town's face, and the red, white, and blue monster of Savertown USA loomed over it like a cancerous lesion. But advertising couldn't detract from the town's intrinsic beauty and worth.

Clear Falls, Em decided, was a town worth fighting for. She may talk shit about her town, and sometimes she might even believe some of it, but in her heart of hearts she knew she could never just disown her past, like Roger had done. Em would leave eventually, but not before tying up all loose ends and doing it right. She owed her family and the people of Clear Falls that much, at least.

She sprinted the rest of the way to the store, black men's jacket flapping out behind her like a cape. She paused at the end of the parking lot and pulled out her phone. *I'm here. Where are you?*

No reply. Em turned the volume all the way up and lit a cigarette.

A group of vest-clad employees were clustered around the dumpsters, sharing a joint. Em peered closer, but didn't detect the entity's presence. She wondered if she should shoo them away from the store, but realized it was pointless. As far as they knew, she was just another happy customer. She couldn't risk them calling the cops, or the new store manager, whoever had replaced Pendleton.

Shit, where's Roger?

Taking a long drag from her cigarette, Em thought about what might be going on in the store right now. Was Roger held up? Did the entity get him? No, couldn't be. She should go inside. Em crushed the butt underneath her sneaker heel and turned toward the store. Just then, Roger came puffing out.

"Come on," he said, "we've gotta go." He tugged at her arm, pulling her toward the service door.

"No, I'm going in from the front."

"There's no time for tactics. It's Judy Nguyen. She locked herself in Pendleton's office five minutes ago and she's not coming out. We have to save her." Roger tossed her one of the hair dryers. He wasn't even trying to conceal them.

This is it. This is where it all comes together.

Em and Roger shoved against the manager's office door with all their might, spilling into the room. Em winced when her palms met hard tile. She looked up to see Judy Nguyen standing tip-toed on Pendleton's chair, threading a rope through the light fixture.

"Mrs. Nguyen, no!" Em screamed. She took the noose away from Judy's neck. "Don't kill yourself! You have so much to live for."

Her ex-supervisor turned to face her. *A zombie*, Em thought. *That's what she looks like. Her spark's been vacuumed out.* Judy Nguyen's eyes were glassy, and her skin seemed sticky and translucent. *Not human at all.* She opened her mouth, but all that came out was a soft moan.

"Get her out," Em said, pointing at Roger. "Take her to a safe place. Then come find me."

Roger did as Em said, dragging Judy Nguyen out of the office by her slackened arms. Stress gave his flab the power of muscle. "Where will you be?"

"Trying to get in touch with that little asshole Escodex." She walked backward toward the sales floor, one eye on Mrs. Nguyen. "If anyone tries to attack you, shoot them."

"But what if they're not the entity?"

"Shoot them anyway. It's just a hair dryer."

Em slipped the energy weapon inside her father's coat and stalked to the toy section. She picked up a plastic-sealed container of Matchbox cars. "Escodex? If you're here, now's the time to speak up."

The voice on the other side of the interdimensional boundary was crackly, but audible. "Em! You must find the nerve center. The code approaches."

Em rolled her eyes. "I *know*. Where is the nerve center? Where is Agnes?"

"In the jewelry department. You must hurry, Em. The nerve center is amassing forces against you."

Em tossed the package of factory-made junk on the floor and stepped on it. Two old women pushing buggies stopped to watch her. Clearly, they either didn't know or didn't care about the strange "disease" emanating through the store.

"Defective merchandise," she said, keeping the hair dryer tucked neatly inside the coat. She went off to find Agnes.

It wasn't unusual for the store to be this deserted on a Thursday morning. Yet, the hairs on Em's arms rose. She should have run into at least one employee by now, infected or not. *Where is everyone?* The store had been decorated for the regional manager's return, but not as garishly as before, as if even the employees knew that such frippery would be meaningless. Em kicked at a mound of bunting and shook her head clear.

No time to think. She raced through the toy section and past Fashion Alley. Gemstone Glen was directly past the wall of belts and costume scarves, at the near-center of the store. Under a banner boasting "50% Off Like-Gold Jewelry — While Supplies Last!" sat six workers in a circle, Agnes Walker and Kevin among them. The brown stink of the entity wafted from the circle of evil like some poison cloud.

Em strode forward, only twenty yards from the depraved little coven. She kept one hand on the grip of her energy weapon. The alien-controlled workers didn't look up. They didn't even blink.

It's almost as if they're not even real, she thought. She looked behind her. The two older women were somewhere back there. Would they be able to see what was happening, really see it? Most likely not. Only Em.

Suddenly, a tunnel opened before her eyes, spinning around her as she walked. Sounds from nowhere swirled into a vortex of muddied voices. Em groaned and clutched her stomach with her free hand. It tumbled like a concrete mixer.

The entity's trying to confuse me. It's trying to make me freak out. She had to press on. She held fast to the blow dryer and concentrated on putting one foot in front of the other. Em strained, she made headway …

And stopped. Turned.

Wes Summersby was blocking her path.

"*You!*" Even though her fear of the channel 64 huckster had proven to be ungrounded in reality, he now shone with a devilish inner glow.

"Looks like you're in quite a pickle, friend. Trust in old Wes," he said, chuckling.

Em blinked, her vision clearing. Em's mother and Jackie flanked Wes, surrounded by a dozen others who remained shrouded with the signature mist of the entity's presence. They reached out for her with zombie fingers just like Mrs. Nguyen's, their voices pricking at her ears.

Em sank to her knees and put her head in her hands. "You're not real," Em said. "None of you are real. This is all an illusion." She stretched her right index finger toward Wes Summersby. It came to rest against the fine cotton surface of his three-piece suit.

The television therapist smirked.

"That doesn't prove *anything*." Em raised the blow dryer, cocking an invisible trigger.

The figures crowded around her, hemming her in on all sides. "We only want what's best for you, Em," her mother said. "Why don't you believe us?"

Em squinted her eyes shut and backed into the phalanx of not-persons. But Em had never been strong, and the figures were tougher than any normal humans. *Because they're not. They're phantoms created by the entity.* She looked over at the group of workers, still fixedly staring at the ground, their fingers tracing invisible lines in the air. Sketching this scene out for her wholesale.

Em aimed the hair dryer at the figure closest to her, which wore the face of Reverend Freddy. Blue fire shot from the weapon, forcing her hands backward with the recoil.

Nice work, Roger.

The righteous young man stiffened as the blue bolt slammed into his chest, but he straightened himself out with a calculated grin. The phantom knocked the hair dryer from Em's hand.

"You should be ashamed of yourself," her mother said. "Such a nice store. And you're *ruining* it like you ruin everything else in your life."

"Shut up, Mom," Em said as she searched the ground for her weapon, barely spotting it in the clouds of brown mist.

Dr. Slazinger stepped forward. He wore a white doctor's coat instead of his usual casual wear and carried a clipboard. "You've had a relapse, Em. You're a very sick girl. How does that make you feel?"

Em knelt to retrieve the blow dryer, bringing a new wave of nausea. "No! You can't trick me like this. You're finished." Em shot another energy bolt into the avatar of Dr. Atchison, her first psychiatrist. He slowed but did not fall, his gaze a fishhook on her mind.

She plucked a piece of costume jewelry from the stand at the counter and held it to her ear. *Escodex, are you there?*

"We're just trying to help you, Em," her false sister said.

"Oh, blow it out your ass," Em said, returning the blow dryer to the pocket of her coat. Clearly, it was worthless against these beings. *Crazy-ass Roger didn't follow the plans.*

As Em surveyed the figures, she was painfully aware of who was *not* among them. Roger was not there, and neither was her father. Maybe their minds were just too broken for the entity to recreate.

Sometimes knowing isn't enough. Isn't that what I learned about my hallucinations? Just knowing this is a product of the entity doesn't make it any less real when I'm in its grip.

Well, if this was going to be her reality, she was going to have to learn its rules. The figures, as much as they nagged at her, seemed to do no real damage. Except for Reverend Freddy's swipe at the stun weapon, none of the figures had affected her in any way. Em studied the phantom that looked like her mother. It remained in place, a nasty grin frozen on its hardened face.

They're all a bunch of robots, she thought. *They're programmed to say a few very specific things designed to stall and weaken me, but they can't interact with me. Just a bunch of big wind-up dolls.*

Em drew breath. She leaned toward the mother figure. Gripping the phantom's shoulders, she unleashed a scream into its ear canal loud enough to shatter glass.

Nothing.

Just a bunch of big dumb robots made out of pseudo-flesh and stuck into this splintered reality. And Em thought she knew how to beat them. She sidled up to her old friend Denise.

"Hey, Denise," Em said, wiggling her fingers in front of the dumb beast's eyes, "over here." Denise lunged forward in a robotic march, as did the figure opposite her, Mr. Pendleton. The Denise phantom didn't even notice when Em put a hand on the back of its head. With a resounding crack, Em drove Denise into Pendleton. Both beings collapsed on the swirling tunnel floor.

One by one, Em picked off the other phantoms, until only the one of her sister remained. It took less time than she'd have thought. They seemed to weaken as she lessened their number.

The dull monster with Jackie's features stared at her blankly, not noticing or caring that its fellows were piled in a heap at its feet. "Are you going to murder me, Em? Murder me like you're going to kill poor old Agnes Walker?"

Em took in the scene. Jackie was the only one left. There were no bodies left to attack her with. "Get outta my way, sis."

The figure, dressed in Jackie's former Pilgrim getup, tut-tutted like some sort of old-timey schoolmarm. "You destroyed our family. You ruined your own life. And now you're going to doom the world."

Em sighed and stepped around Jackie's phantom. The figure glowered at her with uncanny eyes, but it couldn't stop her from approaching the circle of recruited employees and the nerve center herself. Em didn't need to destroy her sister's phantom. She just had to walk away.

"God is going to be so pissed at you."

"Gotta work on your voices, Agnes." Em turned and fired a useless blue bolt into the phantom. "I wasn't buying this one for a second."

THIRTY-ONE

When Em was in her senior year of high school, she'd had a terrifying experience at a grocery store. She'd been pacing the aisles, sticking gum and candy into her jacket pockets, when suddenly all the colors seemed way too bright. The fluorescent lights shined down on her like a baking-hot alien sun. Their buzzing filled her ears until her head felt crammed with static. She'd barely made it out alive.

Em knew now that it was an early manifestation of her schizophrenia, an unheeded warning siren. And as she approached Agnes Walker, she had the same sense of *fullness*, of her senses ramping up on her, of everything becoming just a little too defined, a little too sharp.

Everything becoming real.

Em plucked a necklace from a spinner rack on the jewelry counter and looped it around her ear. The rack looked odd in the transformed store, a prosaic reminder of what had been there before, and now might not ever be again. *Escodex, are you there?*

"I am watching this through your eyes, Em. The nerve center is straight ahead. You must hurry."

"I *know* that." Em looked down at the circle of entity-touched workers. They moved in syncopated harmony, twiddling their fingers and releasing their small puffs of gas, odorless to the nose, but deadly to the eyes. Agnes, her eyes and hair animal-wild, towered just a little higher than the others, almost as if she was levitating.

Scratch that — she *was* levitating. Agnes's borrowed mouth muttered in a language that Em was certain had never been spoken in Clear Falls. Maybe never spoken in the *world*.

"Don't move." Em held her blow dryer up to Agnes. It covered most of her face.

The old woman — scratch that, the *entity* — smiled its slimy grin. "Too late. The code approaches."

"I'm still here. That means it's not." Em looked over at Kevin. What would happen to these people, to the entity's army, once she fired on Agnes? *Escodex, what should I do?*

"You shoot her! You destroy the entity!"

But what's going to happen to them? To her?

"Do you really care?"

Em thought about it while the employees still attempted their useless magic spell. "Yes."

A sound drifted through the dimensional boundary that was almost a sigh. "Don't tell me it's getting to you too. You shouldn't be an attractive target to it."

"It's *not* getting to me! I just don't want to kill anyone."

"You'll kill *everyone* if you don't discharge that energy weapon and transfer the entity into my dimension before the code arrives. Do it, Em. *Now*."

Em looked down at the wretched husks of humanity on the floor. They were all staring at her now. Some, like Kevin, only held traces of the entity. A light sheen of brown glazed their faces, hollowing out their features only slightly, making them appear like shift workers running on a considerable amount of sleep deprivation.

Agnes, far more wizened, rose to meet her. She wobbled on unsteady legs. Em reflexively stepped backwards. "I'll do it, Agnes. I will."

"You don't have it in you, girl." Agnes bared her teeth. A thick wave of the brown gas escaped from between them, and Em swatted it away from her eyes.

It can't hurt me. I'm not what it wants.

"I can make it work," Agnes continued, her lungs still expelling clouds of the entity. "I've had worse meals."

Em gritted her teeth and shot a bolt of energy into Agnes's face to weaken it in preparation for the transfer, just as Escodex had told her. The blue light flashed, but the nerve center still advanced.

It's not working! She fired again. And again. "Why won't you *die?*"

In the corner of Em's vision, something glimmered, a bright light. She turned, but couldn't make out the source. Heat rose at her back.

It's the code. The regional manager. He's in the store.

"That's right," the entity said. "I *will* rise to the next level." A tendril of brown smoke wafted from Agnes's mouth and made a beeline for Em's mouth. Her nose. Em gagged.

"Escodex, help me!" But Escodex was only a voice. He couldn't help Em.

As the brown smoke reached down into Em's body, she felt an overwhelming feeling of — control. Of peace.

"What's happening, Em? I've gone dark!" Escodex's flat voice was as frantic as it ever sounded, but Em couldn't reply. All at once, she loathed the voice in her ear. She *wanted* to help the entity rise above this dimension.

One of Agnes's clawed hands grabbed at Em's wrist. She twitched it away and kicked at the old woman's shins with the last of her own power, and hated herself for doing so.

"I told you it was too late," the entity said, still smiling.

You were right. I was wrong.

The second claw reached out and grabbed the blow dryer. Em watched herself release it, powerless to retain the broken weapon with the all-pacifying subroutine of the entity working its way into her mind.

This is what's supposed to happen, Em thought. *It's good. It's right.* Tears coursed down her face, but she couldn't fight back. She didn't even *want* to.

The heat at Em's back grew larger, took form. Em held her breath, her entity-soaked breath, and waited for the marriage of alien and code that would lead to the true destruction of all things.

"I need details!" Escodex shrilled. Em wanted to bat the sniveling voice away, but even that was beyond her power now. She'd been tranquilized, gutted. Nothing left. Em looked at Agnes, her mind straining to concentrate through the molasses-thick filter of the entity.

The brown haze still coated Agnes, but it was dulled. The old woman's human face shone through for the first time since Em had slowed it down weeks before.

I'm too much for it to handle, Em thought. *It can't control me and Agnes at the same time.* She felt its energy subdivide over and over, again and again, its attention pulled in five different directions at once, as it struggled to incorporate its "bad meal."

Open-mouthed, Agnes turned to Em. "I did all this."

Em could only nod.

Agnes shook her head. *Do you see what I see?* Em wanted to ask. *The brown mist, the pile of discarded phantoms lying in a pile? Do you see the code, advancing?*

The old woman looked at the hair dryer still clutched in her gnarled hand. "I'm so sorry, girlie." She raised it to her head, around which the brown mist was already starting to reform, enlarge.

"No!" said Em, unsure if it was her voice breaking through the haze or that of the entity.

Agnes pulled the trigger.

Agnes staggered backward against the Lucite casing of the jewelry counter. Twin threads of red ran from her nostrils. She smiled, faintly, and collapsed. Around Em, Agnes, and the entity-touched employees, customers were coming back to life.

"Agnes!" Em propped the old woman up and pressed the side of her head — the side without Escodex — to her chest. It rose and fell softly. *She's alive.*

Em looked over at the circle of employees, slowly coming out of their stupor. She locked eyes with Kevin. Then he looked over at Agnes.

"Em … what did you *do*?"

Time hung in the air like a soiled blanket. The other workers stared at her too, and a few customers. So many eyes. "Agnes is sick! You need to help her!" She pointed to another of the workers. "And you." She sprinted toward the employees' lounge, pausing momentarily to eject the memory card from the base of the blow dryer and tossing the makeshift weapon into the home goods section.

I'll sort this out later, she thought. Right now, she had to get to Roger.

Escodex yammered in her ear as she ran. "What happened? Em, you did not fire the weapon. All is lost!"

Shut up, she told him, not unkindly. *She fired it. Agnes saved us all.*

"And what is your reason for not uploading the entity's wave pattern to me?"

Em tore the piece of costume jewelry from her ear and stuck it in the pocket with the memory card. "There! Fucking *kiss*!" She pushed through the set of double doors that led to the employee lounge.

Roger sat next to Em's old supervisor, one arm supporting her. "Em! What happened out there? You've only been gone five minutes."

"I'll tell you later." She knelt next to Mrs. Nguyen. "How are you feeling?"

Judy wiped the back of her hand across her face. "Better now. Like something was there, and then it was gone." She sniffed. "I think I caught that disease they were talking about on the news."

Em held one of Mrs. Nguyen's hands in hers. It was ice cold, but the color was starting to return. "You probably did. But you're okay now. Everyone's going to be okay now."

Fists pounded on the door. Em's eyes widened. *Oh shit.* "Roger, go see what's out there."

Roger lurched for the door, but it swung open before he reached it. One of the Savertown rent-a-cops muscled his way in, heading straight for Em on the lounge bench. "Are you Emmeline Kalberg?"

Em's heart froze in her chest. She pointed a finger at the barely conscious woman next to her. "No, she is."

"We need you to come with us." The cop stared Em down until she sighed, dropped Mrs. Nguyen's arm, and left the lounge.

Out on the floor was a too-familiar sight: customers cordoned away, while a paramedic loaded Agnes Walker's body — still alive? — onto a gurney. Em swallowed the lump in her throat and followed the rent-a-cop through the store, to where the still-confused workers were gathered in a crowd.

"Wait here." He pushed Em into the throng of employees.

She locked eyes with Kevin, who quickly looked away. The Savertown USA workers were still pale, but the color was swiftly returning to their cheeks as their life force flowed back into them. Nobody spoke. Another guard watched them, presumably to make sure nobody split.

Finally, Em couldn't take it anymore. She turned to the second cop. "So, what, are you going to arrest us?"

"Miss, pipe down."

Em crossed her arms and slouched against a display, causing some of the items to cascade to the tile floor. "*Fine*," she said, loudly. Kevin slapped his hand against his face.

Finally, the first rent-a-cop came back. He shook his head. "The cameras didn't pick anything up. Everything's static."

"Is the old lady talking?"

"A little. She said it's nobody's fault."

Kevin stepped over the invisible cordon that separated the employees from the guards. "That's bullshit. I saw Em attack her. We all saw it." He looked around at the gathered employees, but nobody backed him up.

"Son, I'm gonna need you to step back." The man glared at Em. "You were told not to come back to the store."

"That's right."

"But you're in the store." His forehead wrinkled. "Right now."

"That's right." She met his gaze. "I needed some tampons."

The second security worker coughed. "You're free to go. But we'll be watching you, Emmeline Kalberg. You're on our radar."

"That's okay. I wouldn't be caught in this shithole again anyway." She slid her hand into the pocket that contained Escodex and the memory card and rubbed them with her thumb. *It's over. Almost.*

Em crouched in a drainage ditch, her father's coat dipped in the mud, the RFID chip-containing necklace held to the side of her head.

"Escodex? Talk to me, you little piece of shit."

Agnes's gurney rolled toward a waiting ambulance, pushed by a paramedic. Em held her breath.

"I did what you wanted. I did everything you wanted."

Across the parking lot, one of the rent-a-cops spoke quickly and passionately into a cell phone. Nobody looked toward the drainage ditch where a crazy girl in a too-big jacket spoke into nothingness.

"Oh god, none of this was real, was it? Agnes shot herself for nothing."

Why wouldn't he *talk*?

Static gave way to a distant voice. "Em! Rough times here. We could feel the entity straining at the nexus point. It nearly broke through. Have you captured it?"

"Uh, yeah." Em shook the memory card at her ear, although she knew it was futile. Escodex couldn't see her. "In here. I have it in my hand."

She felt the familiar prickling sensation of Escodex plumbing out of her brain toward the memory card. "Very good. Thank you for your service."

"Wait! What about my dad?"

"What?"

"My father. The reason I did this thing for you. You said you'd tell me where he is. So where is he?"

"You'd have never done this otherwise."

"What are you saying?"

"I don't know where he is. I just don't have that kind of information. I'm sorry."

Em's vision went red. A low moan escaped her lips and she dug her free palm into the muck. "You lied to me."

"You saved the world, Em. Congratulations."

Her teeth chattered, developing into a full-body shake that threatened to jolt the memory card from her hand. "You *lied* to me."

"I took the necessary steps to preserve my world and yours."

"You made me think I was going crazy again. You made the last four months of my life a living hell. *You lied to me.*"

"Look at the bigger picture, Em."

"Fuck. You." She balled the fake gold necklace in her fist until the tiny links broke. "You're probably not even *real*. I'm talking to air. I'm so fucking stupid and crazy."

"We thank you for your service."

An absence formed in Em's ear, an unplugging. The distant static that had accompanied her almost every day left, and the silence burned. Suddenly, for less than a second, Em saw before her a limitless expanse, a plateau crammed with impossible shapes superimposed across a multihued sky. Some of the figures were humanoid and their long limbs extended like branches that touched the edges of her vision. The humanoid figures spoke to one another in chiming patterns that layered over one another to create songs that were also words, voices that never stopped talking. Even if she could see and hear in surround, she wouldn't be able to take it all in. She didn't have the proper eyes to see with, the right kind of ears to hear with. She came from a lesser world, or maybe just a different one.

This is his world. This is what he sees every day.

Em hated the vision with every fiber of her being. She threw the memory card into the muck and ground it out under her toe.

Slowly, the low hum of static returned, voices not from another dimension.

After what could have been minutes or hours, she peeked out of the drainage ditch. The paramedics were gone. The rent-a-cops were nowhere to be seen. It was just her, a half-dozen cars, and Roger.

"Escodex lied to me, Roger." Em couldn't help it, she was crying. "He *lied*."

Roger reached down and patted her on the shoulder. "You expected something different?"

Em bit her lip. "I guess not. Everyone lets you down eventually."

"Not everyone."

She looked at the piece of pilfered costume jewelry in her hand, glittering in the bright winter sun. No voice would come from it, not ever again. Escodex had gotten what he wanted from Em's Earth. "They weren't really so different. They both used us to get what they wanted."

"The entity was trying to *kill* us, Em."

"No, it was trying to use us as … a springboard, Escodex called it. To get to a higher dimension. Maybe we wouldn't have died, who knows? Maybe life would have been better."

Roger shrugged. "Well, it's over now. I guess we'll never know."

"Empty platitude, Roger." Em dropped the necklace into the mud next to the shattered remains of the memory card. "Can you drive me home?"

Roger shook his head. "Can't. I have my shift. Judy can take you. She's okay now."

Em still wasn't ready to share a car with her old supervisor. "That's all right. I'll walk. I'm used to it." She brushed a few stray twigs from her pants. "See you around. Stay crazy."

Then she walked the three miles home, along the highway's edge, as she'd done so many times before.

Em found out about Agnes Walker's death in the newspaper, the latest casualty of the "mysterious epidemic" having been picked up by the *Pittsburgh Post-Gazette* and shared on Facebook, amid inane quizzes and listicles.

Just another nameless hick, Em thought. *Just another story.* Savertown USA had been closed down, possibly on the recommendation of the regional manager who'd never learned how close he'd come to bringing about the end of everything. The lines about the store's closure had taken up more column space than the lines about Agnes's death, which really didn't surprise Em at all.

"Low prices, all the time," Em muttered under her breath as she killed the screen.

There would be no funeral. Nobody had given a damn about Agnes in life, and nobody cared about her in death. Em didn't feel great about this. What parts of Agnes's personality were her, and what parts were the entity? Escodex had said there was nothing of her left, but Em *knew* that was a total lie.

Just like so many other things he'd told her.

Em stole a glance around the deserted drugstore. When she knew nobody was watching, she plucked a box of aspirin from the shelf and held it to the side of her head.

Nothing.

You expected something different? Em thought, echoing Roger. *It wasn't different the last fifteen times you tried.* As she stuck the aspirin into her pocket, a familiar voice spoke up behind her.

"Em?"

She spun around. "Kevin."

"Put that back."

She stared at him for a minute, then sighed and put the aspirin back on the shelf. "I know how much you love ratting people out."

"I already apologized for that. I don't know how else to make it up to you."

The section of surveillance video that should have showed Agnes's seizure — Agnes's *whatever* — contained nothing but static. Whether that was Escodex's last gift to her, or a result of the entity's time-warping effect, Em didn't know. The cops had never come to her house for a follow-up visit, and that was all she cared about. "You don't *believe* I wasn't responsible for Agnes's death. You think I killed her. Somehow."

"It doesn't matter," Kevin said.

"Well, at least you got another job," she said, eyeing his work smock. "And nothing happened to *you*. Yet." Em cocked an invisible gun at him.

Kevin's face hardened. "That's not funny."

Em put her hand back in her empty pocket.

"Anyway, I need to get back to work. It was great talking to you."

"But not really."

"No," Kevin said, "not really."

Em shrugged and left. *Some thanks I get for saving your life,* she thought. She knew she'd do it again, though. If she had to.

A few days later, Em got a text from an unknown number, asking to meet at the Starbucks at the local mall. Em never went to the mall, and she really never went to Starbucks, but she found herself borrowing Jackie's bike and riding to the edge of Clear Falls to meet the mystery messenger.

Mrs. Nguyen was there waiting for her, dumping a packet of sweetener into her Frappuccino. Em's heart caught in her throat. The older woman still looked pale from her experience with the entity, but she was alive. And she wanted to talk about Roger.

"He didn't tell anyone where he went," Mrs. Nguyen said. She took another sip of coffee. "I just went over to his house one day and all the lights were out. All his stuff was gone."

Em had tried to call Roger multiple times, though she never learned where he lived. She guessed Mrs. Nguyen got his address from the employee records or something. "Why would he just leave?"

"Creepy man." Mrs. Nguyen caught Em's eye. "But nice. Creepy *and* nice. Are you sure you haven't heard from him, Em? You two were awfully close."

"I don't know where he is, Mrs. Nguyen."

"I told you before, girl, call me Judy. I'm not your damn supervisor anymore."

"Do you think they're ever going to reopen the store?"

Judy shook her head. "Nobody's going to go back there. They're tearing it down. Putting in another strip mall, I think."

Like we don't have enough of those here, Em thought. "Are you feeling okay? Since you … got sick?"

"No money for doctors. I'll be all right. Roger saved me that day, you know. From whatever that thing was." Judy wrinkled her nose. "That's another thing I wanted to ask you about."

"What is?"

She slurped down another gulp of not-coffee. "I think you know more about this than you're letting on. I think you always did."

Em crumpled the paper from Judy's straw between her fingers. "How much do you *really* want to know, Judy?"

"Is it going to happen again?"

"No."

"Then nothing. I don't want to know anything."

After brushing her teeth and taking her night-time meds, Em went into her bedroom and removed a large wrapped package from her closet. She crept downstairs.

"Mom?"

Bea Kalberg rested in her rocking chair, a magazine opened on her lap. She glared at Em over the rim of her glasses. "Yes?"

"Do you have a minute? There's something I want to show you."

"The news is on."

Em turned down the volume. "I bought you something. Here, open it."

Her mom set aside the magazine and ripped the old Christmas wrapping from the box, revealing a complete box set of Wes Summersby's television broadcasts on DVD.

"Oh, Em, I can't take this. It costs too much."

"I had the money," Em said. "I guess you know I stole your set."

"I figured as much," Mom said.

"So, anyway, here you go." Em smiled. "Brand new. I promise not to throw them in the river this time."

After a moment of silence, Em turned to go. She had reached the foot of the stairs when her mother called to her.

"Get back here."

Tentatively, Em went back to her mother's side. Setting aside the box of DVDs, Mom wrapped her arms around Em's middle and squeezed.

"Love you, kiddo."

"You, too," Em said, and meant it. After all she'd put her family through, they still loved her. She wasn't going to be sent away. She wasn't going to have to cut off all ties, like Roger had. *Not that Mom would let me*, Em thought.

After she returned to her room, Em opened her desk drawer and removed an envelope. Nestled inside was a report sent by a private detective she'd hired with the last of her Savertown USA wages.

David Kalberg had been linked via dental records to a John Doe found strapped inside a rented Chevy Cavalier at the bottom of Tampa Bay six months after abandoning his family. A bureaucratic mix-up had prevented the local police from connecting the cases. The records had sat, unseen and uncared-for, for eleven years.

Em had concealed the letter for a week. Would it help her mother to know that her husband was dead? Would it help Jackie? It hadn't helped her to know. She imagined her father's pain in his last moments, what must have been his confusion. Had he been chased by demons in those final moments, beset by voices? Or had he driven beyond the steaming Florida coastline fully cognizant of what he was doing? She could never know, just like she could never know what fate waited for her. *There's so much of him in you*, her mother had always said. Was this going to be her fate, too?

Many times over the past week she'd sat with the letter dangled over an unlit lighter. More times still, she'd carried the letter downstairs, fumbling with it until her mother or sister had shown an interest. "Just something from college," she'd lied, before burying the envelope back in her desk.

Now, she put it back inside. One day, she'd upset the balance, give Mom and Jackie the closure they may not even want. But not tonight, not now.

Em stretched out in bed and let the reality of dreams overtake her.

Ackwowledgments

The book you just finished reading took ten years to write. Well ... kinda. I came up with the idea in 2004, while working in this reality's version of Savertown USA. Two years later I wrote it down. Then, soon after I finished what was then the final draft, I just stopped writing for a long time. Pretty dumb, right? But obviously I came to my senses, and not long after I started seriously publishing fiction again I returned to this novel. I want to think the story is better for that extra-long period of digestion.

I'd like to thank Mike Hodges for fixing this book with a single comment and Soren Lundi for unearthing my mid-'00s anachronisms. I'd also like to thank the WorD writing group in Pittsburgh and Shae Krispinsky for suffering through a much earlier version of this story. (I'm so sorry, guys.)

Much of this book is autobiographical, but one important aspect is not: Em's schizophrenia. I want to show appreciation for all of the memoirs and blog posts I've read over the years by people with schizophrenia, who are some of the strongest people in the world.

In addition, I'm indebted to the Codex Writers Group for emotional support and good business advice. I'm grateful for all the short fiction editors who have published me, and also my most patient editors/publishers Jason Sizemore and Lesley Conner. And I wouldn't be a writer today without Nick Mamatas, who's believed in my writing from the start, way before I ever did.

One last shout out goes to my spouse and in-house editor Rob Mc-Monigal, who's been there through this whole thing.

ABOUT THE AUTHOR

Erica L. Satifka is a writer and/or friendly artificial construct, forged in a heady mix of iced coffee and sarcasm. She enjoys rainy days, questioning reality, ignoring her to-do list, and adding to her collection of tattoos. Her short fiction has appeared in *Clarkesworld*, *Shimmer*, *Lightspeed*, and *Intergalactic Medicine Show*. Originally from Pittsburgh, she now lives in Portland, Oregon with her spouse Rob and an indeterminate number of cats. *Stay Crazy* is her first novel.

APEX PUBLICATIONS NEWSLETTER

Why sign up?

Newsletter-only promotions. Book release announcements. Event invitations. And much, much more!

SUBSCRIBE AND RECEIVE A 15% DISCOUNT CODE FOR YOUR NEXT ORDER FROM APEXBOOKCOMPANY.COM!

If you choose to sign up for the Apex Publications newsletter, we will send you an email confirmation to insure that you in fact requested the newsletter and to avoid unwanted emails. Your email address is always kept confidential, and we will only use it to send you newsletters or special announcements. You may unsubscribe at any time, and details on how to unsubscribe are included in every newsletter email.

VISIT
HTTP://WWW.APEXBOOKCOMPANY.COM/PAGES/NEWSLETTER

SING ME YOUR SCARS

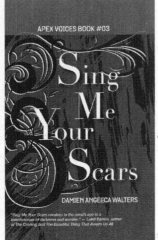

In her first collection of short fiction, Damien Walters weaves her lyrical voice through suffering and sorrow, teasing out the truth and discovering hope.

BY DAMIEN ANGELICA WALTERS

"*Sing Me Your Scars* revolves in the mind's eye in a kaleidoscope of darkness and wonder."
Laird Barron, author of *The Croning* and *The Beautiful Thing That Awaits Us All*

"Anatomies of dreams and nightmares, Walters is a writer to watch."
John Langan, author of *The Wide, Carnivorous Sky and Other Monstrous Geographies*

ISBN: 978-1-937009-28-1 ~ ApexBookCompany.com

Made in the USA
Charleston, SC
09 September 2016